The Pirate

of

Janaconda Island

Also by Warren Firschein

Out of Synch (2015)

The Pirate of Janaconda Island

WARREN FIRSCHEIN

CHAPTER TWO PRESS ◇ SAFETY HARBOR, FL

Summary: In 1949, 12-year-old twins Lucy and Paddy Hendricks
attempt to solve clues to the location of hidden pirate treasure
while spending their summer on a Caribbean island.

Library of Congress Control Number: 2017914991

First Edition: December 2017
10 9 8 7 6 5 4 3 2 1

Printed in the United States of America.
Cover Illustration by Sarah Ort
The text type was set in Georgia.

Dedicated to everyone who has ever spent their time searching for lost treasure.

PROLOGUE

The man looked sick, as if allergic to the heat. He stood on the cracked tarmac in front of the private twin-engine propeller plane dabbing his forehead with a white handkerchief, his pale face shielded from the sun by an old-fashioned bowler hat.

Noticing his presence, Manuel Vargas pushed open the glass doors of the small two-room airport terminal and stepped into the humid air. As he approached the plane idling on the lone runway, he tilted his head in greeting.

Nodding back, the pale-faced man pocketed the handkerchief. "Are you Manuel Vargas?"

"*Si*. I'm sorry I'm late."

"No matter. My pilot made unexpected time."

"You wired my office and asked for me to meet you, but did not explain the purpose of your visit. What can I do for you? Mister—"

"I came to deliver a message. In response to your inquiry of several months ago."

Now Manuel understood. He felt his breath catch in his throat. "Wouldn't the mail have been simpler?"

The man shrugged. "Safety and privacy are more important to my client than cost." He stuck a cigarette in his mouth and lit the end. "I understand there would be children involved."

"Twelve years old, both of them. Hardly children."

"Still," said the pale-faced man. "They could make a mess of things. Cause mischief."

"No, no. I am sure they've been raised properly. After all, their father is a—"

"A scientist, I know." The man took another puff from the cigarette. "Still, my client has concerns."

Manuel nodded. "I took the liberty of hiring a private investigator for such a possibility." He pulled a sheet of paper from his inside jacket pocket and unfolded it. "He reported no—what is the phrase?— blue flags."

"Red flags."

"*Si*. Red."

The two men stood in awkward silence, Manuel holding out the letter from the investigator and the pale-faced man refusing to take it. Finally Manuel said, "I would not have contacted you had there been another option. It will only be several months. I am confident they will not make problems."

"So you will vouch for them?"

Manuel hesitated before responding. "*Si.*"

"Okay then." The man took a drag from his cigarette. "We had reached the same conclusion regarding their upbringing, but I was required to ask nonetheless. For confirmation. My client requested this. He questions whether it is appropriate for children to—well, you understand. Given the history."

"I understand."

The man nodded before reaching into his briefcase and pulling out a sealed envelope with the words 'Boggs & Patterson, Attorneys-at-Law, Belize City, Belize,' printed prominently across the front in blue ink. "Go ahead, open it."

Manuel nervously tore the envelope open. Inside was a handwritten note on a single sheet of white unmarked stationery. He read:

Yes.

But they are not to learn of the controversy surrounding the previous owner.

And nothing inside the house may be touched, painted, or moved.

The letter, Manuel noticed, was unsigned.

The attorney broke the lengthy silence. "Is everything satisfactory?"

Manuel nodded, folded the letter back into thirds, and stuffed it inside his jacket pocket. "*Si.* Thank you."

The pale-faced man snuffed out his cigarette with the heel of his shoe. "Good. The family will need this, too, I think." He handed over a long silver key, then added, "Make sure those children adhere to the rules. Or you will be out of a job."

And without another word, he turned and ascended the short flight of stairs back onto the plane.

June 1949

ONE

"**U**gh," said Lucy Hendricks as she climbed out of the taxi. "It's much too hot here."

She brushed back her brown hair, her fingers coming away moist with sweat. Although she loved the way her locks hung down to her shoulders, right now she wished she didn't have any hair at all. Twelve years old and bald. She'd look funny, but at the moment she was more focused on her comfort.

"Maybe air conditioning hasn't been invented here yet," said her twin brother Paddy, who had followed her out of the cab. "Now *that* would be something to complain about."

Lucy swiped at a pair of mosquitoes buzzing around her face. "I can't believe we have to live on this stupid island for the whole summer."

"Yeah," said Paddy. "There probably won't be any other kids here."

"And if there is, so what? We probably don't like to do any of the same things anyway."

Paddy sighed. "Just a crummy rock heap in the middle of nowhere."

The twins stared up at the old house looming over them, ugly and square-shaped, constructed from blocks of dark gray stone now peppered with mildew stains. A film of dirt and grime coated the windows on the second floor, bordered by two sets of peeling black shutters, making it appear as if the house was slowly opening its eyes after an extended slumber. A distinct gloominess hung over everything.

"We're really going to live here?" Paddy asked, shaking his head. "This is the worst house I've ever seen. It looks like a jail."

"Yeah," added Lucy. "This place is disgusting." She looked back toward their mother, who had followed them up the driveway. "Is this really the house they got for us?"

"I'm afraid so." Margaret Hendricks put down her luggage and adjusted her wide-brimmed hat, shielding her eyes from the sun. "I had hoped for something more modern, but we'll just have to make the best of it. At least the lawn is mowed."

"We can always turn around and go back to Maryland," said Paddy. His full name was Patrick Brennan Hendricks, but everyone called him Paddy after a long-dead Irish ancestor no one knew anything about. "Pretend we were never here."

"We discussed this before we left," said their father as he lifted the remaining bags from the trunk. "We'll only be here for a few months."

He picked up Lucy's suitcases and set them near the front door, adding, "I think you'll love it here, once you give it a chance. Not many kids get to live on a tropical island. There will be lots for you to do, you'll see. I'll bet you'll even end up missing this place when we return home."

"No chance of that," Lucy muttered. She watched the taxi pull away and back through the open wrought-iron gate surrounding the property and onto the road, where an old man had stopped to watch them. She opened her mouth to say more, but was interrupted by the loud whine of an engine as a car careened around the bend. A string of angry honks followed; the cab slammed on its brakes and the speeding car swerved onto the grass, narrowly avoiding a collision, before racing on.

"Some drivers!" said Mrs. Hendricks.

Then they heard a siren as another vehicle raced around the curve and into view. It was a police car, quite clearly chasing the vehicle that had just sped by. But the policeman didn't have the skill of the other driver, or maybe he simply wasn't as lucky. There was a long screech, followed by a dull thud and breaking glass as the police car slammed into the back of the cab. The hood of the police car popped up and a geyser of steam escaped into the air with a hiss.

"My goodness—is anyone hurt?" said Mrs. Hendricks, flinching.

As the family watched, the policeman stumbled out of his car. Now the taxi driver was on his feet, too, and the men began to argue. After a minute the officer wrote a ticket and handed it to the cab driver, who reacted by making wild hand gestures in obvious protest.

"Looks like they're fine to me," Mr. Hendricks said as the officer banged the hood shut, got in his car, made a tight turn and drove off in the opposite direction. "I wonder what that was all about."

"Who knows," said Mrs. Hendricks, as the old man standing on the road spoke briefly to the cab driver before opening the door and getting in. Moments later the taxi drove off. "We'll probably never find out. Maybe this place isn't as safe as we were led to believe." Then she went up the path to the house, avoiding the uneven bricks that jutted from the ground. As the rest of the family trailed her, she tore open the envelope that had been left for them at the airport security office and removed a long silver skeleton key that looked like it had been made a century earlier. She inserted it into the lock, twisted it two-and-a-half times, and pushed against the heavy wooden door, which swung forward with a loud creak.

As they crowded around the entrance, the breeze suddenly picked up, blowing a cloud of dust through the opening and causing their father to sneeze twice.

"Allergies," he muttered, rubbing his nose with the crook of his arm. "We'll have to do something about that."

Paddy squinted at his sister through his splotchy lenses and sighed. "Another great family trip."

"No kidding," Lucy replied. "Wonder what our friends are doing right about now."

"Oh, summer camp, swimming, playing baseball . . ." His voice trailed. "You know, fun stuff."

She slapped her arm and squashed a mosquito between her fingers. "Well, we might as well go in before the bugs finish us off." Grabbing one of her suitcases, she stormed into the house, the rest of the family following behind.

"Whoa," said Paddy.

"It's a little dirty," mumbled their father.

"We'll freshen it right up," said Mrs. Hendricks with a long sigh. "Some sweeping and dusting will do wonders for this place. She brushed the stale air away from her nose. "Open some windows . . . maybe get some fresh flowers . . ."

"It's horrible," Paddy said.

A thin film of dust and dirt covered everything: Turkish carpets, with barely-visible geometric patterns; dark wood floors, nearly black with age; thick drapes covering the wide picture window. But beyond the grime, the house was unlike any they'd ever seen. The room was plastered with faded antique floral wallpaper. Dozens of odd paintings were fastened to the walls, nearly all crooked one way or the other. Tarnished chandeliers hung from the ceiling, their arms connected by strands of silvery cobwebs.

Along the walls stood a collection of life-sized bronze statues of African animals, floor lamps with yellowed shades, and grandfather clocks that each displayed different times, clicking faintly. The furniture was covered with white sheets that were stained and moth-eaten.

It was as if they had taken a wrong turn and accidentally entered an antique shop that had closed down twenty years earlier.

"What *is* this place?" Lucy asked.

"It's giving me the creeps," said Paddy, nudging up to his sister, who pushed him away good-naturedly. "Like it's haunted or something."

"I can't believe this old mansion was available at such short notice," said their father, looking around. "It's huge! And we were worried they wouldn't have a place big enough for us. I guess you never know what you'll find in these out-of-the-way spots."

"It must have been beautiful when it was new," agreed their mother. "I wonder why no one has been living in it."

"Maybe because it's filthy and smells like old people and there are sheets on all the furniture," Paddy said. "I'll bet no one has lived here for like fifty years."

"Perhaps we need a little more light," said their mother. She pulled open the drapes, revealing a perfect view of the sparkling ocean. The room brightened immediately, making the dirt and clutter all the more noticeable.

"There's nothing wrong here that a little elbow grease won't fix," said their father, brushing aside a thick web with his hand. "But we can clean this up later. Come on, let's go upstairs and take a look at the bedrooms."

The second floor was in no better condition. At the top of the staircase, a central corridor branched into five dusty bedrooms. One was larger than the others and would be for Lucy and Paddy's parents. One was locked, and would be no one's room, at least for now.

Lucy considered the remaining three options and chose a room where the wallpaper wasn't peeling. Affixed above the doorframe was a rectangular white ceramic tile with the word 'EAST' on it and, in blue ink, an image of the blowing wind.

Their father came up behind her as she stood in the doorway, causing her to jump involuntarily. "That's odd," he said, pointing at the tile. "That way's south, not east. You can see the ocean through the windows. Whoever placed the tile there must've made a mistake."

"Or been crazy," said Lucy.

Paddy was less picky about the décor and the view. He took the room directly across the hall from his sister solely for reasons of comfort. The window opened without much effort, and he figured a breeze would cool him down at night. There was a tile above his door, too: a handsome image of the sun, with the word 'SOUTH' inscribed along the bottom in the same blue color.

"That's weird," he mumbled.

☠   ☠   ☠

The family soon unpacked and began to clean, using brooms, rags, and an old feather duster they discovered in one of the bathroom closets, until their work was interrupted by the deep clang of the doorbell.

Thankful for the interruption, the twins rushed to the top of the stairs and watched their mother descend and open the heavy front door. Standing on the porch was a tall skinny man, probably around twenty-five years old, wearing a raggedy red cap.

"Yes? Can I help you?"

"Mrs. Hendricks? We spoke on the telephone after receiving your telegram. I see you picked up the key." The young man extended his hand. "Manuel Vargas. I'm here to welcome you to Janaconda Island, and to make your stay with us as pleasant as possible. May I come in?"

"Of course." She stepped aside and closed the door after him.

"You must be Dr. Hendricks," Manuel said as the twins' father came down the stairs.

"Yes." He grasped the young man's hand. "Glad to meet you, Mister—"

"Please, call me Manuel. We are quite informal here. We were glad to learn you were coming. It is not often that a renowned marine scientist such as yourself visits our little island."

"Unfortunately, this isn't a vacation for me, but I'm sure our children will enjoy themselves while we're here."

Manuel glanced around and frowned. "Please excuse my negligence in failing to clean up before your arrival. This house has been vacant for a long time. Unfortunately, these were the only accommodations available on such short notice for the length of your stay."

"It's no trouble," answered Mrs. Hendricks. "This will be perfect for us. Frankly, we're surprised no one lives here."

"Ah, well, that is a thing that cannot be explained."

"He's lying," whispered Paddy as the twins crouched behind the railing at the top of the stairs. "Did you notice how he fidgeted and looked at the ceiling? There's a reason no one lives here, and he knows what it is. Maybe someone was murdered here or something."

"Oh, stop," retorted Lucy. "That's ridiculous." But her brother was right about one thing—their visitor *did* seem uncomfortable when discussing the house. *Why,* she wondered.

"There you are," said their mother. She made a quick motion with her hand. "Come down and meet our guest."

"How old are you two?" asked Manuel, after the twins introduced themselves.

"Twelve," Paddy answered.

"I'm older," said Lucy. "By eight minutes. And taller, too."

Manuel smiled. "No doubt you wish to learn of all the fun things to do here."

"That would be great," said Paddy, perking up.

The man's smile disappeared. "Unfortunately, I cannot think of anything at the moment."

"Great," said Paddy. "Just great."

"I've heard there are some old ruins on the island," their father prompted. "I'll bet they're fun to explore."

Manuel nodded. "An ancient temple, deep in the jungle. But it is not well marked and the stone is crumbling in places. I would not recommend they go by themselves. However," he added, "Santa Elena is safe for them to explore on their own. They can bike to the center of town in twenty minutes or less."

"We don't have any bikes," said Paddy.

Manuel glanced back and forth with a confused look. "I apologize. I will be right back." He left, returning a minute later with two bicycles, each with metal wire baskets attached in front, which he wheeled into the house.

"I have another pair for your parents, which I will bring later. They are the best way to get around the island. There is not much use for a car here unless you have a lot to carry. Although the town isn't large, you can purchase everything you might need there. There are several grocery stores and pharmacies, as well as some wonderful restaurants."

"Thank you," said the twins' mother. "You've been very helpful."

"I will let you finish unpacking. If you need anything, you can always contact me through City Hall." Manuel opened the door to leave, but stopped and turned before stepping out. "I almost forgot—there is one other thing. It is . . . silly. Please forgive me for mentioning it. Although the owners of this house were kind enough to let you stay on such short notice, they insist that you agree to a particular condition first."

"Sure," said their father. "What is it?"

Manuel appeared visibly uncomfortable. "You are not permitted to rearrange any furniture, remove any of the fixtures or pictures, or paint any of the walls. You may certainly clean the house," he said, glancing around, "but everything else must stay exactly as it is. And I do mean *exactly*. That is their condition for staying here, and if you are unable to abide by it, I have been asked to request you find other lodgings."

"That's nuts," whispered Lucy to Paddy. "I wonder what that's all about?"

But their parents didn't seem to think it was unusual. "Certainly—that isn't a problem at all," said their mother, waving her hand in the air like it was nothing. "It's quite normal to have reservations when someone you don't know stays in your home."

Manuel seemed satisfied. "Then I will inform the owners that all is settled." He nodded. "A groundskeeper comes every few weeks to mow the grass and check on the property, but I have instructed him not to enter the house while you are here. If you leave the front gate unlocked during your stay, he will not bother you."

"Thank you," said the twins' mother, taking the key. "We will."

Manuel smiled. "Now, please, enjoy yourselves. Nothing is off limits. You may go anywhere in the house, other than any rooms that are locked, of course, and are welcome to use the boat tied at the dock."

Lucy's eyes widened. "Boat? Neat!"

TWO

During the next few days the Hendricks family dusted and cleaned, brushing away years of neglect with a whirlwind of brooms and mops until the house eventually breathed with new life.

Paddy stopped flinching whenever he heard an unfamiliar sound, and he began to wonder about the people who used to live there and what had happened to them. From the look of things, they had simply left one day and never returned, abandoning their old life for a new one somewhere else.

And what a life it must have been, spent in a mansion with huge rooms and high ceilings situated on a bluff overlooking the sea. Why would anyone leave this house, filled with a lifetime of belongings? Why had no one bothered to clean up, or moved in themselves? The mystery of it caused Paddy's head to throb. Maybe they committed some terrible crime and changed their name and ran off to hide from the law. Maybe they went crazy and ran off to live in the jungle. Maybe they drowned in the ocean or were eaten by sharks.

Maybe they really were murdered, in this very house.

At times like these, Paddy wished he had a normal imagination instead of the kind that would bang on the inside of his brain late at night with such ideas. The intrigue was irresistible. Maybe there were human bones in one of the closets, waiting to be discovered. So, with these macabre thoughts running through his head, he decided to perform a closer inspection, hoping to put his mind to rest.

He began on the first floor, near the front door, and progressed clockwise into the living room. He glanced at the antiques and animal statues crammed in the corners, but spent the most time studying the collection of paintings that filled the walls.

There were scenes of horrible, bloody battles and portraits of people dressed in old-fashioned clothes; ships at sea, sailing against the beating waves; the stars and moon; the crumbling remains of a medieval castle on top of a cliff overlooking the ocean. Others were images of life on an island: coconut trees bent over a lagoon; a pier, bustling with colorful boats; people walking the streets of a small village.

He deduced that these probably illustrated different parts of Janaconda Island and wondered who had painted them. The initials 'T.S.' appeared in a lower corner of most of the artwork, but a full name was never spelled out.

Like the house itself, the furniture must have once been a grand spectacle. Two leather couches, both still comfortable, were arranged in an 'L' shape in the living room, flanked by end tables with ornately-carved ivory legs and Asian characters inscribed with jet-black ink. A mahogany table, long enough to seat eight, was positioned in the middle of the dining room adjacent to a matching hutch containing a set of crystal goblets and a collection of elaborately engraved dishes from Holland.

As Paddy moved between rooms, the floorboards creaked and groaned under his feet like an old man rising after sitting too long.

"It's almost as if the house is trying to say something to me," he mumbled, dragging his fingertips along the wood molding that stretched along the middle of the walls. As he crossed under the archway separating the dining room from the hallway, he felt something rough under his fingers. Stepping back, he noticed numbers and formulas etched into the wall, as if someone had been in the middle of a particularly difficult math problem and ran out of paper. His senses heightened, he found equations scratched into some of the other walls, too, algebraic functions that had been left unsolved and appeared to be nonsense, with foreign symbols mixed among numbers, the sort of thing found in prison cells or left behind by shipwreck victims as they gradually went insane.

"Weird," he said.

Returning to the hutch, he opened each drawer and felt around. In the last one, he discovered a framed faded photograph of an old man, his white hair gathered in a ponytail behind his head. But his eyes were mesmerizing. They stared straight into the camera, his mouth curled in a hint of a smile. He eased the photo from its frame and flipped it over, yet there was no indication who the man was or when the picture was taken, so he put it back as he found it.

As Paddy continued to explore, the place reminded him more and more of old mansions that often are the setting of horror stories. Soon he was convinced that hidden passages snaked through the walls and led to secret rooms. All he was able to find, however, was a little closet underneath the staircase that didn't seem to go anywhere. When he showed it to his parents, they remarked that it would make a terrific place to store the empty suitcases, and that is how it was used.

By far, though, the most interesting room was a little library in the rear of the house, where the walls were lined with floor-to-ceiling bookcases crammed with dusty tomes and old maps. In the center of the room was a huge Steinway grand piano, the kind usually seen in museums and concert halls, although this one sported a jagged crack across the soundboard and its keys were yellowed with age. On one shelf was a small collapsible telescope, which Paddy took for himself, thinking it might be fun to look at boats from a distance and momentarily forgetting the rule not to remove anything.

All of this did nothing to quell the mystery growing in the back of Paddy's mind. Who had the paintings and furniture belonged to? What had happened to them? Why would anyone leave all these things behind?

In contrast, Lucy expressed little interest in such questions. She considered the answers irrelevant; it was unlikely that these people, if still alive, would reappear and demand their things back. So what difference did it make who it once belonged to? She listened to Paddy's theories, but kept her thoughts to herself.

☠   ☠   ☠

By the end of the weekend, the house finally felt livable. Lucy and Paddy knew each creaky floorboard and had claimed their favorite spots on the living room couches. They went out to the backyard and walked down to the water's edge, searching for fish and even going swimming twice. Their parents had made several shopping trips into Santa Elena, and their kitchen was now fully stocked with food.

During breakfast on Monday morning, their father announced he would be going to the lab for the day to start work on his research project. The lab was part of a regional ocean monitoring station, which had agreed to provide space for him during their stay on the island.

"Are you going, too?" Lucy asked their mother.

"Of course."

"But you're not a scientist."

Their mother bristled. "I'm serving as your father's assistant this summer. And without a full-fledged lab here on the island, he'll need all the help he can get. We should be back by dinnertime."

"We're going to be spending a lot of time there," their father said as he collected his things. "So you two will need to get used to being on your own."

"It looks like a beautiful day," their mother added, glancing out the window at the cloudless sky. "Why don't you take your bicycles into town? There must be something fun to do there. Maybe you can even make a few friends."

"Yes, let's," said Paddy. "I'm tired of being inside this stuffy old house."

"I guess," said Lucy without enthusiasm.

"Just don't go anywhere that seems unsafe," said their mother.

Lucy rolled her eyes. "*Mom*," she said. "You heard Manuel. This place is perfectly safe. We ride our bikes around the neighborhood at home, don't we? Nothing to worry about."

"Worry is a mother's prerogative."

"If you want us to try to have a good time here, you'll have to keep it to yourself," said Paddy. "Just saying."

Their mother sighed. "Just make sure you're home in time for dinner."

"Promise," said Lucy. "We'll return as soon as we get bored. That'll probably be in about an hour. If even that long."

After their parents departed on their bicycles, the twins climbed on their own and pedaled toward Santa Elena. The road hugged the shoreline, providing an unbroken view of the ocean as it glistened under the glare of the morning sunlight. The other side of the pavement was bordered by dense bushes and tropical plants, with occasional dirt paths leading into the jungle. Ignoring these turnoffs, they continued forward and soon reached the outer boundary of the town.

Now on the left there was no jungle, but a network of narrow streets lined with shops and businesses. Lucy and Paddy went along further until they reached a small marina. Here, the road widened into a rectangular plaza. Along the water's edge stretched a wooden boardwalk that connected a series of piers. From there, the twins watched fishermen unload their catch from a pair of fishing boats. Off to one side was a huge scale where the fish were weighed and then sold to people wearing white aprons.

Within fifteen minutes the twins became bored of this spectacle. They remounted their bicycles and continued into the heart of Santa Elena, riding aimlessly along the sidewalk until they spied a playground adjacent to a small brick school.

After leaving their bikes leaning against the wall of the school, they wandered on foot and soon stumbled upon a picturesque square bordered by shops and cafés. An old man sat at one table, reading a newspaper. Tucked away on one side was a paved court where older kids were playing basketball. A few benches were arranged in the grassy center of the square, set among marble statues of people who must've been famous for one reason or another. Near the benches, a musician sat cross-legged on the ground, strumming a guitar.

"Let's go listen," Lucy suggested. "We can sit in the shade. I wouldn't mind getting out of the sun for a bit. This heat is horrible."

"Sounds good," Paddy agreed. It had gotten hotter since they left the old house, and dark sweat stains had formed on the front of his shirt. How those kids could play ball in this weather was beyond him.

As they crossed the street, something slammed against Paddy's arm, hard. Knocked off balance, he fell in the middle of the square, scraping his hands and knees on the pavement. He let out a squeal, the sound of pain mixed with surprise.

"Hey, watch out," said a high-pitched voice. It belonged to a boy, probably about the same age as the twins, but a little shorter than Paddy. He wore a baseball cap and looked tough.

"You're the one who walked into me," Paddy retorted, still on all fours.

The boy stared down at Paddy as if he was getting ready to swing his fist or lash out with his foot. Then he laughed and extended an arm. "Sorry, *amigo*. My fault. Wasn't watching. Let me help you up, *bueno*?"

Exhaling in relief, Paddy grabbed the boy's hand and felt himself pulled to his feet.

The boy was skinny, with dark hair that poked from under his cap. He wore an old shirt that was too big for him, and a frayed blue knapsack was slung around one of his shoulders. On his feet were a shabby pair of leather sandals, which looked like they were about to fall apart. He rocked back and forth on his toes as if he was getting ready to run off, and kept glancing around the square like someone was chasing him.

But he didn't run off. Instead, he looked back at Lucy and Paddy and said, "Hey—you're new here, *si*? You on vacation or something?"

Paddy shook his head. "No, we're here for the summer. Our dad is a scientist and he's doing research at the marine lab."

"Oh." The boy bobbed his head up and down. "Sounds like you're gonna stick around awhile, then. My name's José—José Flores. But everyone calls me Chi-Chi. I'm like the mayor of this town, you know?"

"No, I don't," said Lucy. "Why do you say that?"

"Well—just that I know everything that goes on around here. *Comprende*?"

After the twins introduced themselves, Lucy said they had just arrived a few days earlier. "We just finished unpacking and decided to look around this place. Is there anything fun to do around here?"

"Lots! You wanna see something neat?"

"Sure!"

"*Vamos*—follow me!"

Chi-Chi turned and ran down the street, disappearing around a corner. The twins were amazed that he could move so fast while wearing such an old pair of sandals, especially in the stifling heat. And with a knapsack—well, the kid must be some kind of crazy athlete.

Not knowing what else to do, they took off in the same direction. Their chests heaved as they struggled in the humid air. They turned the corner and caught sight of Chi-Chi as he headed down a different street and out of sight once again. The twins ran on, but couldn't gain any ground. Then, when it seemed they couldn't go any farther, they turned one final bend to find Chi-Chi standing with his hands on his knees, laughing hysterically.

"That was fun," said Chi-Chi. "Didn't think you'd keep up."

"We . . . almost . . . didn't." Paddy paused between words to catch his breath. "I thought . . . we were . . . lost."

Chi-Chi laughed. "You really *are* new here. Can't get lost in Santa Elena—not enough streets! Come on—this way."

"But no more running," Lucy demanded.

"We walk from here," Chi-Chi said with a grin. "Promise." He pointed ahead, where the paved street connected to a narrow trail that led into the jungle.

"Where are we going?" asked Lucy.

"You'll see. I'll show you a place where people don't go no more. Don't be scared."

After exchanging a nervous glance, the twins followed Chi-Chi onto the dirt path. The trail had been well tended, and the sunlight pierced the veil of leaves that draped the treetops, illuminating the ground. Soon, though, the trees grew close together. The air became stuffy and smelled of rotten fruit. Now the path was no longer dirt, but mud, and small animal footprints were visible among the scattered puddles.

Chi-Chi pressed ahead and the twins struggled to keep up. "Slow down!" Paddy gasped, sucking down air.

"Let's go, *amigo*," Chi-Chi said.

"Come on, Paddy," said Lucy. "I don't want to miss this."

"I'd like to see how he does in the snow," Paddy grumbled.

As they hiked, Paddy felt his anxiety rise. Withered vines hung from the trees and insects buzzed around his face, biting his neck. It seemed no one was within miles of them. Now they had to brush branches out of the way, and were forced to climb over moss-covered trunks that had fallen across their path. Where was this boy taking them? What if he left them out here, alone, to find their way back on their own? Unfamiliar birdcalls rang out from deep in the shadows, taunting him. What direction was the town in, anyway? He glanced up at the sun, almost directly overhead. No help.

The heat rose and sweat dripped down their cheeks as they climbed upward, their legs throbbing with exhaustion. Chi-Chi forged forward, singing, seemingly unbothered by the conditions. Paddy continued to lag behind, nerves frayed, and often Lucy hung back when the trail forked so he'd know which way to go. He looked at her with a questioning expression, trying to communicate his uneasiness, which she either ignored or didn't understand. Then just when Paddy thought he couldn't hike any farther, the jungle opened into a vast clearing across a rocky plateau.

"*¡Bravo!*" Chi-Chi proclaimed. "You just climbed Mt. Alta Vista. Hard way, too. Not bad for a couple of American kids."

The twins glanced around and discovered they had hiked up a small mountain.

Paddy exhaled with relief, his worries about their safety vanishing. "The island looks a little like a giant peach from up here," he said, walking to the edge of the ridge and looking down.

"No, no—not a peach. The head of a snake!" Chi-Chi picked up a stick and drew the shape in the dirt. "See? That's why the island was originally named Anaconda Island, until a mapmaker made a spelling mistake. New name stuck."

Chi-Chi pointed south to the town harbor, where three fishing boats were now docked at the pier. The ocean beyond was featureless, except for a yellow boat anchored a short way offshore.

Paddy extracted the small telescope, which he had brought with him, and saw the boat had a curvy blue stripe along its hull like a wave.

"Look," said Lucy, pointing. "There's our house!"

Paddy turned and trained the telescope on it. "It doesn't look too ugly from here."

"You're staying there?" asked Chi-Chi, shielding his eyes from the sun. "I thought that house was condemned or something."

Lucy laughed. "Might as well be, from the way it looks inside."

Chi-Chi gestured at a group of gray buildings on the far end of town, near the water. "Your father's lab is over there. What's he doing, anyway? Looking at fish?"

"Not any fish," said Lucy proudly. "The *heliomanth.*"

"Helium man?"

"Not helium man. *Heliomanth,*" Lucy corrected. "It's a very special fish. Everyone thinks they all died centuries ago, but our dad thinks some may still be living around here, so he came to try to find out for sure."

"Someone thought they saw one at a fish market on the island, and Dad found out about it," said Paddy. "He's really excited about finding one alive."

"He'd be famous, too," added Lucy.

"Just another fish to me," Chi-Chi replied. "I don't care what they call 'em, so long as I can eat 'em." He rubbed his stomach and grinned.

"Do people come here to catch fish?" asked Paddy.

"Not much anymore." Chi-Chi pointed at the yellow boat floating in the bay. "Maybe them. That boat's been around for weeks, but they're way too close to the reef to catch anything big. If they're trying to catch fish, they don't know how."

Chi-Chi continued, "People once came here for regular vacations, too. Not just for fishing." He pointed down into the jungle about halfway to the town, where some bungalows were half-hidden in a clearing. "That was a tourist hotel. A fancy one. My grandmother took me there once, to play at this old playground there that looks like a giant ship, like Noah's Ark or something. It's all abandoned and grown over now. No one wants to come here anymore. Not since before I was born."

"Why not?" Lucy asked.

He shrugged and kicked at a rock, silent. Then he motioned the twins over and gestured toward the shoreline on the far side of the marina. "Down there is a cable line strung through the trees. You climb a ladder and attach a harness, jump and—*whoosh*! It's like flying. It goes along about a mile." He dropped his hand to his side. "There's a small office building at the start. Can't really see it from here. Too far."

"Wow," said Paddy. "That sounds really neat. Have you done it?"

"Sure, lots of times. I found an old harness and used it plenty. Don't tell my mom, though. She says it's not safe, that's why it closed down. Someone fell and died or something."

"Can I try sometime?" Paddy asked.

"Yeah, sure. But there's only one harness, so only one of you. I always leave it on top of the first platform so it's there for next time. So if you go, put the harness back where you found it, okay?"

"Okay!"

"It's really fast," said Chi-Chi, talking faster. "Everything goes by like a blur."

"Paddy, be serious," Lucy said. "That sounds way too dangerous. Besides, Mom and Dad would kill you if they found out you went on something like that." She pointed to the island interior, close to the base of the mountain, where the square top of a stone building peeked above the treetops. "What's that over there?"

Chi-Chi followed Lucy's gaze. "That's the temple. Like a pyramid. Built by people who lived here a long time ago."

"We heard about that," Lucy said. "I want to see it. It sounds neat."

"Not really. There's not much of it left. Just a ruin now and hard to get to."

"Oh," said Lucy. "Can we explore it anyway?"

"Why?" asked Chi-Chi. "They make us go there on school trips. There's nothing to do there. Ancient history. Come on. We'd better go. It's getting late. Need to get back through the jungle before it gets dark."

☠ ☠ ☠

When the twins got home, they found their mother in the kitchen cooking dinner. "So what did you two end up doing today?" she asked.

"Nothing much," said Paddy.

"But I think we're going to go back to the village again tomorrow," added Lucy with a grin.

THREE

Over the next several weeks, Lucy and Paddy biked to the village each day to spend time with their new friend. They'd ride through the streets until they reached the school playground, where Chi-Chi would be waiting, hopping from one foot to the other.

"How do you always know when we're coming?" Paddy asked once.

"I know what everyone's doing around here, *amigo*," Chi-Chi replied with a wink. "That's why they call me mayor of Janaconda Island. I've got eyes and ears everywhere." But that wasn't true, as the twins soon discovered.

It happened in the early afternoon, after an eventful morning at the pier. Chi-Chi had taught the twins the proper way to throw his homemade net so it didn't bunch up when it hit the water. Lucy caught a small stingray, which they tossed back and watched swim away, unharmed. Now they were sharing a bowl of guava-flavored ice in the square.

Paddy noticed first. He leaned across the table and whispered, "Don't stare, but I think that guy sitting in the corner is watching us."

Lucy casually turned her head, pretending to brush the hair from her eyes.

"That geezer with the dark shirt? You're wrong. He's just drinking something and reading the paper." As she spoke, the man brought his mug to his lips and met her gaze. Lucy quickly turned away, embarrassed at being caught.

"I keep seeing him everywhere. I think he's been following us or something."

"That's ridiculous. Why would somebody follow us?"

"I don't know," responded Paddy, "but he gives me the creeps. I think he was watching us when we moved in. Remember the old guy who got into the cab after the accident in front of our house? I think that was him." He turned to Chi-Chi. "Know who he is?"

Chi-Chi glanced over his shoulder. "Dunno. That *hombre* looks a little familiar. Think I've seen him around. Never spoken to him or nothing like that." He swallowed the last bite of their snack. "Come on, let's go," he said. "We're finished."

"Well, I still think he's been spying on us," Paddy insisted.

"And I think you're imagining things," said Lucy. "And I'm going to prove it."

"Lucy—no!" cried Paddy, but Lucy had already risen and was walking toward the old man. Paddy and Chi-Chi ran after her.

The man looked up as they approached, and Paddy noticed that his weathered face was marred by a scar across his chin and part of one ear was missing, as if it had been torn off. Sticking out from under the legs of his worn trousers were a pair of brightly-polished black steel-tipped shoes, like the kind policemen wore back home.

"Hello," Lucy said in her sweetest voice. She stuck out her hand and tried not to react to the sight of the man's disfigured ear. "My name is Lucy. What's yours?"

"You're those kids living in the Stephenson house," growled the man, not taking Lucy's hand.

"Um, no." Lucy jerked her hand back, surprised at his lack of manners. "I don't know what you're talking about."

"The old house up on the hill," said the man. "I know you're staying there. Don't deny it."

"Maybe we are, and maybe we aren't. It's just a stupid run-down house anyway."

"Run down?" The man looked surprised. "A groundskeeper trims the bushes twice a week. I'll bet it's just as well taken care of on the inside."

"Uh, sure," Lucy hedged. "It's gorgeous. Chandeliers and everything. Why do you want to know?"

The man laughed. "Academic interest. I've tried to see it for myself, but the gate's always locked, and the groundskeeper says he doesn't have permission to let me in."

Lucy was beginning to get creeped out. "What's so special about it?"

The man looked surprised. "Don't you know? That was old Thomas Stephenson's house. Built it himself, with stone imported from Scotland. That's where he spent the last forty years of his life. He even died there, in one of the upstairs bedrooms." He paused to light a cigarette.

Paddy gulped. "That's got to be the room next to your bedroom," he blurted before he could stop himself. "The one that's—"

"*Shh!*" Lucy interrupted.

"So, you *do* know what I'm talking about," continued the old man, exhaling smoke through his nose and leaning forward. "So what's it really like in there? What's in that house?"

The twins glanced at each other, not sure how to respond. Chi-Chi began to rock on his feet, getting antsy.

Breaking the momentary silence, the man added, "I'm merely curious. He was a famous man a long time ago, in a sense."

Lucy took a step back, surprised by the turn this conversation had taken. "Um, there's nothing in the house," she stammered. "Really. It's empty. We painted it, too. Bright orange, with little pink polka dots."

The man let out an empty laugh. "I've read the will," he said. "No one's allowed to paint the house or change any of the furniture, it said, until . . ." Here he paused, and the twins noticed an odd, faraway look in his eyes, as if he was trying to remember something that happened a long, long time ago.

"What is he talking about?" Paddy muttered.

"Come on, let's go," said Lucy. "He's some old kook."

That seemed to snap the man from his thoughts. He took another deep puff on his cigarette and said, "You know, a lot of strange things have happened in that house over the years."

"What sort of things?" Paddy asked.

"Weird things. Dangerous things. Some people think the place is cursed." He rolled his deformed ear between his thumb and forefinger. "Wouldn't want something to happen to you or your family."

He sent a smoke ring across the small table, pausing until it dissolved into nothingness. "I can help make sure the place is safe. Why don't you let me come by and take a look around?"

"I don't think our parents would like that," said Lucy.

The man nodded and flicked some ashes from his cigarette. "Then maybe you can describe it to me. There's probably some stuff there that you think is odd, like signs or symbols or strange paintings. Maybe something carved on the walls."

"How did you—" Paddy started to say.

"*Shh!*" Lucy said again.

The man smiled broadly, making the twins shiver, which was probably the opposite effect than intended. "Why don't you sit down and tell me about it? I can buy you each another bowl of ice. I won't bite."

"We already ate," said Lucy, backing away.

"Why would any of that stuff be unsafe?" asked Paddy.

"I won't know until I see it," began the old man, tugging on his ear again. "But it may be part of a curse, or a spell. Voodoo."

"Voodoo?" Paddy gasped.

The old man smiled and snuffed out his cigarette. "You kids know about that stuff, right? Voodoo, curses, spells. It used to be big down here in the Caribbean. From Haiti."

"Is that how that guy died? A voodoo spell?" Paddy asked.

The man shrugged. "That's what some people believe."

"And you think there's still something there? Something that could hurt us?"

The old man smiled like he knew some dark secret. "Like I said, I won't know unless I can take a look around. I can make sure the place is safe for you and your parents. You wouldn't want anything bad to happen to them, would you?" He scratched at his chin, along the white scar. "What if something bad happened and you could've done something about it?"

At that last remark, Lucy grabbed her brother by the arm. "Come on, let's go," she said. "There's no such thing as voodoo. He's only trying to scare us."

"Bah!" said the old man. "Listen, you kids find anything, no matter how small, you come back and tell me. I'll be here—and I'll keep an eye out for you in case you forget." Then he laughed, a short, staccato chuckle that burst from his chest like small explosions.

But by then the three friends had already turned and run off, and were soon out of hearing range.

FOUR

"That was nuts," Paddy said, gasping.

The three children had bolted through the streets, and this time Lucy and Paddy had no trouble keeping up with Chi-Chi's sandal-clad feet.

When they reached the playground, they collapsed on the cool grass, exhausted. "What do you think that creepy geezer meant by all that voodoo stuff?" Lucy asked. "Chi-Chi, who was that guy he mentioned—Thomas Steph—Stephenson?"

"*No se.* I don't know. That house you're staying in has been empty a really long time. He was probably talking about something that happened years ago."

"He sounded pretty serious," said Paddy. "Maybe there's still something dangerous in there."

"Don't tell me you're still thinking about that haunted mansion stuff," said Lucy, shaking her head.

"I thought you were over that. It's just a run-down house with a lot of junk in it. There's nothing to be scared of."

"I'm serious. There's definitely something strange about that house, even if you don't believe what that creepy guy said about voodoo and curses. You heard him. Someone *died* there."

"It's an old house, Paddy. Lots of people have probably died there."

"Well, whatever happened, I'll bet it's the reason no one's been living there. If that doesn't freak you out, I don't know what would."

Lucy remained silent as Paddy's words sunk in. She had to admit it seemed like he was on to something. It was definitely odd that the house had been vacant for so long, the furniture covered with dust. Maybe somehow this explained it. Sometimes his thoughts and ideas sounded crazy, but he could connect different pieces of information like a jigsaw puzzle. That was one way they were different.

"You're right, Paddy," she said at last. "It does sound like something weird is going on here. A mystery, even."

Chi-Chi scoffed. "Mystery? That's *loco*. Nothing interesting ever happens here."

"Well, *something* is going on," Paddy insisted. "That old man wanted something from us. And he was about to say more, but stopped before he got to it. Remember? He said no one can change anything in the house *until*. Until what? He didn't say. That's *definitely* a mystery."

"Should we tell Mom and Dad?" Lucy asked.

Paddy shook his head. "No. They're too busy. Besides, they won't believe us."

"You're right," said Lucy.

"We can't do nothing. We need to find out something about that Thomas Stephenson fellow. Maybe then we can figure out what that old guy wants from us. Be better prepared next time we run into him."

"Good luck with that," said Lucy. "Not even Chi-Chi has heard of him."

Chi-Chi shrugged and tossed a small rock into the bushes.

Paddy snorted. "If someone died from voodoo or something bizarre like that, it probably would've been in the newspaper. It's a small island, right?"

Lucy shot a look at Chi-Chi.

"Yeah, there's a newspaper. Only about ten pages long. Printed once a week. Not surprised you haven't seen it."

"Was there a paper fifty years ago?" asked Lucy.

"Sure. One is hanging on the wall of my house, from when my grandparents got married. They put stuff like that on the front page back then."

"See?" said Paddy, gaining momentum. "Libraries usually keep copies of old newspapers around. There's *got* to be a library on this island somewhere."

"Of course there's a library," said Chi-Chi, sounding impatient. "They've got tons of books. Don't like to go there, though—reminds me of school."

"Is it close?" Lucy asked.

"Everything is close here," Chi-Chi said with a laugh.

"Well . . . can we go now?" Lucy pressed.

"Yeah, I guess. Come on."

Chi-Chi led the twins down a few narrow streets, past rows of brightly painted shops, until he stopped in front of a one-story, peach-colored concrete building splotched with dark mildew stains. A wooden sign affixed to the wall identified it as the Janaconda Public Library, established in 1927. The 'J' was partially scratched out.

"Here it is," said Chi-Chi. "Have fun."

"You're not coming in?" Lucy asked.

"Nah," he said. "Got better things to do. See you tomorrow." He waved and ran down the street, as if he was in a hurry to get somewhere.

"Well, I guess it's just us then," said Lucy, pushing open the door. "Watch the time—Mom and Dad will be furious if we're not home for dinner."

They let the door close behind them, but before it latched shut a small brown monkey ran through the narrow opening, past the twins, and scampered down an aisle of books.

"Oh! Not again!" A woman in high heels teetered past in pursuit of the creature, who was now hooting loudly. "That one is such a nuisance!"

As the twins stood near the door not knowing what to do, they heard a series of bumps, some loud screeches, and then the monkey ran toward them, still being chased by the woman. The monkey jumped and grabbed onto Paddy's arm. Paddy shrieked as the monkey climbed up to his shoulder, where it sat hissing.

"What do I do?" said Paddy, standing stiff with his arms at his sides.

"Take it outside," the woman said, waving her hand like she was shooing away flies. "It will run off."

As Lucy held open the door, Paddy slowly exited the library while keeping his upper body as still as possible, worried the monkey might bite him. But when he got outside, the monkey refused to leave its perch near Paddy's neck.

"And you thought you'd have trouble making friends here," said Lucy, giggling.

"Very funny. Go," he said, then louder. "Go!"

The monkey chattered its teeth but still refused to move. Then a man walked around the corner carrying a bag of fruit. The monkey immediately hopped down and scampered off after him.

The twins reentered the library, making extra sure to latch the door shut behind them this time. As they walked inside, they were approached by the same woman as before.

"*Gracias!* Thank you for removing that horrible creature! He is nothing but a nuisance. I do not understand why he always insists on coming in the library, but I cannot seem to get rid of him."

"I think I know why," muttered Paddy, getting a whiff of the woman's strong fruit-scented perfume.

"Yes? Tell me the reason?"

Lucy elbowed Paddy in the ribs as he said, "Maybe he likes to read."

"I didn't know the island had monkeys," Lucy said quickly, changing the subject.

"Many years ago, a man brought several monkeys from the mainland. To be a tourist attraction at his hotel. But they escaped when their enclosure was destroyed during a bad storm. Now they are a plague on our island. Most live in the jungle, but that one— that one stays in the streets."

She straightened her blouse. "Now," she said, "may I assist you in some way? I am the librarian." She fussed with her hair, which had fallen out of place while chasing after the monkey.

"We're only here to look around," Lucy replied. "We're visiting from Maryland."

The librarian smiled. "It is always refreshing to have visitors. Here, I have something for you. As a reward for your assistance with that—that creature." Moving behind her small wooden desk, she reached into a drawer and took out a folded piece of paper. "Take it," she said. "Do not be shy."

At Lucy's urging, Paddy stepped forward and accepted it. The words 'Janaconda Island—Your Path to Paradise' were scripted across the front flap among pictures of people sailing and fishing in the sea, and of a hotel compound set in the middle of the jungle. It must be a very old brochure, Paddy thought.

"It is a map," the librarian said. "A map of the entire island. It will help you get around during your visit, so you do not get lost. Keep it with you. All the roads, important buildings, and tourist attractions are marked."

"Uh, thanks," replied Paddy. Chi-Chi had already shown them how to navigate through the streets, and he was always available as their guide if they needed one. But he politely took the map from the librarian anyway and stuffed it into his back pocket.

"You are very welcome," she answered. "Enjoy yourselves, and let me know if you need anything." She turned to the pile of papers on her desk and began to rifle through them as she hummed a melody in an off-key pitch.

"Come on," whispered Lucy. "We don't have much time."

"Why don't we ask her for help?" Paddy whispered back.

"No," said Lucy. "For all we know, she might be friends with the geezer from the square. Maybe she'll spy on us for him. We can't tell *anyone* what we're looking for. We've got to do this by ourselves."

Paddy reluctantly agreed, and so the twins began to wander through the library in search of old newspapers or other local historical documents. They crossed through the aisles, glancing at the shelves, until Lucy discovered a machine with a large screen tucked away near the reference section.

"Wow—it's a microfilm reader," she said. "This is really modern. We don't even have one at school. I wonder how they were able to get one here."

"Do you know how to use it?"

"I think so. We saw some at the Library of Congress during our class trip earlier in the year. Don't you remember?"

"I must not have been paying attention."

"Just need to find the filmstrips." She ran her fingers across the side of a nearby cabinet before resting her hand on one of the many small bronze handles. "Janaconda Island Gazette, 1893-1948," she read off the label. "This has to be it."

She pulled on the narrow drawer, exposing a collection of several dozen filmstrip canisters, each with a year printed on its lid. She picked one at random. "Well, we have to start somewhere."

"I don't know about this," said Paddy, eying the microfilm reader. "It looks awfully complicated."

"Don't worry all the time," she said. "How hard can it be?" She flipped a switch, causing the screen to light up. "I think the film gets fed through here."

"And those big knobs?"

"One must be to advance the filmstrip, and the other to focus. Simple."

"I think I have just the thing for you," said the librarian from directly behind them, causing the twins to flinch with surprise. She motioned with a thick finger before tottering off on her high heels. "Come with me."

"She must've been watching us fiddling with the machine," whispered Lucy, "and is trying to stop us. She's probably afraid we'll break something."

"She's probably right," Paddy whispered back.

Lucy sighed. "Go see what she wants. I'll start going through the rolls."

Paddy accompanied the librarian to the front of the room while Lucy popped open the first container and pushed the film roll on the spool to begin feeding it through the narrow slit. As they approached her desk, the librarian said, "I notice you located our microfilm reader. I am proud to say it is the only one among the islands."

"We're just—we're interested in learning about your history, and thought we'd look at some old newspapers, that's all. Why do you even have one, anyway?"

"It was a gift from an anonymous donor after the war. We are very lucky." She smiled. "But if you wish to learn about our homeland, perhaps this book would interest you." She pulled a thick volume from a nearby shelf. "This volume describes the history of Janaconda Island, from the very beginning. For instance, this land was created when a great volcano erupted tens of thousands of years ago." She flipped through the pages to an illustration of what the eruption must have looked like. "Interesting, yes?"

Paddy eyed the thick book. "Thanks, but I really don't think we have the time to read something like that."

The librarian made a clicking sound with her tongue. "Not exciting enough for you? Well, well. I will bet you do not know that pirates sailed these waters during the eighteenth and early nineteenth centuries. Famous pirates, too. You can read about them in chapter six."

"Oh?" said Paddy, perking up. Now *that* sounded interesting—at least more interesting than looking through old newspapers. He glanced in Lucy's direction, and heard the faint whir of the microfilm reader. She must've figured out how to use it.

"Yes," the librarian continued. "Pirates had much to do with the history of this island. For many years, the cove near the marina was one of the few ports in the region safe from pirate ships. Matter of fact, this town was originally established as a safe place to trade and sell goods. That was more than a hundred years ago. There are artifacts from that period in the town museum."

"That's neat. Why didn't the pirates come into the harbor?"

Her face opened in a toothy smile. "Not far offshore the water is shallow and peppered with sharp reefs, like the teeth of a serpent. Many ships have gotten stuck there over the years and sank. Today there are maps showing how to navigate the maze of reefs, but back then the way through was a secret among merchants."

The librarian continued to leaf through the book, stopping on a page brightly illustrated with a double-masted wooden ship flying a black flag.

"Ah, here it is," she said, thrusting the book into Paddy's hands. "Lots of information about pirates here."

Paddy scanned the page with growing interest, then flipped through the rest of the chapter. He paused at a drawing of a stern-looking man with a hawk nose and a ponytail, which vaguely reminded him of the person in the old photo he had found in the hutch. "Who's that?"

The librarian glanced down. "That is one of the minor pirates from the nineteenth century, one of the very last. His name was Jean-Pierre Le Moyne." She scanned the passage and shook her head. "Sometimes I wonder why he is mentioned at all. I often suspect this book was written more to promote tourism than as a serious work."

Perhaps it was the dark eyes, or the luxurious deep blue coat he wore, but Paddy was fascinated by the portrait staring back at him. "What does he have to do with the island?"

She sighed. "Some folks believe he spent the latter part of his life here. In fact, there used to be an exhibit on him at the museum, until thieves stole part of it a few weeks ago. Silly, really, when you think about it. Why would a pirate captain come here of all places? To Janaconda Island, to live in secret under a fake name? There has never been any proof. It is just a local myth that people like to repeat. That poor old man, Thomas Stephenson, probably spread the stories himself just to get some attention. People do things like that all the time."

Paddy nearly dropped the book at the name. "What?" he said. "Who?" Then he collected his composure and said, "Thank you; I think I'd like this book after all."

She shook her head. "I cannot believe you are interested in that crazy story. Oh, well. But it is a reference book and must remain in the library. However, you may sit at one of the tables and read it for as long as you like."

Paddy nodded and carried the book to one of the empty tables. His hands trembled as he turned to the chapter on pirates and began to read:

Long after the Caribbean's so-called "Golden Age of Piracy" during the late 17th and early 18th centuries, pirates continued to plague the waters around Janaconda Island. The last of these was Jean-Pierre Le Moyne (1821 - ?), more commonly known as "Bully Blue-Coat" for the long velvet blue jacket he often wore during attacks on merchant vessels from his ship, the Miner's Revenge . . .

FIVE

“Here you are,” Lucy said as she approached Paddy's table. “I've been waiting for you to come back for twenty minutes.”

Paddy looked up from the history book. “Sorry. You won't believe what—”

“It doesn't matter,” she interrupted. She pulled out the chair next to him and eased into it with a sigh. “It's hopeless. Half the microfilm canisters are empty, and some of the filmstrips are torn and won't feed through the machine. What's that you're looking at?”

Before Paddy could respond, she grabbed the book, flipped it around, and skimmed through the first few paragraphs of the open page. “You're reading about pirates? Really? I'm working hard, and this is what you're doing?”

"It's him," Paddy whispered. "Thomas Stephenson."

"What are you talking about?"

He flipped to the page with the portrait. "His real name was Jean-Pierre Le Moyne. He was a pirate captain."

"Oh, come on. You're saying that we're staying where a pirate used to live? That's crazy."

"Not just any pirate, a great one. Everyone was scared of him."

"All pirates were thieves and murderers. That doesn't make him great. Just mean."

"Successful, then."

Lucy twirled her hair as the librarian started humming again from across the room. "Was he killed in our house? Is that the big mystery everyone's afraid of?"

"It's more amazing that that. The book says he mostly targeted merchant ships, until he decided to go after a ship carrying gold to Spain from Venezuela. Not just any shipment, either. A ton."

Lucy's eyes widened. "A *ton*? Isn't that a lot?"

"Yeah. They think it was the largest haul ever stolen by pirates up to that point. He got away with it, too, but it was a mistake. He shouldn't have done it. Until then, he was just a nuisance and no one really paid attention to him, but suddenly he became the most wanted pirate in the Caribbean. The British navy chased after him for almost a year."

"Then what? Was he caught?"

"Well, no one knows for sure. Some people think his ship was sunk by the British, or he was captured and was either hanged or spent the rest of his life in prison. But this book has a different theory, and it's why he's included in a crummy book about the island's history."

"Let me guess." She licked her dry lips. "The British never caught him, and he lived the rest of his life on Janaconda Island under a fake name. Is that it?"

Paddy nodded. "Thomas Stephenson."

"But there's no proof?"

"No. In fact, the librarian doesn't think they were the same guy. She thinks Stephenson lied to get attention. But I think it's true. I found a photograph in a drawer of an old man that looks like the portrait in this book."

"Wow," said Lucy. "That's some story. To think that horrible pirate could have lived in our house!"

"Pretty wild, huh?"

"Yeah. Does the book say what happened to the treasure?"

"That's the second mystery. No one knows. It's never been found. Some people think his ship hit the reef and sank."

"So the gold could be in the water offshore?"

"If he didn't carry it off his ship first. Listen to this." He turned to the last page in the chapter and read the final paragraph:

There have been numerous claims over the years that Le Moyne did in fact escape the British Navy and lived out his remaining years on Janaconda Island under the fictitious name of Thomas Stephenson; and that he hid his treasure there, leaving obscure clues to its whereabouts. Even his grave is believed to hold a clue to its location. To this day, treasure hunters continue to search for the Venezuelan gold. In 1916, a man named M. Chittenden approached the Janaconda Island Historical Society with what he claimed was Le Moyne's journal written during the latter years of his life. Some believe that the journal contains the location of the lost treasure, although others contend it is a forgery and of marginal historical importance. The journal remains on display at the Janaconda Island Museum. This continues to be one of the most fascinating and enduring mysteries in the history of Janaconda Island.

Lucy's eyes widened. "The geezer from the square must also think Thomas Stephenson and the pirate captain were the same person, and that he stashed the gold somewhere in his house."

"*Our* house," corrected Paddy.

"Fine, *our* house. That's got to be what he wants. The treasure!"

"Or a clue to where to find it."

"Of course! That's got to be why no one is allowed to paint or change the inside of the house. There must be clues leading to the treasure!"

"Unless Thomas Stephenson was just a crazy nut looking for attention."

"I don't believe that. I don't think he was crazy, just smart. Very, very smart. He was smart to avoid being captured, and he was smart enough to live here undetected. The question is whether we're as smart as he was."

"What do you mean?" asked Paddy.

"There's only one thing to do. We will have to find the treasure ourselves."

Paddy shook his head. "People have been looking for it forever, Lucy! How will we find it?"

"You're forgetting two things," she said. "Number one, we're the first people to live in his house since he died. If there are clues no one has ever seen, maybe we can find them and figure them out."

"What's the second thing?"

"What else are we going to do for the rest of the summer?"

SIX

C aptain Jean-Pierre Le Moyne watched from the deck of the *Miner's Revenge* as a thick plume of black smoke rose from the burning merchant ship less than a half-mile away. He felt a rush of satisfaction. Everything had gone perfectly once the lookout stationed high in the rigging had spied the beat-up old sloop sailing along the horizon. After that, it was only a matter of time. The *St. Augustine* was no match for Le Moyne's streamlined schooner; the pirate ship was built for speed, and in a few hours the *Miner's Revenge* overtook the smaller boat, fired a couple of warning shots across its bow, and rammed it broadside. Then it was easy, ridiculously easy. His men jumped aboard from the nets strung from the masts, firing their pistols into the air.

At first the crew of the *St. Augustine* tried to fight back, clawing with their hands and swinging pipes and wood planks and whatever else they could find littered across the deck. It was always like that. But once the sailors saw the tall man pacing along the deck in his infamous long blue coat, all the fight went out of them. It was always like that, too. With their hands lashed behind their backs, the captured sailors were dragged across a wooden beam that was temporarily secured between the vessels.

Then it was time for the usual theatrics. Two large pigs were brought onto the deck where they were slaughtered and sliced into chunks, the blood pooling on the rotted planks. Le Moyne grabbed the nearest hunk of meat and tossed it overboard into the swirling water. Within minutes the smell of flesh and blood attracted half a dozen hungry sharks, which quickly devoured the free meal and continued circling the boat for more handouts. That got the *St. Augustine*'s crew positively quaking. They swore their allegiance to Captain Le Moyne; they promised to do anything for him, *anything*, so long as he didn't throw them into the water, too. Things had played out this way a dozen times, more, always with the same ending. After a few months of service, he'd let the sailors off on some island, each with a bag of gold coins. From there, they'd be able to return to their homes and families, wherever they might be. Other than his closest officers, the rest of his crew was exclusively comprised of such temporary help. *Familiarity breeds mutiny*, he thought grimly.

Now the goods—cotton and coffee beans—were stowed safely aboard the *Miner's Revenge*, where they would be brought back to Haiti for trade. The *St. Augustine* had been set aflame, filling the air with the pungent smell of coffee and burning wood.

Jean-Pierre Le Moyne paced the deck, basking in the aftermath of a day gone right. None of his men were injured, and his ship had not incurred any damage. That's what you get, he mused, when you choose your targets carefully. These poor sailors were underpaid and treated worse; why would they risk their lives for cargo that didn't belong to them? He listened to the rhythm of the ropes slapping against the masts as the sun began its descent toward the horizon.

He stopped and peered over the water. What was that tiny shape way off in the distance? There was nothing there a few minutes earlier. He frowned and reached for the telescope that he kept in his inside coat pocket. Approaching quickly from beyond the burning sloop was a frigate, its many sails unfurled in the growing wind. They must've seen the burning vessel and were coming to investigate. *Maybe I shouldn't have set the ship on fire after all*, he thought. He looked through the telescope one more time, and made out the British flag flying from atop the middle of the frigate's three masts.

"Shall we raise the sails?" It was Jack O'Brian, the second mate. "We can still outrun her."

"No," said Le Moyne, shaking his head. "They'll be on top of us before we can hoist the sails. Besides, we've got nothing to fear from the British; we've never attacked an English ship." That was intentional. *If we don't bother them, they won't bother us*, the strategy went, and so far it had worked. Live and let live. "As far as they know, we're a simple fishing boat that came to the aid of this poor burning sloop. Toss out some nets, and we'll wait for them to arrive."

It was a decision he would soon regret.

SEVEN

"All right," Lucy said the next morning. "Let's take this one step at a time."

The twins were sitting on Lucy's bedroom floor with their backs against the wall, ready to begin searching for clues to the location of the treasure, but unsure how to go about it.

"Let's ask Chi-Chi to help," Paddy remarked. "He knows the island better than anyone. Maybe the clues will make more sense to him."

Lucy shrugged. "He doesn't seem interested. He wouldn't even go into the library with us. Besides, it's our house. We have to do this ourselves. We can always ask him for help later if we need it."

"Okay. So how should we do this?"

Lucy cleared her throat. "We need to approach this like real detectives if we're going to figure out where the gold is hidden. They always have a casebook with them to write down notes that might help later. We should do the same thing." She picked up the notebook that was on the floor next to her and held it up. "I brought this from home to use as a diary of our trip, but this is a better use for it." She tore out the first few pages, which contained some writing and ink drawings and balled them up. "I'll write down everything we discover, no matter how unimportant it seems. Then we will have all the clues together in one place to analyze later. We don't know how much we might find. There may be clues everywhere."

"That makes sense."

She opened the notebook to the first remaining page and began to write. "Thomas Stephenson," she said as her pen moved across the paper. "Is that with an 'e' or an 'o'?"

"Two 'e's and one 'o', I think."

"I will just write T.S. for short. It's easier that way. Besides, if someone finds our notebook, they won't be able to figure out what we know. That's what real detectives do."

Paddy nodded in agreement. "You know," he said, "I sort of feel sorry for him."

"The pirate? Why would you feel sorry for him? He was a thief who got rich stealing from others and killed people just for fun. You should feel sorry for all the people he robbed and terrorized instead."

"It's just that I can't imagine what it must be like to live out your life in secret. He was probably afraid to leave the island."

"He deserved it. He was probably cruel to everyone he met."

"You don't know that."

"All pirates were cruel."

"Still," Paddy said, "it's weird to think he sat in this very room." He stretched out his legs. "What do you have so far?"

"Let's see . . . we know that T.S. lived on the island for the last forty years of his life. The creepy man in the square told us that." She began to write.

"In this very *house* for forty years," added Paddy. "That old man said he built it himself with stone from Ireland or somewhere like that."

"Scotland. I wonder why he went to all that trouble. Must've cost a fortune."

"This place is built like a fortress. Maybe he wanted to be safe if there was ever a hurricane." He watched his sister write in the notebook. "Or maybe he was worried something would be stolen. Something precious that he wanted to protect."

Lucy put down her pen. "If the treasure was ever here in this house, it was probably moved somewhere else long ago. The question is where. And for that, we'll need to find those clues he left behind."

Paddy nodded. "Okay. So, where should we start? That old man said there might be symbols carved in the walls. Should we search each room?"

"Before doing that, let's make sure we've considered everything we know so far."

"What do you mean? We don't know anything yet."

"For one thing, that history book in the library said his journal was on display in the town museum. Maybe it says what he did with the gold. I wonder if we're allowed to read it."

"It's probably a forgery," Paddy answered. "Besides, the librarian told me part of the exhibit had been stolen. I'll bet that's what was taken. But the book also said there might be a clue at his grave."

"Do you want to look there first? We can search the house another time."

"Fine with me."

Lucy nodded. "Okay. There's got to be a town cemetery somewhere. Shouldn't take too long to find it."

"Not if we use this," said Paddy, reaching into his pocket to remove the brochure the librarian had given him. Lucy snatched it away and unfolded it. One side showed the entire island, with major attractions identified, while the other side provided a detailed street map of Santa Elena. Lucy flipped it so the town view faced up and spread it across the floor.

"There," she said, pointing. "It's on the edge of town, next to a church. Come on, let's go."

Paddy grabbed the map and the twins rushed down the stairs, only to be stopped by the sound of their mother's voice. "Where are the two of you going in such a hurry?"

"Uh . . . nowhere special," said Lucy, as her brother elbowed her in the ribs.

"We're going down to the harbor to see the fishing boats," Paddy said, hoping the story would stick. Often his cheeks turned red whenever he lied, but maybe she wouldn't notice.

"Well, come in the kitchen first, and I'll pack you a snack."

The twins obliged and discovered their parents bent over the oval table, studying a large sheet of paper covered with lines, circles, and numbers.

"Aren't you going to the lab?" Lucy asked.

"It's Saturday," their mother answered. "The lab's closed, at least until we get our own key."

"But that won't stop us from working at home," said their father, straightening up.

Lucy leaned forward. "What are you looking at?"

"It's a map," said their father.

"Neat," answered Lucy. "Where's our house?"

"It's not a map of the island, dear," replied their mother. "It's a map of the ocean floor. The numbers show the water depth. Marine scientists use maps like this to identify where different fish and plants might live."

"Haven't you found that fish yet?" Paddy asked.

"Not yet," answered their father. "We've gone out in the research boat several times over the past few weeks, but haven't had any luck. I'm beginning to think this whole trip was a waste of time."

"Well—we can't leave yet!" exclaimed Lucy.

"Oh, are you finally enjoying yourself?" asked their mother, smiling. "Don't worry, we aren't giving up. Sometimes it takes a long time for scientists to find something, and we've still got the rest of the summer. Part of the problem is that your father knows almost nothing about that fish, such as whether it lives in deep or shallow water, or whether it hides in nooks along the reef. If we knew that, it would be much easier to plan the search."

"Maybe you should ask the fisherman who caught the first one," suggested Lucy.

Their father sighed. "That's another problem," he said. "No one seems to know who he was."

"Well, I'm sure you'll find one," said Lucy. "You're a great scientist. And with Mom helping, you can't fail."

"Thanks, Lucy," said their mother. "Here you go." She gave each of them a bag along with a canteen filled with water. "Remember, stay safe. And don't stay out too long. Paddy, your face is looking flushed, and I don't want you to come down with something."

Nearly three hours later, the twins sat on the grass of the cemetery, resting their aching legs.

"Argh," grumbled Lucy. She wiped the sweat from her face. "We've gone down every row at least four times and still haven't found his grave. This is so annoying."

"Let's try over there again," said Paddy, pointing toward the oldest section, which held graves dating back over a hundred years.

"It's no use," said Lucy, her voice cracking with exhaustion and frustration. "Maybe the grave is unmarked."

"It's not unmarked," countered Paddy. "The book said there was a clue there. That means it's definitely marked."

"Then you find it." She crossed her arms. "I'm not moving."

"Fine, I will. But my way." Paddy rose and marched off toward a small brick office building near the entrance. Opening the door, he discovered an old man sitting behind a desk, reading a magazine.

The man looked up. "Can I help you?" he asked, sounding annoyed.

"Yes," said Paddy, taking a deep breath. "I hope so. I'm interested in pirates and I heard a famous one was buried here somewhere."

"Ah, you mean old Bully," said the man, putting down his magazine.

"Yes, that's him. I'm having trouble finding his grave. Do you know where it is?"

The man grimaced. "He's buried on the island all right—but jus' like I told your pop and his buddy, you won't find him here."

"What?" Paddy jerked his head back with surprise. "I'm pretty sure my dad hasn't been here."

"You sure?" said the man behind the desk. "A tall guy, skinny as a string bean, came in here a few days ago with a friend and asked me the very same question. Was American and had dark hair, like you. I told him where the burial site is. He didn't send you back here when he couldn't find it?"

"No, my pop's kind of pudgy. I'm just here with my sister. Honest. Why isn't he in the cemetery?"

"Well, there's a funny story 'bout that. You gotta understand that people don't think too highly of pirates, not even if he's their neighbor. Oh, Bully kept to himself and didn't cause any trouble. But even so, the church wouldn't give him a plot 'cause of all the bad things he'd done previously. Told him he'd have to make other arrangements for when he died."

"So what happened?"

"Well, old Bully had no choice in the matter. He didn't want to be buried at sea, you know, the way most pirates are. He said he had put his piratin' life behind him and wanted to be treated like a regular fellow. So he bought a piece of land a few miles out of town to be buried on when his time came. Funny thing was that he was mighty stubborn about that specific location, and he paid a pretty penny for it, let me tell you."

"How do you know all that?"

"Just so happened that he purchased that land from my very own father," said the man. "I was only a boy at the time, but my pop told me all about it. And, oh yes, I see that look on your face. There's no question Tom Stephenson was Bully Blue-Coat. He told stories that would chill your skin, accordin' to my daddy—he was the real deal, all right. Anyway, my pop didn't want to sell the property—he was plannin' to start a banana farm out there, he told me—but old Bully wouldn't take no for an answer. He kept offerin' more and more money, as if he'd already decided to be buried there. Strange, given how far out it is. Middle of nowhere.

Eventually my daddy took the money and sold. If I had a map, I could show you where it is."

"I've got one." Paddy pulled out the tourist brochure and handed it to the man, who unfolded it across his desk, flipping it over to the full island view.

"Let me see . . .," he began. "It's right around . . . oh, look at that. It's already marked."

"Huh?"

"See?" said the man. "There's a little brown number '6', and if you read the legend at the bottom, it says it's the final resting place of Thomas Stephenson." He pointed to a spot northwest of the center of town, where the coast of the island began to curl. It was located directly west of the old tourist hotel they had seen from the mountaintop, which was marked with a small cartoonish image of a building. "You always have to read maps carefully, son. They're more than lines and colors. There's a lot of hidden information buried inside 'em."

"Uh, thanks," said Paddy, embarrassed at not having seen the legend himself.

He took the map from the man and headed out. After leaving the office, he found Lucy still sitting in the same spot where he'd left her.

"Did you find the right grave?" she groaned. "What did it say?"

"Yeah, I found it. We're in the wrong place. Get up. We've got some more riding to do."

☠   ☠   ☠

The grave rested on a small knoll in the middle of a field, a beautiful, peaceful spot and not at all the sort of place where one would expect a ruthless pirate to be buried. The twins left their bikes near the bottom of a short flight of stone stairs, and, their excitement growing, climbed to the top of the hill. The peak of Mt. Alta Vista loomed over them to the northeast. In the other direction, they could see over the treetops all the way to the sea, which heaved and swirled under the darkening rain clouds.

"Look," said Paddy, pointing. "It's that kooky-looking yellow boat with the curvy blue stripe. That's not where it was before. I wonder what it's doing out there."

"They're probably vacationers, like us," guessed Lucy. "Anyway, I don't like those clouds. Let's take a quick look before it starts to rain and get out of here."

Together the twins approached the grave as a bolt of lightning flashed in the distance, followed by a roll of thunder. The slab of gray marble faced the sea and was ringed by a thick hedge, a humble monument to a man possibly once feared by thousands—even tens of thousands, perhaps. Etched across its face was a lengthy inscription:

"Wow," said Paddy after he had finished reading the verse. "If you didn't already know he was a famous pirate, you wouldn't figure it out just from his gravestone. I guess the lion refers to him, but I don't understand the rest of it. Why would someone say their own heart is cold as stone? And those symbols—three stars and four moons. What do you think it all means?"

"I think," said Lucy, furiously copying the poem and symbols into her notebook as the first raindrops began to fall, "I think it means we have our very first clue."

EIGHT

T he rain was short-lived, and by late afternoon the clouds had cleared. The good weather lasted two days. Tuesday morning, though, the twins awoke to a steady downpour pounding the roof with a raucous *rat-a-tat* that echoed through the house like a thousand drummers. Dark gray clouds stretched across the sky, suggesting the nasty weather would last at least half the day. With nothing else to do—and no excuses—the twins agreed this was a good time to begin searching the house itself for clues. They convened in Lucy's room to discuss how to proceed.

"Let's move all the furniture and bang on the floorboards," Paddy suggested. "I'll bet there's a trapdoor. That's where I'd hide a big treasure, if I had one."

"Trapdoor? Be serious."

"I *am* being serious. This house is awfully weird, when you get right down to it."

"It's just old, Paddy. Old and filled with junk. The treasure probably isn't even here, just some clues where it was stashed. I once read a book where a note was taped to the bottom of a drawer. There could be a clue hidden anywhere. That's what we're more likely to find, not the gold."

"So how do you think we should go about it?"

"We need to be organized or we might miss something important. Let's look through each room as carefully as we can. Then, when we're finished, we'll move to the next one. You can search for the clues, and I'll make sure you don't miss any spots and jot down whatever you find in my notebook. Okay?"

"That sounds like I'll be doing all the work," Paddy complained.

Lucy frowned. "Directing the search and taking notes is hard work. But if you prefer, when we get to the next room we can switch jobs. Personally," she added under her breath, "I'd rather do the looking, so I can take all the credit if we find anything."

"On second thought, you can do all the writing," said Paddy. "It's probably better if all the notes are in the same handwriting."

She resisted a smile. "If you insist. Are you ready now?"

"As ready as ever." He took a deep breath. "Let's start by looking inside the dressers and cabinets. Then when we're done, we can move them away from the wall to check behind them."

Lucy frowned. "We promised not to rearrange anything."

"Oh, don't be a twit."

"Don't call me a twit!"

"You deserve it. I'll put everything back where we found it, okay? Don't be afraid of breaking the rules all the time. No one will ever know."

She sighed. "I guess so."

So Paddy opened the drawers, seeking hidden compartments and false bottoms; studied the wallpaper for coded messages in the floral pattern; felt for cracks in the walls for secret panels; rummaged through the closet; and examined the floor for loose boards where a key or compartment might be concealed. He dragged the dressers to the center of the room to search behind them. He slid under the bedframe, emerging a minute later with dust balls stuck in his hair.

"Well, I guess that was a waste of time," he said when finished, plopping down on the mattress. He glanced at the notebook and saw his sister had written 'Lucy's Room' at the top of the page. The rest of the page was completely blank.

"I can see now that it's just as much work to write everything down," he said sarcastically.

As Paddy watched, Lucy wrote, 'Paddy examined everything.' She underlined the sentence twice, then added, 'No clues of note were discovered.'

"Well then," she said, "are you ready to do the next room?"

Grumbling, Paddy stood and walked into the hall.

"Aren't you forgetting something?" Lucy called after him, pointing at her furniture. "This all has to go back where it came from."

Paddy turned and tensed his jaw. "Lucy, I—," he started to reply, and then stopped. "We forgot about that weird engraved tile over your door," he said, gesturing above the doorframe. "It's got a picture of the wind and the word 'east' printed on it. That could be a clue, right?"

"It's only some stupid decoration," she said, entering the hall. She looked up to study the tile as Paddy slipped behind her. "But I should probably write it down anyway, to be safe." She turned toward her bedroom and glanced inside. "Hey—where's my notebook?"

"I'll write it down," Paddy said, emerging through the doorway. He held up the notebook as he brushed past her. "You move the furniture back. I'll be waiting in my room when you're ready to continue."

☠   ☠   ☠

In Paddy's room they uncovered some silver coins, a book on insects, and an old shirt hanging in the closet, which they guessed must belong to the groundskeeper. Some excitement occurred when Paddy noticed a series of brown spots on one of the walls, but Lucy quickly informed him it was caused by mold and wasn't a coded message.

Their search of the empty room next to Paddy's bedroom also proved fruitless, so the twins next tackled their parents' room, which had more furniture than the others. This too yielded nothing of value, and as they moved everything back into its original place, their talk turned to the strange poem on Thomas Stephenson's gravestone.

"It's not much of a clue," said Paddy as he dragged a cabinet across the floor. "I'm starting to understand why no one has ever found this treasure."

"Didn't pirates often leave treasure maps behind?" Lucy asked. "You know, 'X' marks the spot, and all that."

"That's only in the movies. But if I happen to find a map with the letter 'X' written somewhere on it, I'll let you know."

"Any letter on a treasure map would probably work just as well."

"Funny."

"We're down to the final bedroom," said Lucy, walking into the hall. She tried to turn the knob before remembering the door was locked from the inside. "Now what?"

Paddy nudged her aside and tried to peer through the keyhole. "I wish we had the key."

"Maybe it's above the door. That's where Mom and Dad keep them in our house."

He looked up at the doorframe and jumped, swiping his fingers along the top of the molding and sending bits of dust floating down onto their heads.

"Nope," he said, coughing. "Nothing there. Maybe we could pry the lock open with a screwdriver or something."

"Too risky. We could break it."

Paddy sighed, frustrated. "That's the only locked door in the whole house. There must be something in there no one is supposed to see. We've got to get in somehow."

Lucy rolled her lower lip between her teeth. "How do you propose we do that?"

"I don't know, and I can't think any more. We've been inside this smelly old house all day. My head hurts."

"Let's take a break," Lucy suggested. "It looks like the rain stopped, and the market is open for a couple more hours."

☠   ☠   ☠

The Outdoor Market was held twice a week, on Tuesdays and Thursdays, in a small field near a pavilion. Chi-Chi had brought them here the previous week to buy fresh vegetables for his family, but it was more than a food market: there were stalls where crafts and artwork were sold, along with trinkets and souvenirs for the few visiting tourists. The three of them had spent over an hour running between the aisles, people-watching, and just hanging out. The twins loved the multitude of smells that bombarded their senses, the sounds of customers negotiating prices, the striking colors of the rugs and clothes for sale. Everything was so different from the markets back home in Maryland. It made them feel like they had really traveled someplace far away.

Paddy was removing a guava from a bag of mixed fruit he'd bought when a brown blur rushed toward him. Before he realized what was happening, he felt the fruit wrenched from his hand.

"That crazy monkey!" he exclaimed, watching it weave through the crowd.

"He really likes you," Lucy laughed as the monkey paused to chatter in their direction.

"I don't care. I'm getting my fruit back."

He started off, but after taking a few steps someone ran into him for the second time since arriving on the island. This time Paddy managed to stay on his feet, but the rest of the bag's contents spilled all over the dirt.

Paddy looked up with a sharp glare, ready to launch into a tirade, but immediately swallowed his words—for standing in front of him was the old man with the torn ear. From this close distance he appeared strong and imposing. Intimidating.

But instead of becoming angry, the man smiled at Paddy like they were good friends. "If it isn't my pal from the town square," he said, his keys jingling from his waist. "Sorry about your fruit. Let me buy you some more."

Paddy backed away, shaking his head, trying not to stare at the old man's deformity. "No—that's all right."

"You sure? I can get you another bag. We can sit somewhere and enjoy it together. It'll give us a chance to talk some. If I recall, you promised to tell me about anything interesting you discovered in that old house. What do y'say?"

By now Lucy had run up. "No," she answered. "We haven't found any clues to the pirate treasure. Why don't you leave us alone?"

The old man smiled. "Not so loud, not so loud." His eyes darted around, easily, as if he was used to being watched. Then he nodded. "So you know about the treasure. I should've figured some smart kids like you would learn about it. It's no secret. People have been looking for it for decades. Why should you be any different?"

"Except we're going to find it first," said Lucy, lifting her chin.

"Good for you, good for you. Nothing wrong with a little friendly competition, is there?" He laughed, but somehow it didn't make the twins want to laugh along with him.

"I don't suppose you're interested in sharing any information, are you?" the old man pressed. "We could work together. I could help make sense of anything you find in the house. Things you might not understand yourselves."

"Never," said Paddy. "We'd never share anything with a dangerous man like you."

"Dangerous?" The corners of his mouth angled down in a frown. "I'm not dangerous—at least, not like those two." He pointed toward one of the covered stalls, where two men were in the process of stealing some round fruit. The taller one was lean and angular, a stark difference from his partner, who had broad shoulders and thick arms. From their clothes and manners, it was obvious they didn't belong. They pushed past the owner of the stall and headed through the market while the merchant shouted after them in Spanish.

"Who are they?" Paddy whispered.

"Dangerous men. That's all you need to know." He turned back toward the twins and leaned down so he could talk without anyone overhearing. "Listen to me. I know you don't trust me, and that's okay by me. But believe me about this. Stay away from those two men. They're nothing but trouble—big trouble. They'll hurt you and take what they want. This isn't a game to them. If they're following you or harassing you, you come and find me. You hear?"

The twins nodded in silence, taken aback by what they'd seen and the old man's warning.

"Okay, then." The man smiled again, as if nothing had happened. "Now that we're all buddies here, let me give you kids a free tip. I've been searching for that treasure for quite a while, and I've learned some things about the way the old pirate's mind worked. If there are clues in that house of yours, they're not going to be obvious. No, not by a long shot. I'm sure of that. So you're gonna have to look for something unusual or out of place. Like a secret code or a symbol that looks like one thing but means something else entirely different."

"How do you know all that?" Paddy asked.

"Simple deductive reasoning. He *wanted* the treasure to be found by someone if he couldn't spend it himself, so there's gotta be something there, you just have to find it. But he didn't want it to be easy. He didn't write down instructions or directions. No, nothing like that. He wanted to make sure the person—or people—who found it were worthy. Make them work hard for it. That's where I can help you kids. I can help make sense of whatever's in the house."

"No way," said Lucy. "You're not coming into our house."

He sighed. "Then let's work together. You let me know what you find, and I'll figure out what it means. That's what I'm good at. My specialty."

"If you know so much, why haven't you found the treasure yet?" Lucy asked.

"Yeah," said Paddy. "Why?"

The old man grimaced. "That house was never intended to be closed off to the public. It was supposed to be open to everyone. It was a mistake by the administrators of the estate. I think the answer is there, waiting to be found. You two have access, and I've got the expertise. A perfect team. If we find anything, we can split it, fifty-fifty. I'm not greedy. There's plenty of gold to go around. What do you say?"

"We'll think about it," said Lucy. "Come on, let's get out of here." She took Paddy by his wrist and dragged him away until they were out of sight.

"Did you really mean that?" Paddy asked. "That we'll think about telling him what we find in the house?"

"Geez, no! I just wanted to get out of there. Paddy, listen—something he said made me think. He said we should look for some sort of symbol. Do you think those painted tiles above each bedroom door are clues after all? I think we only wrote down one of them."

"I guess it's possible. Let's go back and take a closer look."

Back at the mansion, they climbed the stairs and stood in the hallway, studying each of the decorative tiles in silence. They were all different. In addition to the image of the blowing wind above the entrance to Lucy's room, there were images of the sun (over Paddy's door), a wave of water, and a picture of a small island with a palm tree growing on it. Each tile had one of the four compass directions inscribed in block letters, although, as their father noticed when they first moved in, none were correct. The tile above the door of the locked, fifth bedroom was of a gold coin floating in the starry sky. Unlike the others, this one did not include a direction.

Lucy's eyes sparkled with recognition. "I get it now. Those first four tiles represent air, fire, earth, and water. Those were considered the four elements of the ancient world. That last tile, though . . . I don't know what it stands for. Maybe he only put it there because he didn't have any other tiles."

"Maybe the fifth tile is the clue we're looking for. It doesn't belong, and it has a gold coin on it. Maybe it stands for the treasure."

"Maybe," said Lucy. Then a new idea popped into her head. "Maybe the key to the room is hidden behind that tile."

"Let's find out."

Paddy disappeared down the stairs and returned carrying a knife and a step stool from the kitchen, which he placed in front of the doorframe and climbed. Reaching up, he dug into the wall with the blade, tracing around the border of the tile until he could pry it off with his fingers.

He peered at the newly exposed plaster. "Nope, nothing here. I guess we were wrong."

"Pass me the tile anyway," Lucy said. "I'll copy the engraving into my notebook in case there's something about it we can't think of yet."

"Okay," agreed Paddy, placing the rectangular tile into her outstretched palm. "Then we'll need to find some glue before Mom and Dad get home."

NINE

The following morning, the twins turned their attention to the room that had fascinated Paddy from their arrival: Thomas Stephenson's personal library. This was a treasure of a different sort.

"There was more to this guy than people know," said Paddy, pulling several books off a shelf. "Look! Here's *The Three Musketeers* and some books by Charles Dickens. I would never have thought a pirate would be interested in books."

"Or music," said Lucy, nodding toward the piano in the middle of the room.

"Yeah." Paddy stacked the books on the floor and walked over to look at the piece that still leaned against the music rack. "It's called *Variations on a Ballet Air from "Castor & Pollux,"* for piano," he said. "Someone drew asterisks in the margins and sketched a boat around part of the title."

"Castor and Pollux were twins in ancient mythology. Like us."

"Oh yeah? That's pretty neat."

"You think you could play it?"

"After three years of piano lessons? I can try." Paddy sat on the bench and studied the notes. Then he placed his hands on the keys and a simple melody filled the air.

When he was finished, Lucy said, "That wasn't bad."

"I skipped to the easy part. I wonder if there's anything else to play." He stood, swung open the top of the piano bench, and lifted out a thin booklet entitled *Bach for Beginners*. Thumbing through the pages, he saw some of the pieces had been marked with fingering instructions. "He was very different from what we first imagined."

Lucy examined the spines of the books on the nearest shelf. "Maybe he wasn't the cruel pirate captain everyone's made him out to be."

"Oh? You're the one who said he was nothing but a thief and a killer."

"I don't know what to think anymore. Look, here are books on astronomy. Some of the pages are dog-eared." She pulled them out, one by one. "It's like he lived two different lives."

"Hey, look at this one," said Paddy, reaching for a book with a worn, brown cover. "It's about pirates."

"Really? Let me see." She grabbed it away and flipped to the table of contents.

"It's a book describing pirate life," she concluded. "That might be interesting. Maybe you should read this." She handed it back as they heard a loud knock.

They ran to the front of the house and opened the door. There on the porch stood Chi-Chi, hopping back and forth on his toes as if he were about to run back into town.

"*Hola, ¿Qué hay?* Where you two been?" he asked. "Not sick of me, are you?"

"No, of course not," said Lucy, moving aside to let him in. "We've just been busy."

Chi-Chi strutted into the living room and looked around. "Whoa. Look at all the pictures in here."

"That's not all," said Paddy. "Remember the guy who we learned died here a long time ago? He was a pirate captain. All this stuff was probably his."

"I guess that's neat," said Chi-Chi. "Used to be lots of pirates around here."

"You know about the pirates?" Lucy asked.

"Sure, of course. They have that festival every year."

"What are you talking about?" asked Paddy. "What festival?"

"Best part of summer. Carnival rides, music, food—lots and lots of food. There's a parade, too. People dress up like pirates and walk through the streets. That's what made me think of it. Maybe you'll still be here and you can see it for yourselves." Then changing the subject, he asked, "Hey, that rowboat at the dock yours?"

"We were told we could use it when we moved in," Paddy replied.

"You want to go swimming in the bay? There's a special spot I know near the reef. Can get there in the boat. Not too many people go there. What do you say?"

"Maybe another time," Lucy said. "We're in the middle of something important."

"Trust me on this," said Chi-Chi. "It'll be fun."

Paddy looked at his sister with a pleading expression. "We can always finish this tomorrow. I'm worn out."

"Come on, let's go," Chi-Chi pleaded. "Nothing to worry about. Water isn't deep and it's not far from here. Be able to see land the whole time."

"Oh, all right," answered Lucy. "I guess I could use a break."

Paddy grinned. "Great! Chi-Chi, do you need to borrow a bathing suit?"

"Nah." The boy laughed. "Already got one on."

The twins changed and the three friends ran down to the dock, where the rowboat swayed with the waves.

Paddy climbed in and sat down. "So, we're going to see a reef and some fish?"

"Not exactly," said Chi-Chi with an odd grin.

Lucy stepped in after her brother, and Chi-Chi followed, dropping the end of the rope in the bottom of the boat. "Paddy, you row, okay?"

"Fine with me." Paddy took the oars and inserted them into the oarlocks. "So, where to?"

"Not too far." Chi-Chi pointed off to the southeast. "That way."

The sea was calm and sparkled under the sun. Paddy rowed along the coast, and as the boat glided forward with each stroke of the oars, their house soon disappeared. The water was clear enough for the twins to pick out grass growing on the seafloor in places and fish swimming nearby.

Then Lucy saw something out of the corner of her eye. "What's that?" she asked, startled. "Something huge just swam past the boat."

"Great—we're here!" said Chi-Chi. "You're going to love this."

"There's another one!" called Lucy. "What was that?"

"Stingray," Chi-Chi called back.

"Wow, they're big," said Paddy.

Chi-Chi laughed. "Welcome to Shark Alley. That's what I call it, anyway." He slipped his shirt over his head. "Ready?"

"Um . . . ready for *what*?" Lucy said.

"To go in, *guapa*." With that, Chi-Chi leapt high in the air and landed in the water with a loud splash.

"Chi-Chi!" Lucy yelled. "Are you nuts?!"

"I thought you weren't afraid of anything," he called back from the water.

"I'm not afraid." She sniffed. "Look! There goes a big one! Aren't they dangerous?"

"Nah." Chi-Chi swam farther from the boat and paused, treading water. "You coming or not?"

"If Chi-Chi is doing it, I'm going in, too," Paddy said.

"Suit yourself," Lucy said, shrugging. "I'm remaining right here in the boat." She saw Paddy make a face. "Well, *someone* has to. We don't have an anchor, and the rowboat will drift off if someone doesn't stay in it."

"Hmm," said Paddy. "That's a good point, but I still think you're chicken."

He pulled off his shirt and shoes, removed his glasses, and before he could lose his nerve, stepped over the edge of the boat into the water. Something grabbed hold of his leg and Paddy shrieked.

Chi-Chi giggled from behind him. "Super, no?"

"That's not the first word I thought of."

"You should feel lucky. Not too many people know about this spot anymore. My mom and dad say there used to be boat tours here all the time. The guides would throw bait in the water to get them to come close. No need, though—they're always here in the middle of the day. The water's real shallow and warm from the sun. They like that."

"What should I do?"

"Don't be afraid. Put your face in the water and look around."

Paddy did as Chi-Chi suggested. Once his face was underwater, he could see a hundred feet in any direction, even without his glasses. The beige sand, littered with conch shells and seaweed, sparkled from fifteen feet below. Then something brushed his leg again.

Paddy lifted his head. "Chi-Chi, it's not funny anymore," he started to say, but then he realized this time it wasn't his friend who had touched him, but a huge gray stingray, its wings nearly six feet across.

Paddy put his head back under and saw a half-dozen huge stingrays cruising nearby. As he watched, Chi-Chi swam toward one and stroked it with his open palm before surfacing nearly a minute later.

"Did you see that?" Chi-Chi exclaimed. "You try it, they don't mind if you touch them. Gently. Otherwise they might sting you."

"I guess that wouldn't be such a good thing," muttered Paddy. "Here goes!" He took a deep breath and dove under the surface. Kicking hard, he descended farther as the pressure built in his ears. Still, he kept kicking until he reached two stingrays floating motionless at a depth of about ten feet. Swallowing his fears, Paddy gently stroked his palm across their backs until he could no longer resist the urge to breathe, and he surfaced, gasping for air.

"What did you think?"

"They're really soft. I thought their skin would be rough, like a lizard's. But it was smooth, like rubber." He turned to the boat. "Lucy, did you see that?"

"I did," she replied. "Be careful!"

"I'm going down again," said Chi-Chi.

"Wait!" cried Paddy. Another shape had darted past, but this one was long and narrow. "That's a shark! Come on, let's get out of here!"

"I said this place was called Shark Alley. What did you think we'd find here?"

"I thought it was some kind of joke."

"Don't worry; no more dangerous than the stingrays. Watch!"

Chi-Chi kicked his feet and dove toward the sea bottom. Plunging his face under the surface for a better look, Paddy saw him swim in front of the shark and hold out his hand. The shark glided past, brushing against Chi-Chi's outstretched palm with its entire body. Then Chi-Chi gave Paddy the thumbs-up sign and surfaced.

"See? No problem."

"Whoa," said Paddy. "Aren't you scared?"

"Nah. Lots of different sharks. These aren't dangerous. They're nurse sharks."

"Whatever it was, it was *huge*," said Paddy. "That shark was bigger than you!"

"That one, maybe about seven feet. Try it! They feel different than the rays."

"I don't know, Paddy," called Lucy.

"Are you sure they aren't going to bite me?"

"Nah," Chi-Chi replied. "Just don't pull on their tails or anything like that."

"Okay—here goes!"

As Lucy watched, Paddy disappeared under the surface once more. Twenty seconds later he popped up with a big grin on his face.

"That was neat!" he said. "You're right, they do feel different, almost like sandpaper."

"But not as rough."

"Yeah. Bumpy, but not rough. Maybe sandpaper isn't a good word for it. They're really something when you get up close to them."

For the next half hour, they dove over and over, playing with the sharks. Chi-Chi liked to swim to the bottom of the ocean and hover there for well over a minute, watching, before ascending and taking his next breath. Paddy had never seen someone hold their breath for so long. "How do you *do* that?" he asked.

"No big deal. Lots of people can do it. Just takes practice. My cousin can stay down almost four minutes. He catches loads of fish that way. I'm not nearly as good."

They stayed in the water for ten more minutes. At one point Paddy counted fifteen sharks and about a dozen stingrays nearby. Then, when his arms got tired, he waved to Lucy, who rowed over to him. Paddy hauled himself over the side, with Chi-Chi following.

They sat in the boat, basking in the hot sun as their bodies dried. "Thanks for bringing us here, Chi-Chi," said Paddy. "That was a lot of fun. Lucy, you should have gotten in. It was super!"

"Good thing I didn't," she replied. "I think I found something." She pointed toward the shore, past the entrance to the town harbor, where a tall cliff jutted into the water like the prow of a ship.

"What is it?" asked Paddy. He put his glasses on and shielded his eyes from the sun's glare.

"Lion Rock," said Chi-Chi, glancing up. "Ships used to look for it when they were sailing here. You can see it for miles."

"It does look a little like a lion," agreed Paddy. "I see ears, and a mane on the side. And that dark splotch could be its mouth."

"It's really called Lion Rock?" Lucy asked. "Paddy, don't you get it? Remember the poem on the gravestone?"

"Of course—the lion! It's guarding the treasure! It must be up there!"

This got Chi-Chi's attention. "Wait a second," he said, sitting up in his seat. "What's this about treasure?"

"We should probably tell him," Paddy said.

"Tell me what?"

"You know that pirate who lived in our house?" Paddy started.

Chi-Chi looked up. "Yeah?"

"He had a treasure."

"—a big one," Lucy interrupted.

"—like a ton of gold he stole—"

"—and he hid it somewhere on the island—"

"—and no one has ever found it—"

"—but he left clues to where he put it—"

"—and a poem he left mentions a lion—"

"—a lion and a stone—"

"—and we're going to find it—"

"Wait, slow down. You think treasure is buried on the island? At Lion Rock?" Chi-Chi laughed. "Impossible. Even if someone could climb up there, there's no way they could carry a big treasure with them."

"Yeah, I think he's right. I don't think it's up there, either," Lucy said. "I think it's a sign people would see from far away. The poem mentions a lion watching from a throne. I think it only means the treasure is somewhere on the island."

"To let us know we're on the right track," agreed Paddy. "That makes sense."

"What it means," Lucy concluded, "is that this isn't a hoax after all. There actually *is* a treasure to find." She looked at her watch. "We better get back. We have a lot of work to do."

TEN

Jean-Pierre Le Moyne rushed under the dizzying maze of sails and rigging that swayed in the wind above his head as he was led past the mizzenmast and across the quarterdeck of the British frigate, the *H.M.S. Vanguard*. With a distinct English accent, the British officer escorting him had identified himself as Lieutenant George Pope, courteously stating that Le Moyne's presence was requested by the captain—and so here he was, racing along the deck in an effort to keep up with the officer's long strides.

Lieutenant Pope led Le Moyne down a short flight of stairs and into a large room, where a man stood beside a long oval table, dressed smartly in an officer's uniform all the way down to his polished silver-buckled shoes and a ceremonial sword that hung from his waist. He was about forty years old, and his tanned face was forgettable if not for its deep-set steely blue eyes and a faded scar down one cheek. He ordered Lieutenant Pope to exit, leaving the two men alone in the elegant room.

"My name is Forester," the man said politely. "Captain Charles Forester of Her Majesty's Navy. And you, I take it, must be the celebrated pirate Jean-Pierre Le Moyne. Welcome aboard the *Vanguard*."

Le Moyne glanced around. The captain's study was painted with gold and green stripes, and the sunlight streamed through a pair of windows that were edged by red silk drapes. On the oval table in the center of the room lay a flask and a pair of opaque glasses; Forester poured two drinks, offered one to Le Moyne, and then sat down in the nearest chair, gesturing for his guest to do the same.

"You are mistaken," Le Moyne said at last, deciding caution was the best policy. "I'm just a poor fisherman, not a pirate. And a good thing, too. As a British officer serving in the Caribbean, it is your sworn duty to apprehend all pirates and transport them to the nearest colony to be tried and hanged."

Captain Forester held his glass up in the air. "A toast then. To fishermen who, despite appearances, are not pirates."

Le Moyne took a drink. "What can I do for you, Captain? I doubt very much you brought me here just to share your wine."

"I'd like to make you a proposal," said Captain Forester. "One I hope you'll find impossible to refuse. Roughly three months from now, a ship will leave Venezuela bound for Spain with a ton of gold stored inside her hold. We prefer it not to reach its destination."

"You have something against the Spaniards?"

Forester coughed dryly. "Actually, the Venezuelans."

"Why not attack it yourselves?"

"We require something a little more . . . subtle. Something without our mark on it. You immediately came to mind."

"Oh? I don't know why. As I said, I'm just a poor fisherman."

Captain Forester ignored him. "Francis Drake, Henry Morgan, even William Kidd—these were all notorious pirates who served British interests in wartime as privateers, hired to stop merchant ships of the enemy from getting through. Drake and Morgan were even knighted for their efforts."

"I didn't know that England was at war with Venezuela."

"We're not. We have—how can I say this?—a certain interest in stopping that freighter."

"But not to be blamed for it."

"Now you're catching on. I had heard you were a smart fellow, Le Moyne."

"I am a smart fellow, Captain. Smart enough to know that one needs a Letter of Marque to act as a privateer, and that the practice was abolished almost ten years ago by the Declaration of Paris."

"This would be . . . an unofficial designation."

So it was some illegal scheme. Le Moyne repeated the offer in his head. He was sure he was being played, but couldn't figure out how. Probably best to exit gracefully. "As I said, I'm just a fisherman. I think you want someone else for this."

"And I suppose you know nothing about that sloop burning not a half mile away, with its cargo safely in your hold? I'm not a fool, Le Moyne. I know your history. Come now, there's no need for dishonesty or deceit here; this is a private conversation between two captains. If I intended to arrest you, I'd have done so already."

That was certainly true. "What's in it for me?"

"Stop that shipment from going through—I don't care how you do it—and you can keep all the gold you can salvage. All of it. There'll be more gold on that ship than you could spend in a lifetime. Even three lifetimes."

Le Moyne thought it over some more. He'd be rich; he'd no longer have to attack fishing boats or sell stolen cotton in Central America or on one of the remote islands. "You won't come after us for the gold?"

"My orders do not address the gold," said Captain Forester. "Only to stop the shipment from reaching Spain. So what happens to it is no concern of mine. If it happens to find its way to your pockets . . ." He shrugged. "It's just politics. What do you say?"

"And if I refuse?" asked Le Moyne, even though he was pretty sure he knew the answer.

"Then I'll apprehend you right now on charges of piracy, and take you and your crew to the nearest British colony to be hanged."

"Wouldn't there be a trial first?"

"I suppose so. Not that it would matter much."

So that was it. An offer he was unable to refuse. In one swoop, he'd go from being a minor nautical hassle to the most wanted man in the Caribbean, hunted by both the Spanish and the Venezuelan navies. However, if all went right, he'd have a ton of gold to show for it. And if things went wrong . . . well, it didn't sound like it would be any worse than if he refused the offer in the first place.

"I guess we have a deal, then."

Captain Forester stood and thrust out his arm. "Good luck, Le Moyne. I won't forget this."

That's what I'm afraid of, Le Moyne thought.

ELEVEN

Energized by their discovery of Lion Rock, Lucy and Paddy continued to search the mansion for secret compartments or loose floorboards. They studied the equations scratched into the walls, hoping they were references to coordinates on a map, but the math was beyond them. Next they examined the lamps, grandfather clocks, and animal sculptures, finding nothing out of the ordinary. Paddy showed the framed photograph he had discovered to his sister, who agreed that it was probably a portrait of Thomas Stephenson as an old man. They displayed it on the hutch in the formal dining room as motivation not to give up.

The twins spent hours staring at the paintings that filled all the space on the walls, arguing over which they liked best and which they'd take home with them if they were allowed. Lucy loved the paintings of different locations on the island, while Paddy was partial to the pictures of ships sailing on the ocean because they made him think of adventure. By now they were positive they'd been painted by Thomas Stephenson himself. If one of the paintings revealed where the treasure had been hidden, Lucy and Paddy were unable to figure it out.

☠   ☠   ☠

They were playing outside in the yard when Paddy glanced up at the house. "There's the window to the locked bedroom," he said, motioning up to the second floor. "I wonder if it's open."

"We'll never know without a ladder," answered Lucy. "And we don't have one tall enough."

"That's true . . . but I'll bet I could climb that tree and peek inside." Paddy approached the nearby trunk and soon he was high in the branches.

"I can't see much," he said, trying to stare through the window. "Only a desk and a telescope. That's all."

"Are there any pictures on the wall?"

"Let me check." He shuffled closer, careful not to lose his balance. "Just the same ugly wallpaper that's in the other rooms. Wait a second—there is something. It looks like a bulletin board, and there are papers tacked to it."

"Paddy! What are you doing?"

"I think I can reach the window." He inched along one of the thicker branches, his back stiff like he was walking a tightrope. "Another few feet, and I can jump to the ledge. Then I can open the window and step right in." He moved again, the branch swaying underneath him.

Lucy started to ask, "What if the window's locked from the inside?" but before the words were out, there was a loud crack, the branch snapped, and her brother tumbled to the ground.

"Paddy!" she screamed, running over. "Are you okay?"

Paddy sat up, rubbing his elbow. "Yeah, I think so." He looked up at the tree, which now sported a broken, jagged stub where the branch had been. "I guess we'll have to find another way in. Another day without any progress."

"The day's not over yet," reminded Lucy. "Come on, let's go inside."

They opened the front door and entered the foyer, where they were greeted by their mother from inside the living room.

"I thought I heard a loud noise from outside," she said. "Do you know what that was?"

"Uh, nothing," Lucy answered.

"Yeah," said Paddy, flexing his arm. "I think a branch fell or something."

"Thanks, kids. You know, we've hardly done anything together since we've gotten here. We're going to go home at the end of the summer without any family memories."

"We're not here for fun, Margaret," said their father from somewhere out of sight. "We're here so I can do research, and I've been doing a pretty poor job of it so far."

"Still no luck finding that fish?" asked Lucy, poking her head into the living room.

"No," sighed their father. "The heliomanth doesn't seem to be anywhere! I'm beginning to think it was all a hoax."

"Well, I think we could use a break," their mother said. "It's Saturday. I don't think I've been in the village center other than to buy groceries. Why don't we all go out to dinner tonight?"

☠ ☠ ☠

Several hours later, as the air was beginning to cool, the family rode along the shore road toward Santa Elena. After leaving their bikes by the school, Lucy and Paddy led their parents past the library and into the center of town.

"Look at all these outdoor cafés," said their mother. "It's like a small festival."

Since it was Saturday night, cars were banned from the streets until morning. Many of the restaurants had moved their tables onto the sidewalk, and some of the chefs had wheeled their grills outside for people to see what they were cooking. As the Hendricks family walked along, they passed several musicians, including the guitarist the twins had heard earlier in the town square. A juggler rolled past on a unicycle, somehow managing to keep three bowling pins aloft without losing his balance.

"Mm-mm, something smells delicious," their father said, inhaling deeply. "How will we decide where to eat?"

"I guess we'll have to—" their mom started, when a loud argument erupted from down the block.

They turned to look, and there was the old man with the torn ear. He was shouting at two men in the middle of the street—the same two dangerous-looking men Lucy and Paddy had seen stealing fruit from the market. It was impossible to hear what the old man was saying, but he was obviously angry about something.

Now the men were shouting back. Then, as the twins watched, the taller of the two shoved the old man to the ground and stormed off.

"Come on, we'd better help him," said their mother. "That poor man!"

"No—wait!" cried Lucy, but their parents had already moved forward. The twins rushed after them and nearly froze when they saw their father bend down and help the old man to his feet.

"Thank you," he said calmly. "Don't know what that was all about." Then his eyes landed squarely on Lucy and Paddy, who had caught up and were standing in the middle of the road, feeling uncomfortable. "Huh," he said. "These your children?"

"Yes," said their mother. "This is our daughter, Lucy, and our son, Paddy. I'm Margaret. I hope you're okay."

"I am now," said the old man, brushing some dirt off of his trousers, his keys jingling from where they were hooked to a belt loop. "I must remember to buy Paddy and Lucy some flavored ice next time I see them."

"Oh, I'm sure they would enjoy that very much."

"Not a chance of *that*," whispered Lucy to her brother.

The man glanced at the twins and winked. "Now if you'll excuse me," he said with a slight smile before disappearing into the crowd.

"That was nice of him," said their father. "See what a friendly place it is here."

"Um, sure," said Paddy. He grabbed his sister's elbow. "Lucy, now he knows our names," he whispered.

They walked farther down the street, halting in front of a small but colorful café with an outdoor grill. "This seems like a good spot," said their father. He led them to an empty round table that had been placed in the middle of the sidewalk. Sitting down, they each took a menu, which had been printed in both Spanish and English and featured an illustration of a pretty woman labeled 'Rita.'

Several minutes later, the waitress approached. "Welcome to Rita's Café. What can I get for you?"

"Everything looks so good," said their father, gesturing toward the menu. "What's that on the grill? It smells delicious."

"It's a special delicacy made here at Rita's," the waitress replied. "It is a local fish, grilled tenderly, and flavored with local spices and fruits. I highly recommend it. Go take a look; you can watch the chef preparing it."

Their curiosity raised, the twins and their parents left the table, navigating between the tables and chairs spread along the sidewalk. The chef nodded at them as they looked at the fish sizzling on the grates. Instantly their father's face went white, and he grabbed for their mother's arm.

Margaret Hendricks gasped in disbelief. "The heliomanth!"

TWELVE

It was nearly midnight when the Hendricks family finally got home. First there had been a lot of yelling and shouting, most coming from Lucy and Paddy's father. The cook spoke very little English, and it was almost comical watching the two of them trying to communicate using hand signals, while their father's face got redder and redder. Eventually Rita, the owner, emerged from a back room to sort things out. Unexpectedly, Rita turned out to be a short, stocky man who spoke in a heavy accent.

Initially Rita refused to tell the Hendricks anything. The heliomanth was a rare delicacy, he said, only served at Rita's Café, and he never divulged his recipes, especially signature dishes like this one. Following some more shouting, the twins' father managed to convince Rita he was only interested in where the fish had come from, and didn't care at all about the spices and marinade sauce.

After making the entire family swear they weren't planning to open their own restaurant, Rita admitted the fish was a mystery to him. As he explained it, late one morning several months earlier, a fisherman appeared at the restaurant with one of these big strange-looking fish, and offered it to Rita at a good price. Since then, the fisherman, a man named "Flapper" Bathwaite, had returned a handful of times, and each time Rita had purchased the fish, no questions asked. This morning Flapper had shown up with a pair of them; the first had already been served ten minutes earlier. What's more, Rita had no idea how to contact the fisherman and couldn't predict when he would next show up. All he knew was that Flapper lived somewhere on the other side of the island.

Their father then offered to buy the remaining heliomanth and asked Rita how much he wanted for it.

"No more fish," said the cook with a toothless grin. He made an exaggerated eating motion with his hands.

The Hendricks family stared down at the grill. The heliomanth had vanished; in its place were two yellowtail snapper and a parrotfish. While they had been talking to Rita, the cook had served the heliomanth to one of the other diners!

James Hendricks dashed forward. Springing between tables, he grabbed as many plates that he could, without even bothering to check what they contained.

"Don't eat that! Don't eat that!" he shouted. "It's a scientific discovery!"

The shocked diners stared at him; some yelled angrily, while others tried to snatch their dinner plates back. One woman wondered aloud if he was a physician and asked if they were all going to get sick.

"I'll pay for it; I'll pay for it all," he repeated, over and over again, as he deposited the plates on their now-empty table, but no one heard him over the din.

He was still pawing through the remains when the police arrived.

☠ ☠ ☠

Officer H. Douglas Ernst III had been stuck on night duty since accidentally plowing his patrol car into the rear end of a taxi cab in late June. At the time, he'd been in hot pursuit of a couple of men who had broken into the town museum and taken off with some minor display piece. Why anyone would steal a worthless old book was beyond him. But then again, he had yet to meet a smart crook.

Officer Ernst thought his punishment harsh; it wasn't his fault the taxi driver was backing out of a hidden driveway just as he came around the bend.

Now he had to sit behind a crummy desk each night for the next three months, alone. To pass the time, he had begun reviewing some of the old open case files. Most were petty thefts, but the one he had just reviewed was more exciting. It involved an armed robbery at some old resort in the middle of the jungle, and appeared that it could be the island's oldest unsolved case. He had just put the file back in the cabinet when the call from Rita's came. Putting on his cap, he locked the door and headed down to the restaurant.

Officer Ernst was not fully prepared for the scene that greeted him when he arrived at Rita's. He had seen a lot during his career, but a tourist stealing plates of half-eaten food from other diners? Now that was a first. The guy hadn't had a thing to drink, or so he said, and Officer Ernst was pretty sure that he'd become a laughingstock if he charged the guy with theft as the restaurant owner demanded. After all, it was only half-eaten fish bones. Not knowing what else to do, he marched the entire family down to the police station with an irate Rita in tow.

It took nearly an hour, but eventually Lucy and Paddy's parents convinced the officer that they were *not* crazy; they were scientists, and they needed the fish for research.

This did not make Rita any less angry. "My customers, my customers," he kept repeating. "They will never come back after what you have done."

That's when Margaret Hendricks offered to pay Rita for everyone's food that they had taken, *and* to treat all his customers to a free meal the following evening. That calmed Rita significantly, and he agreed to drop the charges. There was still the matter of creating a public disturbance, which carried with it a $15 fine for each of them—$60 in total. Their mother signed over three traveler's checks, and they hurried back to the restaurant, where they were shocked to discover that the waitress had left all the plates spread on the back table, thinking they might be used as evidence of a crime.

So until Rita's Café closed at 11:30, the Hendricks family poked through the remains of the two dozen or so dishes, while Lucy and Paddy received a lengthy lesson about how to recognize the heliomanth by the shape of its mouth and tail, dark color, extra fins above and below its body, and its bulbous three-lobed tail. By the end of the evening, Lucy and Paddy were close to experts themselves.

Their father later calculated that the night had cost them nearly four hundred dollars—in his estimation, well worth the two half-eaten specimens that they carried back home with them, enough to construct a full skeleton with several bones left over.

☠ ☠ ☠

The incident at the restaurant strengthened the resolve of Lucy and Paddy's parents. Now that they had proof the heliomanth existed, they believed it was just a matter of time before they found one alive. They studied the skeleton for clues, and began spending mornings at the marina, inspecting the fishermen's catch as they debarked from their boats.

The twins were having less luck with their own mystery. A few days later they were sitting on the grass near the school playground discussing how to continue their search, when Chi-Chi strode by. He waved happily and bounced across the field toward them.

"*Hola, ¿Qué hay?* Still treasure hunting?" he asked loudly.

"Shh!" warned Lucy. "Someone might hear you."

Chi-Chi shrugged. "Want to go exploring? I'll show you a secret place no one visits anymore."

"That sounds neat," said Paddy.

"*¡Vamonos!* You don't need bikes. Just your bags."

Chi-Chi led the twins down a narrow street. At the edge of the village, the road transformed into a rugged dirt path that led deep into the jungle that choked the center of the island. They trekked north toward Mt. Alta Vista, which peeked through the branches, until the trail split and they took the right fork. As they hiked east, their surroundings gradually became wild. Moss hung from the trees and water dripped from the leaves. At times the plants were so dense that they couldn't see more than a few feet away. Twice they traversed a flowing stream, where the water rose to their waists. Fighting the current, Lucy slipped and fell during the second crossing, drenching her clothes and cutting her palms on the gravelly bottom.

Chi-Chi pulled her up and helped her across. "Come," he urged. "Not too much farther."

"What could possibly be worth all this effort?" Paddy mumbled.

Chi-Chi grinned. "You'll see."

They trekked on until they reached the wall of a black rocky cliff, which opened to a dark, ominous cave. A murky river flowed into it—quite possibly the same one they had already crossed twice—and on either side, huge human-looking figures were chiseled into the rock face as if guarding the entrance.

The stone idols were crumbling in places; large chunks of rock had cracked and fallen to the river bed where they shone in the harsh sunlight, but that made them no less intimidating. They were wonderful and hideous, fascinating and terrifying, all at the same time. Both had huge heads and scowls on their faces, as if they were intended as a warning, to frighten away travelers.

"This is called the Cave of the Black Rock," said Chi-Chi. "My *abuela* brought me here once. She said this place was sacred among my people. They came to the river here to pray to the Stone Watchers. For good weather, lots of food, stuff like that. This was much before she was born. Her mom showed it to her when she was a kid. There were human sacrifices inside the cave, too. No one comes here anymore—too superstitious."

"Human—sacrifices?" stammered Paddy. "You mean people were killed in there?"

"Long time ago," said Chi-Chi.

"You're not afraid?" asked Paddy.

"Nah—not of dead people. But bats—I don't like bats." He shuddered. "Get in your hair and bite your ears. Drink your blood. The cave is filled with them. Here, watch."

Chi-Chi picked up a small rock and threw it into the mouth of the cave. Almost instantly they heard a fluttering of wings, and a mass of small shapes shot out of the darkness like missiles.

"Duck!" shouted Chi-Chi. He threw himself onto the ground and covered his head with his arms. Lucy and Paddy crouched down as a dozen bats flew past, disappearing into the trees.

"Wow," said Paddy, feeling goose bumps rise on his arms. "So no one has been in this cave for maybe hundreds of years?"

"My mom says twenty or thirty years ago some tourists tried to explore it. But it started to rain when they were inside, and the cave filled with water. People said they drowned. No one knows. Never found the bodies."

"That's just a stupid story to scare kids," said Lucy.

"*Quizas*," Chi-Chi said with a shrug. "Sometimes it rains really hard, and there are flash floods. Thing is . . . supposedly there were no clouds in the sky. Some say the gods punished them for daring to enter the sacred cave. Don't think anyone's been in since."

"And you're not afraid of that?" dared Lucy.

Chi-Chi shrugged again. "Come on, let's go." He turned and started walking up the path. "That's not why I brought you out here. Just thought you'd like to see it."

"We have to come back here later by ourselves," whispered Lucy to her brother as they followed Chi-Chi along the trail. "Did you see what was etched in the rock above the entrance to the cave?"

"No."

"The letters 'T.S.,'" she continued. "And there were three stars, too—three, just like on Thomas Stephenson's gravestone, right where it said not to forget about him. It could be a signal. We *have* to go back and look around."

"Um, by 'look around' you mean go into the cave. You heard Chi-Chi—there are blood-sucking bats in there."

"Forget about that," said Lucy. "Bats don't suck your blood; that's only a fairy tale. But if it'll make you feel better, I'll whip up something that'll keep them away."

"*Vengan*," called Chi-Chi from up the path. "Come on—over here—wild banana trees! Lots of 'em. Island's best-kept secret. Ripe, too."

THIRTEEN

Over the next several days the twins planned their excursion to the cave. Lucy was convinced the treasure was hidden there, reasoning that the best place to stash it was somewhere everyone was afraid to go, and found it hard to contain her excitement. Paddy was anxious for other reasons. He dreamed up all sorts of dangers they were certain to encounter, and imagined witnessing the human sacrifices that Chi-Chi claimed had occurred inside. Still, he knew there was a good chance they'd find something, so he tried to put his fears aside.

There was much to be done. They pored over old maps, including the one in the tourist brochure, but the cave wasn't marked on any of them. It was as if it had been erased from the island's history. As far as they could tell, it was directly east of Thomas Stephenson's grave site, with the old run-down tourist hotel roughly halfway between them. If they were correct, the three locations formed nearly a straight line through the bottom half of the island, forming a triangle with the ancient temple, which was north of the hotel near the base of Mt. Alta Vista. The twins traced the river with their fingers as it wound through the jungle, until confident they could find their way without Chi-Chi's help.

While rummaging through the storage shed near the dock, they found hard hats, a long rope, and several pairs of thick gloves which were caked with soil. All they still needed were a pair of small flashlights, which they purchased in town. With a burst of inspiration, Paddy also bought a roll of medical tape, with which he attached the flashlights to the top of the hard hats so their hands would be free. At the same store Lucy discovered a set of water-tight containers for fishermen, the perfect size to keep her notebook dry.

The night before their expedition, the twins stayed up late to make sandwiches and pack their knapsacks. Paddy remembered the collapsible telescope and included it with the rest of their supplies. Then, after he went to bed, Lucy prepared something extra in secret.

The following morning, as soon as their parents had left for work, they grabbed their bags and raced into town. After leaving their bikes in the usual place, they found the correct path and hiked into the jungle. The sun shone through the canopy of branches above the trail, a good omen. Hopefully the weather would hold.

The way seemed strange and unfamiliar, and the twins wondered if they had taken a wrong turn. But then they reached the stream. Whooping and hollering, they jumped into the cold water and forged across, soaking their socks and shoes. As before, they crossed it a second time. Soon thereafter, they reached the mouth of the cave.

The two human figures carved into the stone face stood at attention on opposite sides of the entrance. To Paddy they no longer seemed imposing—just a little sad, as if wondering what had happened to all the people who used to live there and keep them company. Still, his chest tightened at the thought of crossing their threshold. Who knew what they might find inside? He reached up toward the closest figure and touched its leg.

"Um, hello," he said, rubbing the stone with his palm. "Hope you don't mind if we come in and look around. We're not here to disturb anything."

Lucy gave him a sideways glance. "What are you doing over there?"

"Nothing."

"Oh, come on. I heard you talking."

"I'm just asking their permission to go in, that's all."

She rolled her eyes dramatically. "So long as you don't expect them to answer."

Paddy sighed. "Don't you get the feeling they're guarding something? If we're nice to them, maybe they'll show us where it is."

"And if we're not, then what?"

"Chi-Chi said some people went inside and never returned . . ."

"So you think they'll get angry and we'll end up dead?" She snorted in disbelief.

Paddy glared back. "Forget I said anything." But he whispered to the figure anyway, then patted it on the knee before stepping back.

He glanced up at the rock face above the cave mouth. Sure enough, the initials 'T.S.' had been inscribed there, surrounded by three crudely etched stars.

"Now what?" he asked, even though he knew the answer.

Lucy didn't hesitate. "Into the river, stupid. Come on!" She waved him forward and plunged into the water, which widened into a large murky pool at the cave entrance.

"I can't believe I'm doing this," Paddy said as he jumped in after her. "Ugh—it's freezing!"

"Don't be such a baby." Lucy sloshed several steps before the bottom dropped from under her. She shrieked, startled, and began to dogpaddle, trying to keep the knapsack on her back dry. "We'll have to swim from here," she called.

"How far?"

"I don't know. I can't see much. Too dark ahead."

"I'm going to try carrying mine." Already waist-deep in water, Paddy slipped his knapsack off his shoulders and waded ahead until he came to the point where the ground sloped down beneath his feet. Several steps later the water was at his neck. Holding his bag over his head, he pushed off with his toes and rotated his legs like eggbeaters. Soon his arms ached from the weight and, his legs tiring, he struggled to keep his mouth above the surface. Then, when it seemed he was about to drop the knapsack into the pool, his toes scraped the mucky bottom. He put his weight back on his feet. The ground was solid. Resting the bag on his shoulder, he sucked in a deep breath. "It's shallower here," he called out.

Lucy stopped doing the breaststroke and put her feet down, finding the water was no deeper than her waist. Relieved, she continued into the cave until she reached dry ground on the edge of the riverbank, where she pulled off her knapsack and rifled through it.

"Well, everything's soaked," she said when Paddy reached her. She pulled the sandwiches out of her bag and watched the water drip off the bread. She rummaged around some more and extracted the container holding her notebook. She pried it open, holding her breath. "It's not wet," she said. "Thank goodness."

"Mine's dry," Paddy said with an over-exaggerated shrug. He slipped the straps back around his shoulders. He took several steps and let out a short yelp. Staring back at him was a hideous face carved into the rock, watching over the ancient pool. Its eyes and nose were rich in detail, but the cheeks and mouth were worn away or possibly never carved, as if a scarf was wrapped around its face.

"The Mask of the Rock!" Lucy said, her excitement rising. "Got to be. That was part of the poem on the gravestone—remember?"

"Well," said Paddy, "I guess that settles it. We're in the right place after all."

They continued past the masked stone face, walking in the stream, the water no deeper than their knees. Within a dozen feet the cave became noticeably darker. "I think it's time for those lights," Lucy suggested.

They put on the hiking gloves and hard hats, and flicked on the flashlights taped above their heads. Immediately the tunnel brightened around them. Caught in the beams, a couple of long-legged spiders danced among the rocks and scurried into the shadows.

"Let's go," said Lucy, her voice strong. "We don't have time to waste."

"Aren't you even a little scared?"

"No. Just curious what we'll find. Are you?"

"A little. What if there are other people here?"

"Don't worry; no one's here. Besides, we're only here to look around. There's nothing wrong with that."

"I hope you're right," said Paddy. "This place gives me the creeps."

On they went, following the cold river deeper into the cave, until gradually the passage narrowed into a lengthy tunnel. Water dripped from above. From time to time they heard a faint scraping sound, possibly from mice scurrying among the rocks. Paddy swirled his head around, hoping to catch something in his light. Nothing. He clenched and unclenched his hands as his tension rose.

The tunnel widened again into a long cavern. Narrow streams of light penetrated through small gaps in the ceiling, creating a soft glow.

"Look at those rock formations." Forgetting his anxiety, Paddy pointed up to the ledges that lined the sloped walls of the passage, which rose in tiers like gym bleachers. "They look like an army of little people, watching us. And look at how those stalactites sparkle! There must be some kind of quartz in them."

"Forget about the rocks," sniffed Lucy. "We're not here to sightsee."

"Come on, Lucy. There's no harm in looking around while we're here."

"Now you think you're Marco Polo," she grumbled. "I think I like it better when you're scared."

"This place looks amazing. Would it be so bad to explore a little? We might never have another chance."

Lucy sighed. "We've already been here over an hour, and I doubt we've even gone a half mile. Who knows how much farther we have to go? We've got to get back and cleaned up before Mom and Dad get home or they'll want to know what we've been up to. We can always come back some other time."

"Okay. I guess you're right. But we shouldn't rush ahead without paying attention to everything around us. Maybe the gold is hidden among the rocks."

Lucy turned to face her brother. "I've been thinking about the treasure since we got in here. The gravestone reads, 'Behind mask of rock he watches from earthen throne.' We already found the mask of rock at the entrance. I'll bet the earthen throne is a large rock that looks like a seat. I think it'll be obvious when we find it. This cave is gigantic. I doubt he wanted to make it too hard."

Just then a loud splash came from behind. "What was that?" Paddy whispered.

"Probably a fish. Come on, let's go."

"I hope it's not raining outside," he muttered as he followed his sister. "I can't imagine being trapped in here when the water starts rising." He shuddered.

On they went, in quiet. The passage narrowed again. At times they were forced to climb over rocks and squeeze between boulders crammed so tightly together that they had to remove their knapsacks first and throw them ahead in order not to get stuck.

Lucy started having difficulty breathing. Since she was a kid she had trouble in tight spaces. Until now she'd managed to block it out, but a feeling that she needed to be somewhere else, somewhere in the open where she could breathe normally, overwhelmed her. The lack of sunlight only made things worse. The way Paddy swung his flashlight around when he moved was giving her a headache and making her a little nauseated. She shut her eyes, trying not to panic, and sucked down a deep lungful of air, willing her heartrate to slow.

"Why'd you stop?" asked Paddy, who'd nearly caught up.

Lucy didn't turn around. "Just . . . taking a short break." She sprang ahead, rolled over the boulder blocking the path and slid through a crack in the next. The only thing that would make her phobia worse was if her brother knew about it. "Come on."

The spiders scattered as Paddy followed. He was convinced they must have gone too far; surely, no one could have carried a ton of gold past such obstacles. Once he slipped and fell backwards into the rushing water, scraping his leg against the edge of a sharp rock. When he rose, a thin ribbon of blood oozed from the three-inch gash. But Lucy waded on as if possessed, and Paddy didn't want to lose sight of her.

Without warning the passage opened into a cavern as large as a cathedral. After their trek through the narrow tunnel the wide space was a welcome relief to their senses. A slight breeze blew past them. Lucy gulped down the fresh air, feeling her muscles relax. She'd made it through the hard part.

Together they scanned the cavern. Stalactites at least thirty feet long hung from the roof, dangling over a small lake. Small breaks in the ceiling let in tight streams of sunlight, which sparkled off the stagnant water. In spots, too, the roof and walls had dark splotches on them.

"Could that be some mineral?" Paddy wondered. He looked again. Now the black splotches appeared to be moving. That could only mean . . .

"Aah! Bats!" He reached down to cover his leg, still bleeding. "They'll come for my blood! What'll we do?"

But Lucy was already in motion. As Paddy watched, she unzipped her knapsack, removing a jar of—

"*Strawberry jam?*"

Lucy grinned. "Most kinds of bats like to eat sweet fruits and nectar from flowers. Like hummingbirds."

"How do you know that?"

She shrugged. "Library book. Keep your fingers crossed. I hope this works."

"Me too. Hurry!"

Quickly, she reached into the jar for a handful of jam, which she smeared across a flat rock. As soon as she moved away, a dozen bats fluttered down from the roof and began to feast. She repeated her actions in two other spots, several yards away. Within minutes all three areas were covered with the black-winged creatures.

"See?" she said. "Simple."

"Is that all of them?" asked Paddy, scanning the ceiling of the cavern. His eyes caught sight of something that looked strange, out of place. Curiosity overtook his fear. Retrieving his small telescope, he extended and trained it on a rock spire that shot up from a ledge halfway up the cavern's right wall. Then he smiled.

"What is it?" Lucy asked.

"You better take a look at this." He held the telescope out.

The stalagmite thrust up from the ledge, no different than hundreds of others in the gigantic cavern. But someone had draped a long coat around this particular rock, put a pirate hat on top of it, and wrapped a bandana around the hat like a ribbon.

"He watches from earthen throne," Paddy exclaimed. "That's it! I'll bet that's his actual blue coat."

Lucy steadied her hand. "Too dark to tell what color it is." Then she noticed a smear of color and took a longer look.

"What is it?"

"Just below the hat. Someone painted a face with a scar down one cheek." She handed the telescope back. "He certainly had a strange sense of humor."

Paddy peered through the glass. "Huh. Well, I guess that's where we're going."

They sloshed through the water until they stood more or less below the costumed rock. Looking up, they discovered a narrow step carved into the stone, hidden among the spires. But it was still eight feet above them, well out of reach.

"I'll bet we were meant to go that way," said Lucy. She eyed the inclined wall, which slanted up at a sharp angle. "We need something for a boost. I don't know if we can climb up there ourselves. It's too steep."

Paddy took a couple of steps up the slope before slipping on the smooth rock and sliding back to the bottom. "I have an idea. You brought that rope, right?"

"I don't see how it will help," she said as she removed it from her knapsack and handed it to her brother.

"I think I can loop it around one of the lower stalagmites, and we can use it to climb up to that step. Look! There's one that should work." About fifteen feet above them a thick rock spire jutted out from a ledge.

He eyed the distance. "I'll bet I can toss the rope around there. I just need something heavy to tie to the end."

"Will this do?" Lucy asked, handing her knapsack to her brother.

"I think so."

After tying the shoulder strap to the rope, he swung the knapsack back and forth several times before letting go with a loud yell. They watched intently as the bag flew through the air toward the stalagmite

. . . and grimaced as it hit the rock spire squarely in the center and fell back to the ground with a muted thump.

"Well, at least we know that rock column is solid enough," said Paddy. "It didn't even vibrate when I hit it."

"Come on, Paddy!" Lucy encouraged. "One more try!"

Paddy wound up and once again let the knapsack fly. This time, it was a perfect throw; the bag flew over and around the stalagmite, bounced off the ledge, and fell back down to the ground.

"Great toss!" cheered Lucy. "I knew you could do it!"

"Thanks." He wrapped one end around his waist and arm and leaned back with all his weight. "You go first."

Lucy took the loose end of the rope and began to climb up the steep slope. As she pulled herself higher, she grabbed cracks in the rock with her free hand and jammed her feet between the wall and the spires. In less than a minute she had reached the narrow platform.

"Thanks!" she called. "That worked perfectly!"

"Great. Is there an easier way from there?"

"Hold on." She looked up and nodded. "I think there's a way to climb from here without a rope," she said. "I'm going to try." She dropped the rope to the bottom of the cavern, leaving it looped around the stalagmite. "It'll only take me a minute. I'll go higher and look around."

"Not without me, you won't," Paddy called back. "I'm not going to let you have all the fun."

Down on the cavern floor, he took both ends of the rope and twisted them together into a single thick cable. By pulling himself along the rope and bracing his feet against the rocky outcrops, he made his way up the steep wall like a mountain climber. Moments later he was standing next to his sister.

"That was a smart way to do it," she said.

"Where to now?" Paddy said, gasping for breath from the exertion.

Lucy pointed up the wall. "I think we can make it up using those ledges. They're almost like steps. See?"

"Yeah. A natural staircase. I'll bet Thomas Stephenson carved this first one to make it easier to reach them."

Lucy looked down at the way they had come and scoffed. "You call what we just did easy?"

"I guess his legs were longer than ours. He was probably used to climbing the masts of his ship. This was probably nothing to him."

Together they clambered up the wall, using the stalagmites for balance as they hopped from ledge to ledge. Soon they were standing on a rectangular platform alongside the spire draped with the long coat.

Paddy held up a worn sleeve. "Look—it's blue, just like I thought."

Lucy nodded. "His famous coat. Probably the same one he wore when he was attacking other ships."

"I'll bet we're the first people here since he left it," Paddy said proudly. He peered down to the water, forty or fifty feet below. Around them, the phalanx of spires stood by as if awaiting orders.

"The treasure has to be here," Lucy insisted. "Look around. I can't imagine he went to all this trouble for nothing."

They searched the nearby ledges and niches in the rock face, but it soon became obvious Lucy was wrong. No treasure, and no other clues to be found. "Oh, blast it, there's nothing here!" she finally admitted.

"I guess we came all the way here for nothing," Paddy groaned. He bent down for a pebble and heaved it over the edge, waiting to hear the splash from below. "This whole treasure hunt has gotten us nowhere. It's been nothing but riddles and more riddles. Maybe he didn't want his treasure to be found, or he was playing a big joke on everyone."

"Why would he leave his coat and hat here unless he wanted someone to climb up to get it? It doesn't make any sense."

"You said it yourself, Lucy—there's nothing here."

"I guess." Lucy exhaled slowly. "There's no reason to waste any more time. Let's climb down and look around the rest of the cave until we have to head back."

"I'm not leaving empty-handed," Paddy said. "At the very least, we deserve to take his coat for all the time and trouble he cost us. Besides, I want to try it on." He removed the blue jacket from around the spire and carefully slipped his arms into the sleeves, threadbare in places from the passage of time.

"How do I look?" he asked. "Like a real pirate, I'll bet. Look, it has brass buttons."

But Lucy didn't answer—she was too busy staring.

"What is it?" he asked from the other side of the ledge. "Do I look stupid?"

"We're such idiots," she said. "There's a picture of something carved on the rock. It was hidden under the coat. Come over here and take a look."

A square had been crudely etched into the rock, the corners of which were connected by crossing lines to form a letter 'X.' A small circle was inscribed where the lines of the 'X' crossed, and along the left side of the square were three stars, like those above the entrance to the cave.

"I don't get it," said Paddy, coming close.

"Neither do I."

She shivered; her soaked shoes were starting to bug her, and suddenly she had a burning desire to be out of the smelly cave and back in the warm sun so her drenched clothes could dry.

"You're the one who said pirates always mark the location of the treasure with an 'X,'" Paddy pointed out. "It means the treasure is here in the cave somewhere."

Lucy thought for a moment. "You said yourself that only happens in the movies. I think it's another clue—the reason he wanted us to climb up to this ledge. I wish I knew what it meant."

"There were also three stars on his gravestone," Paddy pointed out. "Maybe they're related somehow."

"I guess it's possible. Let me copy it down, and we can think about it later. But for now, why don't you put that blue coat back where you found it? That way we'll be able to find this rock later if we need to look at it again."

Paddy checked the pockets before he slipped the coat off with a heavy sigh.

"What now?"

"It's just . . . well, I wish we had a camera. I'll never get to see what I look like in that old jacket."

"If we find the treasure, I promise to buy you a full pirate outfit, okay?"

"It won't be the same thing somehow."

"Accept it," said Lucy. "Come on, let's get out of here."

The way down was easier. When they reached the steep part near the bottom of the wall, they bent their knees, leaned against the stone, and slid the rest of the way. Upon reaching the ground, Lucy pulled the rope down and stuffed it in her knapsack to protect the secret of the stairs.

"Should we go back now?" Paddy asked. "It's getting late."

"No," his sister replied. "Not yet. There may be something else deeper inside the cave. Let's keep going. We still have time."

They passed through the cavern until they reached a narrow passageway barely wide enough to walk side-by-side. Here the river came to their chests and flowed quickly; they held to the wall to keep from falling and floating off. This went on for some time, until the walls opened up again to form another cavern, about half the size of the first. They scrambled up onto a wide ledge that stretched along the wall ten or twelve feet above the river, shocked to discover that it was littered with shards of pottery—a few complete bowls and pots, but mostly broken pieces that had probably lain undisturbed for centuries. Here and there, some bones and a few skulls were scattered across the ground. Were these the victims of human sacrifices that Chi-Chi had told them about? Or were they the bones of people who lived here peacefully centuries ago? Would anyone ever learn the truth?

Now that he saw the bones, Paddy realized there was nothing scary about them. He thought of people sitting on that very spot, ages past, cooking food in their clay pots and living a simple life. He wondered what they were like—what did they talk about? What games did they play? What did their laughs sound like? Without quite knowing why, he felt sorry for them— and for himself, because he'd never learn the answers to these questions.

"Leave them alone," Lucy said, stopping Paddy from touching some pottery near his feet. "Maybe someday the islanders will stop being so superstitious and explore the cave, and they should find these things as they were left all those years ago."

So the twins walked past the pottery and the bones, being careful not to step on anything. When they reached the far end of the ledge, they clambered down and plunged back into the river. They forged through two more narrow corridors, continuing forward until they saw a soft light ahead emanating from a fissure in the rock blocked by thick brush.

They pushed their way between the branches and found themselves once more in the open air. They had passed through another entrance to the cave. After hours spent exploring in the dark, the bright sunlight stung their eyes.

"Well, that wasn't so bad," Paddy said.

After their vision cleared they looked behind. The back entrance to the cave was completely hidden by the tall vegetation. Above the entrance, though, the letters 'T.S.' were inscribed on the rock face, surrounded by the same three stars they had noticed on the other side and etched on the rock spire on the high ledge.

"That settles it," Lucy said. "He must've been telling us to look for a clue inside the cave that was marked by the three stars—the square with the 'X'. Now we just have to figure out what it means. Come on. We better hurry back through the cave if we hope to get home before Mom and Dad do."

Paddy glanced around. "Lucy, I think I know how to get home a faster way. The river empties into the sea. If we follow it, we can walk along the shore and we should get to the town marina from the other direction. I'll bet it isn't far; I think I can even smell the ocean from here. What do you think?"

She took a deep breath. "If we can get home without having to go back though that stinky cave, I'm all for it."

They followed the river through the jungle, until the trees suddenly gave way to the beach and the sea beyond. Nearby, on a high precipice jutting out into the sea, was Lion Rock, which they had previously seen while swimming with Chi-Chi at Shark Alley.

Lucy looked out toward the ocean. "There's that yellow boat again," she exclaimed. "You know, the one with the wavy blue stripe."

"That's interesting," said Paddy. "That's not where it was the last time we saw it."

"Hold on." She took the telescope from Paddy's knapsack and trained it on the boat. "I see people walking around . . . Hey! It's those two men who got into the fight with the old man that night we went to the restaurant with Mom and Dad."

"I wonder what they're up to?" Paddy asked.

FOURTEEN

"You went *where*?" Chi-Chi threw the basketball and it clanged off the rim, bouncing toward the grass.

"We told you," Lucy said. She paused to receive the ball from Chi-Chi, who had tracked it down. "We went into the cave and through to the other side." She took careful aim and let the ball fly.

"That's nine for me," she said proudly, as it fell through the hoop. "One more and I win." She tossed the ball to Paddy, who was standing on the other side of the court.

"That's because you're shooting from the easy spots. Try it from here." Paddy dribbled the ball three times and launched a long shot, which bounced softly off the backboard and rolled around the rim before dropping through the hoop. "Six for me," he said in triumph. "Chi-Chi, it's your turn again."

"What's there?" Chi-Chi asked. "Are there really bones of people from a long time ago?" He dribbled the ball toward the basket and took an off-balance shot, missing hopelessly. He chased it down and tossed it back to Paddy.

"Not just bones," answered Lucy. "We found clay pots, too. I think people used to live there."

"What about the bats?"

"They didn't bother us," said Paddy, not mentioning the strawberry jam. "I was even bleeding from my knee, and they didn't attack me."

"Wow. Wish I had gone with you."

"But that's not all," continued Lucy. She took another shot, a longer one this time, which hit the front of the rim and bounced away. "*We found another clue!*"

"To the treasure? Tell me!"

"It was a symbol carved on a rock," said Paddy. "We don't understand what it means. That's seven for me. Your shot, Chi-Chi."

Chi-Chi picked up the ball and carried it to a spot directly in front of the basket. This time, he used a simple two-handed underhand toss, and the ball fell right through the hoop without grazing the rim. "There! I'm catching up!"

Lucy watched the ball roll toward the center of the court. "Do you really mean that?" she asked.

"Yup—only three behind now," he confirmed.

"Oh, forget about basketball for a minute. I meant, do you really wish you had come with us?"

"Yeah, kind of," their friend admitted. "It's starting to sound exciting."

"Good," said Lucy. "Because we want to go somewhere else, and we could use your help getting there."

Chi-Chi frowned. "Where?"

"Yeah, where?" asked Paddy.

"The ancient temple we saw from the mountain."

"But that's just an old building. Why do you want to go there?" He looked at Paddy, who shrugged and shook his head. "Next you'll want me to take you to that run-down hotel with the *loco* playground."

"What's so special about that playground?" Paddy asked.

"I told you, it's like Noah's Ark. Masts and everything. Crazy. You climb up using these long ladders. But it's falling apart and covered with weeds."

"Listen," Lucy said, continuing on. "That treasure is hidden somewhere on this island, right?"

"Right . . .," agreed Chi-Chi.

"And he *wanted* someone to find it. He left clues so someone could find it someday."

Chi-Chi nodded. "Okay, I'm with you so far."

"But he didn't know how long it would take, so he made sure to leave them where they wouldn't be destroyed. Some of the clues are in his old house, which he instructed not to be changed in any way. He left a clue carved in a cave. Another one is on his grave itself. See what I mean? The question we should be asking ourselves is: where else would he have left a clue where he'd be sure it wouldn't be torn down or covered up?"

"The ancient temple," said Paddy and Chi-Chi together.

"You're right," Paddy added. "We've been going about this backwards. We should be trying to think from his point of view. You're brilliant."

"Thank you, Paddy," she said, blushing.

"What made you think of that?"

"While we've been playing, I've been watching those people whitewashing that mural across the street."

Chi-Chi turned. "It's for the festival. They paint a new one every summer."

"Exactly!" Lucy shouted. "They change it every year. I realized he had to make sure his clues weren't lost the same way."

"Okay, so you want to see the temple," said Chi-Chi. "Why do you need me?"

"We need help finding the right road."

"Not really a road. Just a dirt path. Entrance was washed away by a storm a few years back and it's all overgrown now."

"Can you show us?"

Chi-Chi squirmed and glanced around. "Don't know. What about that *hombre*?"

"Is that why you haven't been helping us?" Paddy countered. "Because you're afraid of that old man?"

Chi-Chi looked down at the ground.

"I thought you weren't afraid of anything," Lucy prodded.

"That was before—"

"Before what?"

"Forget it."

The silence lingered as they stood facing each other, their sweat dripping onto the blacktop. Chi-Chi sighed and looked up again.

"Look, you're going to leave at the end of summer. I *live* here. I'll always live here. I don't want him to chase me forever."

"I don't understand," Lucy said.

"He's following me, okay? Watching me. I see him all the time now and it's spooking me out."

"I'm sorry," Lucy said. "We didn't mean to pull you into this."

He shrugged.

"But I don't think you have anything to worry about," she continued. "He's interested in *us*—not you. He'll stop bothering you when we leave—or when we find the gold."

"Still leaves almost a month," Chi-Chi said. "He could be spying on us right now." He glanced around again. "That old guy is *dangerous*. I can feel it. Aren't you scared?"

"A little," Lucy admitted. "But I don't see the point in being afraid of something you can't control."

"Well, I can control it. All I have to do is stop hanging around you two."

"I don't think you really mean that," said Lucy as his words reverberated across the court.

Chi-Chi looked glum. "No, I don't. I'm out here playing ball with you, aren't I? I just don't want him to see me sneaking around with you, that's all. I don't like feeling that he's keeping track of me and what I'm doing."

"Come on, Chi-Chi—just this once. We won't involve you again. We really need your help. The geezer's not here. Let's go now. I have my notebook in my bag. He'll never know."

Chi-Chi's eyes moved between the twins' faces. Finally he muttered, "Can't believe I'm doing this."

"Great," said Paddy. "I'm ready."

"Come on, then." Chi-Chi rocked on his feet while he glanced around the square. "*Vamos. Pronto.*"

"There's one thing I have to do before we go," Lucy said. She walked toward the center of the court, picked up the ball, turned, and fired. She had never taken a shot from this distance before. The three watched the ball rise and then fall through the hoop.

"Ten," she said triumphantly. "I win."

☠ ☠ ☠

The temple was hidden deep in the jungle, in a wide clearing overgrown with thick grass and weeds. To get there, Chi-Chi led them on an unpaved road north, past a turn-off to the run-down hotel he had told them about. The twins pushed through the last curtain of trees and gawked at the huge structure looming over them. Chi-Chi had misled them: this was not a crumbling ruin lost to the ravages of time; no, it was much, much more than that.

Ahead of them, a great pyramid of stone, forty feet square at its base, rose from the open ground. Each of its smooth sides were interrupted only by the two parallel sets of wide steps extending to the top.

"Wow," said Paddy, taking it in. "That's awesome."

"Daddy's *National Geographic* magazine sometimes has photographs of pyramids like this in

Mexico," Lucy said. "I wonder if it was built by the Mayans or Aztecs or someone else."

"Maybe it was used by the people whose bones we found in the cave," Paddy wondered. He looked at Chi-Chi for an answer, but their friend was glancing into the jungle and not paying attention. Probably to see if they'd been followed.

They studied the pyramid, noticing it was divided into seven levels separated by wide walkways. The stone walls above the walkways were carved with designs that were impossible to discern from this distance.

They strolled through the clearing, past some grass-covered mounds. Chi-Chi followed behind, sullen and quiet. They reached the front of the pyramid, which had been built at one of the long ends of a rectangular plaza. Paddy noticed a wooden sign staked into the ground and went over to examine it.

"It's something about the temple," he called out. "Listen." He read:

The Temple of the Moon is believed to have been constructed between 1200-1400 A.D. It was first discovered in 1863 by British naturalist Henry Thibodeaux (1826-1897).

"He wasn't the first," Chi-Chi interjected. "He was the first outsider. People who lived here already knew about it."

"I didn't know you were listening," Paddy said.

Chi-Chi shrugged and turned away.

"What else does it say?" Lucy said. "Anything interesting?"

"Just that he was traveling on a ship belonging to the British Navy when it stopped here. It also says he discovered a small frog that he named after himself."

"Thibodeaux's Jungle Frog," said Chi-Chi. "He didn't really discover them, either. They're everywhere after a hard rain. But now everyone calls them by that stupid name."

"It also says a major excavation of the site is going to happen soon."

"No excavation," said Chi-Chi. "No money for it. Sign's old."

"Then why does it say it?" Lucy asked in an annoyed tone.

Chi-Chi shrugged again. "For tourists like you." He bent down and picked up a small red frog that was hopping around. "See? Now I'm an explorer, too."

"Come on," Lucy said. "Forget about the sign and who was here first. We don't have all day." Without looking back, she strode to the base of the temple.

Paddy rushed behind her and Chi-Chi followed at a half-hearted pace.

"What are we looking for?" Paddy asked once he had caught up.

"I don't know. I think we'll know it when we see it."

Lucy began to climb, pumping her knees to reach each high step. Soon she was out of breath, but she didn't stop until she reached the first walkway, where she paused to rest her aching muscles. Now she had a better view of some of the designs carved in the rock wall, images of people, birds, and large cats that may have been panthers.

"Whoa, look at that," Paddy said after he had caught up again. He pointed at one of the etchings, a human face that appeared to be crying or yelling. "Maybe Stephenson carved that one as a self-portrait."

"Don't make fun," Chi-Chi said from one of the upper steps. "The faces are sacred among my people. They have names. That one is known as *Achurituro*."

"Sorry."

Chi-Chi broke into a huge grin. "Kidding."

"Funny."

"Told you I've been here a bunch of times." By now Chi-Chi had reached the walkway. "That one with the weird expression is my favorite. I once got suspended from school by telling my friends it looked like our teacher." As Paddy stared at him skeptically, he added, "Truth, I swear. Three days. My mom made me write an apology."

"If you two are finished," Lucy said, "let's look in one of those openings. Maybe they go somewhere."

"Okay, but there's nothing there," Chi-Chi said under his breath.

They continued along the platform until reaching a rectangular-shaped archway, about five feet high. It led into a small room with a tiny window carved out of the stone. The walls, dark from soot in places, were scratched with years of graffiti, including names and initials of prior visitors. On a plaque was written 'DO NOT DEFACE THE MONUMENT,' in both English and Spanish. The twins scanned the writing for a secret message, possibly accompanied by the initials T.S., but nothing caught their attention.

They backed out and continued around the edge of the temple. On each side they found a pair of doorways, each leading to another empty, graffiti-covered room.

They continued their circuit until reaching the spot where they'd begun, and climbed higher to the next level, and then the next. At each they paused to examine the walls and small rooms, finding only more graffiti, including some purportedly left by Henry Thibodeaux himself, according to a sign.

The fourth level was partially damaged on the side of the temple facing the open plaza. Here, the blocks of stones above each doorway were smooth and a slightly lighter color, as if the carvings had been removed or chiseled off, replaced by cement.

Soon they climbed above the height of the tallest trees. Not far away, the peak of Mt. Alta Vista hovered over the island. In a clearing toward the south, they could just make out the tops of the buildings of the old hotel. Much farther in that direction lay the town harbor, and past it, the sea. The sun beat down on them, but overhead a dark cloud was forming. They continued upward. Eventually they reached the top of the temple, which had been squared off and left as a small platform. They sat with their feet dangling over the sloped slide of the pyramid and rested, enjoying the spectacular view of the clearing and the jungle.

"Look," said Paddy, pointing down at the large mounds of dirt that bordered the plaza. From the ground, they looked like steep little hills dotting the landscape, but from up here it was obvious they were something else. Something orderly, intentional, man-made. "Something was buried there. I'll bet anything it's the treasure." He stood and danced in a circle. "We have to get shovels. It'll take days to dig it up."

Chi-Chi laughed. "That's not the treasure. Those are other old buildings covered with dirt."

The enthusiasm drained from Paddy's limbs. "Uh . . . really?"

"Really. They tell us stuff like that on school trips. Told you there was nothing here."

"This is just like the sites in Mexico I've read about," agreed Lucy, ignoring Chi-Chi's last comment. "This whole area was probably once a city. I wish it was excavated. Even if there isn't any gold, there could be pottery or antiques under there."

"Then where *is* the gold we're looking for?"

"I don't know. We've been all over this temple." She sighed in frustration. "I was *sure* we'd find something. It made so much sense that he'd leave a clue here."

"Admit it," said Chi-Chi, repeating his earlier thought. "We came for nothing."

"Not nothing!" Lucy exclaimed. "Even if it didn't lead us to the treasure, this ancient temple was worth seeing. You're the one who keeps dragging us to different places around the island. Why didn't you want us to come here and look at it? The people that lived here could have been your ancestors."

"I already know all that," sniffed Chi-Chi. "Besides, the museum is full of old pottery and things from the people who used to live here. No reason to come here for that stuff."

"Maybe we should check it out," said Lucy. "It might be fun. Besides, it would give us a chance to see if that old journal is still there."

"Not me," Chi-Chi answered. "That museum is boring. Who wants to look at old stuff locked in cabinets? Even have to talk real quiet and walk careful. Like a library."

"Well, I think we should go," Lucy said to her brother. "Maybe next time it rains."

"That could be ten minutes from now." Paddy looked at the gathering storm clouds. "We'd better go."

Together they clambered down the tall steps. Back at the bottom, Lucy and Paddy paused in the middle of the grassy plaza and turned to take one last long look at the ancient temple. Then the three friends sprinted through the jungle to avoid the approaching downpour.

FIFTEEN

Jean-Pierre Le Moyne watched as the men plunged the rusty shovels into the ground, over and over, tossing clumps of rock and dirt onto the grass with each swing of their muscular arms. By now the hole was nearly five feet deep, and it wouldn't be long before he could drop the barrels and cover them up.

He turned and looked around, breathing in the salty air. The bluff overlooked the sea; he could hear the waves crashing against the shore. It was unlikely anyone would stumble upon the buried treasure. The island was sparsely populated; the only town of note was several miles away through a thick jungle or along the rocky shore. Maybe someday a road would be built, but by then he'd have dug up the gold and would be long gone. If he wasn't dead first.

That last thought concerned him. He hadn't planned on burying the treasure in some remote place, but then the message from Captain Forester had arrived. Forester wanted to meet with him on some backwater place called Janaconda Island, and gave a date a few weeks off. *I'll bet he wants some of the gold for himself*, Le Moyne thought, and hatched the plan to arrive on the island early and bury the treasure somewhere Forester couldn't find it. It might be a useful bargaining chip, if things came to that. It proved tricky navigating the nasty reef surrounding the island, but he was nothing if not patient, and eventually he discovered its secrets.

He glanced around the bluff, at the two dozen barrels on the grass containing nearly a ton of gold. It had taken a perfect job of piracy to seize it from that Venezuelan freighter—*a perfect job*, he thought proudly, and he was just the one to pull it off. To think he almost gave up as soon as he saw the convoy escorting the freighter to Spain! But no, he stuck it out, waiting for his opportunity. Then it came, on a dark night when the sea was shrouded by a blanket of ghostly fog. Stealthily he approached the last ship in the convoy, and before they knew what had happened, his men had boarded her and commandeered the vessel without firing a single shot. Then it was easy; he was a wolf in disguise among the sheep. No one thought anything was wrong when he sailed the stolen convoy ship alongside the freighter, and by the time the fog had dispersed, it had all been over. An act of wizardry; yes, that was it. Wizardry.

He paused to eye the pit's depth. More than two barrels deep. That should do it. He ordered the men to climb out of the hole and rolled the first barrel to the edge until it passed over the lip and tumbled in. Only twenty-three left. Then it would be time to see what Forester wanted with him.

SIXTEEN

The twins were eating breakfast when their mother entered the kitchen. "I've got great news," she said. "Do you remember Manuel Vargas, the man from the government who welcomed us when we arrived?" She paused until the twins grunted in response. "We ran into him yesterday. He asked about both of you."

"That *is* great news," Paddy mumbled, rolling his eyes.

"No, that isn't the news, and watch your tone. He offered to take you out in his boat today with his niece. She's just a few years older than the two of you. What do you think? It'll give you a chance to see the ocean."

"We can see the ocean from here," Lucy said.

Ignoring her retort, their mother continued, "I told him you would be delighted. He'll be expecting you at the marina at ten."

Lucy absentmindedly curled a lock of her hair around one of her fingers. "Where's Dad today?"

"He woke up early and went to a mangrove swamp on the far side of the island. He thinks it's a promising environment to find the heliomanth."

Paddy glanced up from his cereal. "Still no luck finding that fish?"

Their mother sighed. "Not yet. But he hasn't given up. We have to remain patient."

"But how *do* you know when it's time to give up?" he pressed.

"Paddy," she replied, "a dedicated scientist *never* gives up."

Just like dedicated treasure hunters, he thought.

"You go without me," he said to his sister. "There's some stuff I want to do around here today."

"I suppose that's all right," said their mother. "It'll be good for Lucy to spend some time with another girl. Maybe she can make a new friend."

Lucy exhaled hard and glared at her brother. "You owe me one."

☠   ☠   ☠

At the marina, Lucy found Manuel standing near a large boat parked in a slip reserved for government use. The words 'Janaconda Island Water Patrol' were hand-painted on the hull in black.

Manuel's face lit up as she approached. "Welcome," he said, holding his hands out, palm up. "I am glad you were able to make it."

"This is a huge boat," Lucy responded in awe. "I wasn't expecting something like this."

He smiled. "My duties include making sure no one is fishing in protected areas or conducting illegal activities on the reef. Every few days I take the boat and look around. It's pretty routine and we rarely see anything wrong, but I thought you and your brother might enjoy the trip out. Is he joining us as well?"

"He couldn't make it."

"Ah," Manuel said. "This is fine. I have arranged for you to have company. My fourteen-year-old niece Katarina is already onboard."

Lucy followed Manuel along a short metal walkway onto the deck of the ship. Katarina, a beautiful girl with long dark hair, was splayed on a lounge chair. She was wearing a stylish bathing suit and reading a magazine.

"*Hola*," said Lucy politely, but Katarina just kept reading.

"Katarina is angry with me," Manuel said softly. "She wants to go shopping, but I must do my work first and have insisted she come with me."

Lucy left Katarina alone and stood at the rail on the side of the boat. Manuel soon had the engine rumbling, and the vessel jolted as it pulled into the harbor.

The sea was calm and the hot sun felt good on her face. She sat down on a lounge chair near Katarina as the craft began to steam through the water.

"You're welcome to go wherever you want on the boat," Manuel said over his shoulder. "Make yourself comfortable. There's a kitchen and bathroom below deck."

Lucy nodded and stood up.

"If you're going down, could you bring me a drink and a snack?" Katarina asked without looking up.

"Okay." Lucy pushed open a door, leading to a lounge and a spiraling metal staircase. She descended and discovered the small kitchen, fully stocked. She grabbed two bottles of soda from the ice chest and a container of chips and returned to the upper deck.

"You are very kind," Katarina said when Lucy handed her the chips and one of the drinks. "How old are you?"

"Twelve."

Katarina nodded and smiled, then refocused on her magazine and didn't say anything else.

Lucy turned wand watched the sea roll past as the craft bounced through the low waves. Out of nowhere a pod of dolphins appeared at the surface, effortlessly leaping into the air as they raced alongside.

"You are lucky today," Manuel called from the helm. "Once, maybe twice a month they swim with the boat. Always in this spot."

Lucy stood and returned to her place by the rail to get a better look. From the corner of her eye she noticed Katarina craning her neck behind the pages of her magazine. Their eyes locked momentarily.

Katarina shrugged. "I see dolphins all the time," she said, sinking back into her chair.

After the pod vanished under the waves for the last time, Lucy remained at the rail, wondering what else there would be to see. About ten minutes later, the boat slowed.

"We've reached the edge of the reef," said Manuel over the rumble of the engine. "The water isn't very deep here, and we must be careful not to damage the boat on the sharp coral. We'll speed up again soon. Meanwhile, if you look into the water, you may be able to see fish swimming near the surface."

He picked up a pair of binoculars and swung them in a wide arc. Then his face darkened. "Oh, not again," he grumbled. "Hold on."

The deck tilted as Manuel changed direction. Less than a minute later Lucy was able to identify another craft in the distance. It was the yellow boat with the curved blue stripe.

The government boat approached and pulled alongside, slowing until coming to a complete stop.

"Hey," Manuel shouted. "You can't be there."

Lucy shielded her eyes from the glare and noticed the two now-familiar-looking men standing on the deck. They were peering over the edge, where several ropes and cables dangled down into the water.

"What?" one of the men yelled back. "What did you say?"

"I've told you this before," called Manuel. He moved his arms to emphasize his point. "This is a government-protected marine zone. You have to move your boat. You can't stay here."

The men each waved back. "We'll be going soon," one said.

"You'll be leaving now, or you'll be receiving a fine."

"We need some time to pull up our equipment." From the man's tone, it didn't sound like he was very happy about it.

Manuel shook his head. "I'll be back in an hour. I want you gone by then." Then he turned the wheel once more, and Lucy felt the boat accelerate.

"I've caught those men in this region several times before," Manuel said once the other vessel was out of sight. "They know they shouldn't be there. It's a regulated area."

"Why? Isn't the ocean for everyone?"

"It is very easy to become caught on the reef. We do not have the resources to carry out rescue and repair operations at sea. Several months ago, a pleasure craft like that one became stuck and tore its hull trying to back up. We did not reach it in time. It sank to the bottom and leaked oil for several weeks. Even now the fishermen must avoid that area." He shook his head. "It is easier to prohibit large boats from navigating over the reef."

"But we're going over it," Lucy pointed out. "Your boat is bigger than theirs."

Manuel nodded and smiled. "There are natural channels where the water is deep enough to pass without causing damage. Every boat is given a map when it registers with our office of marine protection. The passages are clearly marked. But those men were drifting over the reef itself. It wouldn't surprise me if they had dropped their anchor, which is illegal."

"Why is that illegal?"

"It will eventually get stuck in the rocks and they won't be able to pull it up. There are probably half a dozen anchors in the reef that had to be cut loose. You can see them from the surface if you know where they are." He shrugged. "They become unmarked hazards to other craft."

Lucy thought of their trip to Shark Alley with Chi-Chi. "Aren't people allowed to go swimming or snorkeling along the reef? To see the fish? Maybe that's all they're doing."

"Of course," Manuel responded. "The coral reef is one of the best places for that. But you must use a small, flat-bottomed boat. These men—they are not here to snorkel or swim. They're treasure hunters."

Lucy was stunned. "Uh . . . treasure hunters?"

There was the briefest of pauses before Manuel continued. "Yes. Years ago, lots of ships sank in these waters. Every now and then treasure hunters come and try to locate one of these shipwrecks, hoping to find something valuable. They bring all sorts of equipment, but even so, it takes a long time and a lot of patience to find anything. These particular men have been here since late spring." He took a sip of water from his canteen. "I'll bet they're searching for that old pirate ship, *Miner's Revenge*. People have been looking for it for years. Hang on, I'm going to open her up now."

The purr of the engine rose as the ship picked up speed. Lucy watched the ocean sparkle under the sun's glare as the boat raced through the sea, considering what she had just heard. So those two men were also searching for the gold, and they must believe it was aboard Le Moyne's ship when it sank. What they would do if they discovered her family was living in Thomas

Stephenson's old house? And that there might be clues there leading to the treasure itself?

Manuel continued his loop around the island, hugging the reef. From time to time they saw a fishing boat. In each case Manuel waved in greeting before they moved on, but he didn't stop. They passed the entrance to several small coves, leaving Lucy to wonder if one was where their father had gone to search for the heliomanth. When they were partway around, he pointed out Lion Rock, before they raced past the entrance to the harbor. When they returned to where they had seen the yellow boat, it was gone.

"Okay, Lucy," Manuel said. "We're done for today. Let's go home."

"It's about time." Katarina shut her magazine and looked at Lucy. "You want to go shopping with me? I need a new pair of shoes."

SEVENTEEN

The following morning their father was in a sour mood. His trip to the mangrove swamp hadn't gone well; not only did he fail to catch a heliomanth, but the boat got caught along the bank and he had to wade into the muck to help push it out. By the time he got home the rest of the family had already gone to sleep, and even now he still smelled funny.

Paddy, however, didn't appear for breakfast—in fact, Lucy hadn't seen him since yesterday when she got home after spending several hours shopping with Katarina. The older girl turned out to be quite friendly and would hardly stop talking, mostly about movie stars and fashion and the older boys on the island.

Anxious to tell Paddy what she had discovered about the two men on the yellow boat, she pounded on his bedroom door until he finally opened it.

She looked around, confused. His room was a total mess. Old astronomy books were spread across the floor, blocking the entrance.

"*What* are you doing in here?"

"I can't find it anywhere," Paddy grumbled.

Shutting the door, Lucy skirted the textbooks and sat down on an empty spot on the floor. "What can't you find?"

Paddy sighed. "The *constellation*, Lucy," he said, flopping on his bed. "I'm trying to identify the *constellation*."

"I'm not stupid," she sniffed. "Stop talking to me like I'm four." Then after a long pause she added, "Um, *what* constellation?"

Paddy pulled up his feet into a cross-legged position. "The constellation on the tile with the gold coin." He rubbed his nose with his palm. "Didn't we talk about this already?"

"Um . . . no." She crossed her arms. "Out with it."

"Well . . . I think I discovered another clue while you were out yesterday."

"What? Tell me!"

"Maybe it's better if I showed you."

He opened the door and stood in the center of the hall, pointing above each bedroom doorway. "Take a good look at what's on each of those tiles. Wind, water, sun, the ground, and sky. Right? Remember that. Now come with me."

Paddy led Lucy downstairs and into the center of the living room. He turned to face the wall opposite the picture window, where five paintings were arranged in three rows: one on top and one on the bottom with three in a straight line between them.

"What do you see there?"

"Is this some kind of test?" she grumbled. "They're all pictures of old ships. Two are in a storm, and three are in a calm sea. So what?"

"Look more carefully. One is of a ship in a storm with a really strong wind. You can tell by the sails and the size of the waves. This one here is in a rainstorm. These two are ships sailing under a bright sun and anchored next to shore."

"And the one in the middle is a picture of a different ship at night," finished Lucy. "Again, so what? They're not very good. I think the painting of the castle is much better."

"Ignore the boats for a moment. The pictures contain the wind, water, sun, ground, and the sky—just like those tiles upstairs! That's got to be intentional."

Lucy silently worked it through. "You're right. They are similar. But that could be coincidence. After all, there are only so many ways to paint a ship."

"That's not all," he continued. "The wind tile over your door has the word 'EAST' printed on it. On a map, east is always on the right. And look—the painting on the right is the one with the strong wind. The directions on the other tiles match their paintings, too."

"One of the tiles upstairs doesn't have a direction etched on it."

"That's the tile with the gold coin and the stars." He tapped the painting of the ship sailing under the night sky. "It corresponds to the one in the middle, so it doesn't need a direction. It all fits, doesn't it?"

"Wow," Lucy exclaimed. He really *had* found something.

"There's one more thing." Paddy's eyes met hers. "You won't believe this, but the constellation in the painting is the same as the one on the tile with the gold coin."

Lucy stared back, mouth agape. "You think the constellation is a clue to the location of the treasure."

"Or somewhere. Problem is, I can't identify it. I found all those old astronomy books in the house, but they're no help. They're more about the planets and different kinds of stars than the constellations."

"Did you try the library?"

"I didn't have time."

Lucy looked at her watch. "Let's go now. It should be open."

"Okay," said Paddy. "Let me get a sketch I made first."

He ran up the stairs, two at a time, and returned a moment later holding a sheet of lined paper, which he folded and stuffed into his back pocket.

After riding to town and leaving their bikes near the school playground, the twins headed to the library on foot. While passing through the main square, though, a familiar voice interrupted their thoughts.

"Well, well. Who do we have here? Paddy . . . and Lucy? Do I have that right?"

They turned around, startled.

The old man smiled over the top of his newspaper. "I believe I promised to buy you each some flavored ice. Why don't you have a seat and I'll get some?"

"Um, that's okay," said Lucy, backing away. "It's a little too early in the day for that."

The old man shrugged and tapped the ground with his steel-tipped shoes. "I thought it was *never* too early for a bowl of ice, but suit yourselves." He toyed with his torn ear with his thumb and forefinger.

"How'd that happen?" Paddy blurted.

"Paddy!" Lucy whispered, nudging him in the side.

"A monkey bit it off." He laughed. "So how's that treasure hunt coming along? Have you discovered anything interesting in that house to share with me?"

Hearing the old man's voice gave Paddy the creeps. "No, not a thing," he said, sticking his hand into his rear pocket and scratching at his hip. "It's a really boring house, like we told you before. But we'll let you know if we find anything." He turned to leave, but the conversation wasn't over.

"Now what's this?" The man bent down to pick up a piece of paper.

"That's mine." Paddy reached to take it. "It must've fallen out of my pocket."

The man pulled his hand back, then unfolded the lined paper and looked it over, frowning.

"You like stargazing?" he asked.

"Huh?" Paddy snatched the paper away and jammed it into his pocket. "No."

"Well, then, why are you carrying around a picture of the constellation Gemini? It's not very accurate, though—the star Castor is misplaced; it belongs farther to the northwest. As drawn, it's much too close to its brother Pollux."

Flustered, the twins stared at each other until the old man broke the silence.

"Oh, I get it." He laughed in short bursts, a strange cackle that sounded a bit like a bird. "Gemini—the two of you are twins—do you carry that around for luck?" He laughed again. "Have a good day, kids. If you find anything you want to tell me about, you can usually find me here each morning."

The twins mumbled a polite good-bye and hurried out of the square.

"So the constellation is Gemini," said Lucy. "We're such idiots—Castor and Pollux. I think that's in the name of the music on the piano. You *played* it."

"Oh. Yeah. There were even stars drawn across the title, but I thought they were just doodles."

Lucy grimaced. "I never thought we'd figure out a clue with *his* help."

"If it weren't for him, we wouldn't have known about the treasure in the first place," Paddy pointed out. "Every time we run into him we learn something new."

He pulled out the sheet of paper and stared at it. "So it's Gemini, huh? I don't get why he thought it was so funny."

"The zodiac sign for Gemini is twins," Lucy answered. "Twins—like you and me. Come on, let's go."

"I guess there's no point going to the library." Paddy said, refolding the drawing. "What should we do? I don't feel like going home."

"It looks like it's going to rain. Let's check out that museum before we get caught in it."

"Fine with me," replied Paddy. "It's got to be close by somewhere."

☠   ☠   ☠

The museum was located down a sleepy side street near the marina, in an old building constructed from dark stone. Upon entering, they first noticed a sturdy desk partway down the hall with a familiar-looking woman sitting behind it. She wore a creased blue shirt, buttoned to the top, with the words 'Janaconda Island Museum of History' sewn over the pocket. One of her arms was encased in a plaster cast, which hung from her neck by a cloth sling.

"Look," Lucy said. "It's the librarian. I wonder what happened to her arm."

The museum lady chuckled. "I see you've met my sister."

"Your sister?" Paddy stared. "You look exactly alike." Even their hair was done in the same style. He took a sniff of the air. Thankfully, they didn't use the same perfume.

"As we should," said the museum lady. "We're twins."

"No kidding," answered Lucy. "We're twins, too."

"But not identical," Paddy added. "Then we'd both have to be boys."

"No, you'd be a girl," Lucy countered. "I would never be a boy."

The museum lady laughed again. "You certainly argue like twins. Not that I have any experience at that."

"When do twins stop arguing?" asked Paddy.

"I don't know. Maybe never."

"Oh. Then I guess we better get used to it."

The woman smiled. "Twins have a strange way of showing they love each other. It's normal." She handed Lucy a brochure, adding, "Ask me any questions while you're here. Enjoy your visit."

"Thanks," Lucy said. "We will."

As Lucy slipped the pamphlet into her knapsack, Paddy rushed off to find the pirate exhibit. It didn't take long. Inside a display cabinet was a small sign that read 'Journal of the Notorious Pirate Jean-Pierre Le Moyne.' The glass was cracked like a spider web, and a fist-sized hole in the center was taped up. A sticker read, 'Exhibit Temporarily Closed' in both English and Spanish.

Paddy peered inside. The cabinet was empty other than an empty book stand, a small model of a sailing ship with twin masts, and a yellowing placard, which he read intently.

Born in Haiti to French immigrants, Jean-Pierre Le Moyne spent much time at sea as a child, most often aboard ships owned by his father, a known trader and smuggler. At the age of seventeen, three years after his father was arrested and hung by local lawmen, Le Moyne fled to southern Mexico, intending to earn an honest living mining silver, quickly becoming disillusioned by the poor conditions and low pay. In 1842, at the age of twenty-one, he was shot by bandits and left for dead while transporting silver ore for the mining company. At the time he had just eleven dollars in his pocket. Soon thereafter, he became a bandit himself, believing it was easier and more profitable to rob others than to perform manual labor.

For the next several years, Le Moyne and his band of henchmen terrorized the area of southern Mexico, Honduras, and British Honduras. Starting with burglary and simple theft, they soon progressed to more serious crimes such as bank and train robbery, avoiding capture by fleeing across the borders between the three countries.

In July 1845, the three governments formed a joint task force to track down and capture Le Moyne and his gang. Tipped off by a local officer, Le Moyne commandeered a 40-ton schooner, the

H.M.S. Santa Lucia, which he loaded with thirty cannon and renamed the Miner's Revenge. Le Moyne soon began plundering fishing vessels and cargo ships, calling himself "Bully Blue-Coat" for the long velvet blue jacket he wore during attacks. For such audacity, he quickly developed a reputation as the most notorious pirate captain to sail the Caribbean during the middle of the 19th century.

"Huh," said Lucy, reading over her brother's shoulder. "That explains the name of his ship."

"Most of that information is in the history book the librarian showed me."

"It's all such a shame. He was kind of forced into being a pirate. If he hadn't been robbed when he was in Mexico, who knows what would've happened to him. All he wanted was to make a living."

Paddy nodded. "And somehow he ended up here." He ran his fingers over the taped cabinet case. "I guess there's nothing here for us to see after all. Might as well leave now."

The museum lady must have been watching, because she said then, "If you're looking for Le Moyne's journal, I'm afraid it's not here at the moment."

"Yeah, we know," said Paddy, walking part of the way back to the front desk. "Your sister told us it had been stolen."

The museum lady frowned. "Did she now?"

"Yeah, she did. She was super nice. She told me a little about the history of the island and gave me a book to read. So what happened?"

The woman hesitated. "Well . . . museum employees aren't supposed to tell visitors about the theft."

By now Lucy had rejoined her brother at the front of the room. "We won't tell anyone—promise."

The lady glanced around, as if to confirm the museum was otherwise empty. "I guess it would be okay to tell you. After all, twins have to look out for each other, right?"

"Right," agreed Lucy.

"I was working the desk," she began, "when two men came into the museum. They walked over to me and asked to purchase the journal. Just like that. Of course, I told them this was a museum, not a dime store, and our exhibits were *not* for sale. They became angry and stormed off. Next thing I heard was the sound of glass shattering."

"They broke the case!" exclaimed Paddy. "Did you try to stop them?"

"I tried, dear. I saw what they had taken and demanded they give it back. One of the men laughed and said if I wasn't going to sell it to them, they'd have to take it for themselves. I tried to block the way, but it did no good! They shoved me out of the way and onto the floor. That's how I broke my arm." She held up the plaster cast and wiggled her fingers.

"That's horrible!" said Lucy.

"I called the police immediately," the woman continued, "but the men drove off and got away when the officer chasing them hit a taxi. I'm afraid the police on this island couldn't even catch a cold."

"Oh." The twins silently remembered the car accident at the bottom of their driveway on the day they moved in. So *that* was who the policeman was chasing.

"The funny thing is that the men only took that old journal," the museum lady added, "and nothing with any real historical value. Especially when there are plenty of valuable artifacts here."

Paddy's eyes shot up. "Why do you say that?"

The museum lady made a quick movement with her good arm. "Most people think it's a fake—a hoax. Someone donated it to the museum some years ago, and he wouldn't say where he had gotten it. He insisted it remain on display. Otherwise, we would have removed it years ago. I suppose we should be thankful the thieves didn't take anything else."

"Do you remember what they looked like?" Lucy asked, even though she had a hunch she already knew the answer.

"Why, sure do," the museum lady said. "I don't think I'd ever forget them. One was tall and thin, and the other was a little shorter, with wide shoulders and big arms. They both had brown hair and spoke in American accents."

"Uh, thanks," said Lucy. She'd heard all she needed. "I think we'll go look at some of the other exhibits while we're here." She grabbed hold of Paddy's arm and dragged him behind one of the larger display cases.

"Paddy," she whispered, "she's got to be talking about those two men that pushed the old man into the street that night in the village. They must think there's something in that journal that will lead them to the treasure."

"How do you know they're looking for the treasure?"

"They're the men on the yellow boat! I saw them when I was with Manuel. They were in a protected spot and he told them to move."

"Why didn't he arrest them?"

She bit her lower lip. "I don't know. Maybe he doesn't know they're the robbers. He's not a policeman. But more important, he told me they're searching for the *Miner's Revenge* along the reef. That's why they're out there. They're looking for the gold, too."

Paddy steamed. "When, exactly, did you think would be a good time to tell me that?"

"I tried! But you locked yourself in your room, and then I forgot when—"

"That doesn't matter! We're a team in this. You—"

Lucy cut him off with a wave. "Hey, look at this," she said, staring into the huge glass cabinet next to them, which contained two rows of pictographs. "It's the blocks that were missing from the side of the temple." She read from the adjoining placard:

These carvings, removed from the Great Temple in 1931, demonstrate the sophisticated craftsmanship of this long-ago culture. Like the other carvings on the temple's façade, one row consists of depictions of animals and human faces, believed to be portraits of high priests and other leaders of the society. The second row incorporates images of the moon in different phases. These are the only known symbols of a celestial object discovered from this ancient culture.

"So that's what happened to those lost stones," she said. "We should have guessed that; it's pretty common in archaeology. The British removed carvings from ancient Greek temples and took them back to England."

"Lucy! Stop talking for once. There are four moons."

"Yes, I know. I just read that."

Exasperated, Paddy tapped the glass case. "Don't you get it? Four moons. The inscription on the gravestone had four moons on it. Remember?"

Lucy's eyes widened. "Paddy—there's something else there, too. Look closely at the carving of the full moon. Do you see it?"

Paddy squinted. "'T.S.' Of course! The temple was a marker after all—we simply didn't know it!"

Also carved next to the four moons was a small square similar to the one the twins had discovered inside the cave: the opposite corners were connected in an 'X', and a tiny circle was etched over the point where they met. Unlike that other carving, though, this one didn't include three stars along its right side.

Lucy rifled through her knapsack and pulled out the pamphlet the museum lady had given her, unfolding it. "There." She held it up so Paddy could see the photo of the four moons. For some reason, Thomas Stephenson's initials and the carved square had been edited out, so Lucy uncapped her pen and drew them in. "That's all we need. Come on, we've got work to do."

EIGHTEEN

Lucy spent the rest of the day alone, thinking about the men who'd stolen the journal from the museum. Why were they searching for the *Miner's Revenge*? Everyone knew the gold was hidden somewhere on the island, so what were they hoping to find? None of it made any sense.

"Maybe they know something we don't," she said. "Maybe the journal isn't a fake after all, and there's something important in it. I wish we could take a look at it."

Paddy sighed. "They're just wasting their time. He stashed the gold around here somewhere; we just have to find it. Besides, if the gold is on the bottom of the sea, it would be the end of our treasure hunt. Not even Chi-Chi could hold his breath long enough to look for it there."

Lucy tightened her lips but didn't respond. She was determined to find out what the men were doing, and why. She only had to figure out how.

☠   ☠   ☠

The answer came a few days later, when Flapper Bathwaite unexpectedly showed up at Rita's to sell several snapper and triggerfish. Remembering his promise, Rita sent a message to Lucy and Paddy's parents, who hurried over to speak with him, the twins following behind.

"Why you want this *pescado*?" Flapper asked in heavily-accented broken English, after listening to their father's description of the heliomanth.

"Science," the twins' father replied. "*Ciencia.*"

Flapper's eyes narrowed. "Science, *si*, I no *estupido.*"

"Well—can you tell us where you catch them?" He paused, then made a reeling motion with his hands. "Where? *Cuándo*?"

"No, no. *Dónde. Cuándo* mean 'when'. *¿Comprendes?*"

"Well—*dónde*, then."

"No, I cannot," said Flapper, shaking his head. "It is secret." He imitated the reeling motion. "Secret spot. Good for fish, not good for *turista.*"

At this point Rita stepped in and a full-blown argument in Spanish ensued. After several minutes of back-and-forth, Flapper threw up his hands.

"Okay, okay. I take you. But must keep spot secret."

Mr. Hendricks exhaled in relief. "Yes. Si. We promise. When can you take us? Uh, *cuándo*?"

Flapper chuckled. "*Bueno*, you learn. I like you. Only catch this *pescado* at night. We go tonight. *Esta noche*. Meet me at dock. Six o'clock. Okay?"

Their mother turned. "Will you two be all right without us? You'll have to prepare your own dinner and put yourselves to bed. We might not return until early in the morning."

"We'll be fine," said Lucy. "Don't worry about us." She smiled with her most innocent expression. Inside, though, she had already begun to hatch a plan.

"We'll be there," said Mr. Hendricks.

"*Excelente*," said Flapper. "No be *tarde*."

That was one word that didn't need translation.

☠   ☠   ☠

As their parents mounted their bikes and pedaled home to prepare for their trip, Lucy leaned close to her brother. "Did you hear that? They'll be gone all night. This is the perfect chance to check out that boat."

"The yellow one with the stripe?" he replied. "No way. It's too dangerous."

"You haven't even heard my idea yet."

"I don't have to."

"Oh, just listen. Tonight, when it gets dark, we can take the rowboat and sneak up on them. They'll never notice us. Maybe we'll find out what they're up to."

Paddy frowned. "That's your silliest idea ever."

"Why?"

"For one thing, that boat could be anywhere."

"We've got the rest of the day to find it. Come on. We can do this. We have to, Paddy. We *have* to. Something isn't right with those two, and I want to know what's going on."

"I know," sighed Paddy, adjusting his glasses. "That's always your problem."

☠   ☠   ☠

It didn't take long to find the boat anchored south of the island, just a few hundred yards offshore, on the far side of the harbor. Through his telescope, Paddy watched the two men walk back and forth on the deck. For a time they stood near the railing, as if gazing into the water.

"I wonder what they're looking for," he said, his voice trailing off. Next to him, Lucy smiled. She knew she had him now.

As sunset approached, they walked down the hill to where the small rowboat was tethered. After Lucy climbed in, Paddy untied the rope and shoved off from the wood dock into the gray sea.

The sun crept toward the horizon, painting the sky with streaks of orange and red. Paddy pulled hard on the oars until his shoulders grew numb, humming under his breath as he rowed. Lucy sat in the front, her attention focused on locating the yellow boat.

"Look!" she whispered as they were lifted by the crest of a wave. "There it is."

Paddy relaxed his arms and raised his head. The boat was maybe a hundred yards ahead. Even in the last glows of dusk, the wavy blue stripe along its hull was unmistakable. With renewed vigor, Paddy continued his rhythmic strokes. One, two, three, four. One, two, three, four. One, two—

"Quiet!" Lucy whispered.

"I didn't say anything!"

"Can't you row softer? We don't want them to hear us."

"I'll try." He exhaled slowly. Now would come the difficult part, the part he'd been dreading. The two men were undoubtedly dangerous, and Paddy knew he'd have to be ready to row hard at any moment if they were detected.

The rowboat floated closer and closer to the yacht ahead of them. A cloud passed in front of the rising moon, temporarily darkening the sky. The seawater slapped against the side of the rowboat with a rhythmic *thump-thump-thump*, and it gave Paddy an idea of sorts. He began to time each of his strokes to the beat of the lapping waves to mask their sound. It seemed to work. He pulled the wooden oars, ignoring his screaming muscles.

Moments later, the rowboat glided up to the yacht. Paddy flicked his left oar one last time, and the rowboat rotated in a tight turn as it floated to a halt next to the larger vessel's hull. From here, the yacht towered above them. Lucy tied their rope to its anchor line to keep from floating off. So far, so good.

"Now what?" Paddy whispered.

"*Shh!* I can hear someone walking around."

Paddy cocked his head and held his breath. Amid the rhythmic thumps of the waves lapping against both boats, he heard movement and the clatter of equipment, then the unmistakable sound of a door opening.

The creak of footsteps. "Here's a couple of aspirin."

"Thanks. I must've risen too quick." The clink of a bottle, the guzzling of a drink. "Water's deeper here, too."

"You were down a long time. Don't know if that makes a difference."

"I would've stayed down more, but the light was disappearing. Not much visibility this late in the day."

"You can go back down tomorrow morning."

"I've seen all there is to see at this spot. There's nothing here. Nothing but fish and sand."

"So we'll pull anchor first thing," said the first voice. "Go to a different spot."

"I don't know. I'm beginning to think we're wasting our time out here."

"It's down there. We just gotta stay patient. We'll find it."

A cough. "We've been hunting for three months. We've got nothing to show for it."

"I never said this was gonna be easy."

"Easy? It's like looking for a needle in a haystack. I think that diary was someone's idea of a joke. And we got suckered."

"It's not a fake!" The voice of the first man rose. "I know a forgery when I see one. I've done a couple myself."

"With a prison term to show for it."

"I'm telling you, this is the real deal."

The silence dragged on for what seemed like minutes. Down in the rowboat, Lucy and Paddy looked at each other, afraid to move.

Then: "We've already been along the entire coast. Maybe we're at the wrong island or something."

"Give me the book," the first voice said angrily. The twins heard paper being ripped. "Look at that! It's definitely Janaconda Island. You see? It looks like a peach. No other island around here has that shape."

"I kind of think it looks like a snake's head, Boss. See? That cove would be its mouth."

"Whatever. The important thing is that this map shows where the ship hit the reef. It's right near here. All we got to do is find where it ended up." He belched noisily. "We paid a lot of money for this boat, and we're not gonna stop until we find that treasure."

"I thought we stole the boat."

"Whatever."

"Did you hear that?" whispered Lucy, the moonlight flashing across her eyes. "That's why they think the gold is on the bottom of the ocean! It's marked on a map."

"Shh! They're still talking."

". . . myself if you don't want to." There was a soft thump, the kind of sound a thick book might make when dropped on a table.

"Ah, forget it. I'm just frustrated, that's all. Maybe we should go into town tonight and blow off some steam."

"That's a good idea. But first make us some dinner. I netted a couple of yellowtail snapper earlier. They're on the stove. I'm gonna be in my cabin."

More stomping around. A door opened and shut. Then everything was quiet, except for the beat of the waves against both boats.

"I think they left the journal up on the deck," Lucy whispered, wide-eyed. "I'm going to try to get it."

"Don't even think about it!" Paddy hissed back, but Lucy was already scaling the narrow metal ladder next to the anchor line.

Paddy watched in horror as she hoisted herself over the rail, disappearing from sight. Then her head popped up and she motioned for him to follow.

"Oh, here we go again," Paddy muttered. He stood, being careful to keep his balance, and grabbed the ladder. Up he went. When he reached the top, he slipped between the two railings that ran the length of the boat and dropped to the deck, where he crouched in the darkness next to his sister.

"I can't believe we're doing this," he muttered.

He glanced around. The deck was littered with cabinets and tools. His eyes fixed on a roundish metal-and-glass helmet near a large wooden box with what looked like a pair of steering wheels attached on opposite sides. The top of the helmet was connected to the box by a long black tube coiled in a pile.

"What's that stuff?"

"It's a diving helmet and an old-fashioned air pump," Lucy answered. "To breathe underwater."

Paddy nodded. "What do we do now?"

Lucy pointed toward a rectangular equipment chest. On the lid was a book with a brown leather cover. "There it is."

Paddy silently eyed the closed door near the chest.

"They've both gone below deck," Lucy said, correctly reading her brother's expression. "I can do it—you wait here."

Exhaling hard, Lucy made her way across the deck, weaving in and out of the shadows. Carefully, very carefully, she took the last few steps while holding her breath, hoping the wood flooring wouldn't creak. Then she held up her arm, grinning. The book was in her hand.

"Come on!" whispered Paddy, still crouched in the shadows. "Take it, and let's go! Hurry!"

But Lucy didn't return, not yet, for on top of a different cabinet near the doorway she noticed a weathered piece of paper. She picked it up. It was the map the two men had ripped from the journal and had been arguing over.

It was definitely a map of the island. There was a mountain drawn in the middle, and an arrow pointing at a spot along the coast labeled 'Lion Rock.' A short way offshore was a red 'X', which could only be where the *Miner's Revenge* struck the reef and began to sink. It probably wasn't far from where they were right now.

Underneath the hand-drawn map and continuing on the back of the page was a lengthy inscription penned in a neat script. Forgetting the danger of the situation, Lucy held it up to catch the moonlight. Then, as Paddy watched, she shoved it inside the back cover of the journal and flashed him the thumbs-up signal.

She took three or four steps toward her brother when a muffled sound rang out from below. Someone was coming up the steps.

"Lucy!" Paddy cried, forgetting to whisper. "Come on! They're coming!"

The door slammed open against the bulkhead and a man stepped out. Her heart racing, Lucy couldn't help herself: she froze.

The man saw her immediately. "Hey—what are you doing here?" He strode toward her. Then he saw what was in her hand and his jaw tensed. "Give me that!" he yelled, grabbing at the journal.

Lucy held onto the book with all her strength, but the man yanked hard and her grip started to slip. Paddy shouted something at her when suddenly there was a terrible ripping sound. All at once the back cover tore off; the map came loose and fluttered into the air; and Lucy flew backward and fell painfully on her hip. The map floated across the deck before landing near the man, who bent to grab it.

That was the distraction Lucy needed. She scrambled to her feet and in a single motion turned and tossed the journal into the air. "Paddy!" she yelled. "Here! Catch!"

It was a perfect throw. Before Paddy could react, the journal hit him squarely in the chest, bouncing to the deck. He picked it up, leaned over the rail, and dropped it into the rowboat.

"Come on, Lucy," he called. "Come on!"

Lucy sprinted across the deck with the man in pursuit. Then good fortune struck as a large wave hit them broadside. The yacht tilted one way, then the other. Losing his balance, the man stumbled and fell, grasping for Lucy's heels as he sprawled across the floor. Lucy didn't stop. She had only a few feet to go—and then she reached the railing, swung her legs over, and started climbing down the ladder to the rowboat, where Paddy was already waiting with the oars in his hands.

"Let's go!" she cried as she jumped the last few feet. The rowboat teetered dangerously, but didn't tip over. "Row—what are you waiting for?"

"We're still tied up!"

Lucy turned in horror. The cord still held the rowboat to the anchor line! She scrambled along the boat to reach it. She glanced up to see the man glaring down at her from the railing's edge. Almost immediately he was joined by another man.

The first man pointed down toward the rowboat. "They've got the journal!" he yelled. "Don't just stand there—get the gun! Shoot a hole in that damn boat!"

"It's in the cabin!"

"Idiot!"

"Hurry, Lucy, hurry," cried Paddy.

By now Lucy had scurried to the other end of the rowboat and was fumbling with the connection. In a moment she had released the cord. They were free!

"Go!" Lucy shouted, as the men climbed over the rail and prepared to leap down.

She took a seat on the nearest bench as Paddy began to row as hard as he could. The rowboat inched away, gaining speed with each pull on the oars.

"They're getting away," screamed the second man as he stepped back.

"Well, swim after them!"

"Why me?"

"You used to be a lifeguard, didn't you?"

The shorter man hesitated. "But the sharks—and those big fish with the teeth—"

"Just go! I'll meet you at the dock. Hurry!"

The man jumped in the water with a splash. He disappeared, but the twins could now hear the sound of his body cutting through the water.

"Quicker, Paddy!" Lucy shouted. "He's getting closer!"

"I'm rowing as fast as I can!" he shot back. But he pushed himself harder, focusing on his strokes. One, two, three, four. He counted each pull, over and over again. One, two, three, four. Now even his back was beginning to ache, and he could no longer ignore the pain shooting through his shoulders. One, two, three—

"My . . . arms," Paddy cried out. "I can't do it anymore. No strength left." He let the oars drop into the boat and sagged, defeated.

"Move over!" Lucy crouched and slunk across the boat, catlike. "I'll take over."

Then there was a rough crunching sound. Still on her feet, Lucy fell forward and landed on the bottom of the rowboat as it came to an abrupt halt. They had run aground on the beach!

"Come on!" Lucy shouted. Grabbing the journal, she jumped onto the sand and started running along the shoreline, toward the trees that loomed nearby. Paddy followed behind. He was exhausted from all the rowing, but he felt a rush of adrenaline as he trailed her across the sand. Behind, he could hear their pursuer reach the beach and tramp ashore. They weren't free yet.

"Stop!" shouted the man. "I ain't gonna hurt you. I only want the book back."

Lucy forged ahead on a wide dirt path that led into the jungle. Paddy, who had gotten his second wind, ran alongside her. Darkness overcame them, and they were forced to slow to keep from tripping over a branch or root. On they went, until they were gasping for breath in the humid air and thought they could go no further.

"There you are," cried their pursuer from behind them.

"We're . . . not . . . going to make it," said Lucy between breaths. "We might as well . . . just—"

"Don't even think it," said Paddy harshly. "I think I know where we are. There's still one more chance for us to escape—follow me!"

He picked up the pace and turned down a side-path marked by a sign Lucy was unable to read. She followed closely, until they reached a clearing in the jungle next to a small run-down shack.

"Now where?" Lucy asked.

But their pursuer had also reached the clearing. "Stop, you miserable brats!" he yelled. Lucy looked over her shoulder and saw the man walking toward them, hands on his hips, breathing heavily. "Let me have the journal, kids, and you can go home without any more trouble. I promise I won't hurt you."

"He's lying!" said Lucy between her teeth as the man continued to walk toward them, his hands palm up. "What should we do?"

"This way!" Paddy strode to one side of the clearing and began to climb up an old wooden ladder affixed to the trunk of a tall tree. Without time to think, Lucy followed him up the rickety steps. There were footfalls behind her, then the ladder shifted. The man was scaling the ladder below them. Lucy glanced up, but Paddy had already vanished among the branches and leaves. She was on her own. She continued to climb. The man's breath got louder and louder when she suddenly reached the top and stepped onto a small platform, bumping hard into her brother.

"There's no place to go," she screamed in a panic. "What are we going to do?"

"Hold on to me," he whispered. Then Lucy saw Paddy was busy fastening the last buckle on a harness that was now attached around his chest and waist. Somehow, he had brought them to the old cable line that Chi-Chi had told them about.

"Tighter," Paddy said. "Legs too." Lucy was amazed at the calm in his voice. She couldn't squeeze tighter, not while she was holding the journal in her hand. Without thinking, she slipped the journal up the back of Paddy's shirt, then wrapped her arms around his neck and squeezed tightly so the book was pressed between them. Praying the journal was secure, she linked her legs across his waist. "Ready?" he asked, clipping the harness to the cable above their heads.

There was no time to answer. Paddy turned, and together they saw their pursuer's head reach the top of the ladder.

"See ya," Paddy said cheerfully, stepping toward the edge of the platform.

"This better work," Lucy started to say—but the words became stuck in her throat as Paddy leapt into the darkness.

A soft *whirr* broke the momentary silence. The air whipped Lucy's face, brushing her hair into her cheeks and eyes, like she was riding her bike downhill. Instinctively she tightened her grip around Paddy's neck. As one they coasted along the cable, illuminated only by the moon, which shone through the canopy like a spotlight. They swung back and forth, at one point twisting completely around, but the cable held and the harness supported their joint weight. After twenty or thirty seconds the ride came to an abrupt stop. They hung in space, bouncing gently between branches as thick as their legs.

"Now what?" Lucy asked.

"You can put your feet down. We've reached the next platform. He can't follow us anymore."

Lucy touched the platform with one foot, then the other. Her legs were shaking. As she stepped away from her brother, the journal fell to the platform with a *thunk*. Lucy laughed in a release of fear and relief. "I guess I didn't remember to tuck your shirt in." She bent down to pick it up, running her fingers across what remained of the rough leather cover as she rose.

She turned around. The first platform was out of sight. She laughed again, then whooped loudly. "We did it. *You* did it."

But Paddy wasn't ready to celebrate. He unhooked the harness from the line. "We have to keep going to the end. There's no other way down."

They were still thirty feet above ground, and this platform had no ladder. "How much farther?" Lucy asked.

"About six or seven more sections."

She nodded. "Okay. Is there a better way for me to hold on? My arms are already tingling."

Paddy thought for a moment. "Maybe. Let me try something." He unbuckled his belt and pulled it off. He looped it around the clip at the top of the harness and then attached the harness to a second cable. He reconnected the belt, then tugged on it. "Try holding that. And you won't choke me around the neck as bad."

"Did I really? Sorry."

Paddy turned with a grin. "It's okay. Ready?"

"Sure—wait. What should we do about the journal? I'll need both my hands."

"Hm. How about I sit on it? The bottom of the harness is like a little seat."

"Sure. Why not?"

She held out the journal, and Paddy wedged it under his backside. He looked back at her and shrugged. "I guess that'll work."

He motioned to Lucy and she jumped on his back once more. When she was in place, she reached up to grab the belt. "Ready."

A moment later he pushed off the second platform, and again they whooshed through the trees.

This time Lucy tried to enjoy the ride. She watched as the leaves and branches flew by, noticed how Paddy extended his legs in front of him to reduce the turning and twisting. She smelled the sweetness of the trees and ferns, heard the flapping of wings as birds flew off, shrieking. She looked down at the reflection of four eyes as two small, raccoon-like animals raced across the ground. Moments later they reached the next landing, where Paddy once again unhooked the harness.

Six more times Paddy unhooked the harness and reattached the clip to the next cable. Six more times

Lucy grabbed hold of the belt and squeezed with her legs as her brother leapt into the air, letting gravity do the rest. When they finally reached the last landing, Paddy was quiet for what seemed like minutes.

"We're right near where we started," he finally whispered. "The cables go in a big circle. There's just one more, and it will take us down to the ground close to where we climbed the ladder."

"Then what are we waiting for? Let's go."

"In a minute. We've got to make sure the man from the boat isn't waiting for us."

"I guess that would be bad."

"Yeah."

The twins listened to the sounds of the jungle, bird calls mostly, which did not seem nearly as dangerous as the man who had been chasing them. Lucy touched his shoulder and nodded. Paddy hooked up for the last time, and with his sister holding on, slid the final length to the ground below.

He reached behind him and pulled out the journal, handing it over without a word. Lucy took it and held it tight against her chest, stroking the remaining half of the brown leather cover as if it were the treasure itself.

Lucy watched her brother unclip the harness. "Paddy," she asked, "how did you know so much about the cable line? You knew right where to go and how to attach the harness. Chi-Chi didn't tell you all of that when we were on the mountaintop."

"Oh," said Paddy, flashing a sheepish grin as he rethreaded his belt. "I came here the other day, when you went on that boat with Manuel."

"You're unbelievable! I told you it was too dangerous."

"I guess you were wrong. Good thing, too."

At that, Lucy was speechless, so she settled for punching him on the shoulder.

"Let's go home," Paddy said. "That man's gone." He pointed down an overgrown trail that wound through the trees. "That way leads to the first platform. From there we can find our way back to the beach."

"Wait—why would we want to do that? Won't it be faster to go the other way?"

"We still have to get the rowboat. Besides, I promised Chi-Chi I'd always put the harness back on the first platform where I found it."

The narrow path did lead back to the small office building. Paddy scaled the wooden ladder, and after planting a big kiss on the harness, returned it.

They found the rowboat upside down, floating twenty feet from shore. The man must have upended it in his anger and left; he was nowhere in sight.

"I hope he didn't put a hole in it," Lucy said, scrunching up the corners of her mouth.

"Only one way to find out. Come on."

Lucy placed the journal on a dry rock and together they waded into the ocean, their feet sinking into the muck and sand. They flipped the rowboat over, spilling out as much seawater as they could. Underneath they found the oars, intact.

Lucy went back for the journal, and then they both climbed in. As she settled into her seat, she flipped through the pages and thought of their two new enemies. "I sure hope it was worth it," she said.

NINETEEN

The next morning, the twins were downstairs reliving the previous evening's adventure, when Paddy turned serious. "What I don't get is why you didn't just take that page with the map when you picked it up instead of stopping to read it. What were you thinking?"

"I don't know. I guess I wanted to look at it."

"Good going. We could be studying it right now."

"We got the rest of the journal," Lucy pointed out. "I'd call that a success." She walked into the foyer and glanced at the small table near the front door. "Um, where is it?"

"You're joking, right?"

"No. I'm sure I left it here when we got home, before we went upstairs to bed."

Paddy grimaced. "I didn't take it. Maybe you're just remembering wrong."

They rushed around the living and dining rooms, frantic, before Lucy found the journal resting on the kitchen table, holding down a piece of paper with writing on it.

Paddy slid it out. "It's a note from Mom. She says she hopes we had a peaceful evening by ourselves." He looked up. "They really have no idea what we've been doing all summer. Peaceful? We could've gotten killed last night."

"But we didn't. Does it say anything else?"

He scanned the script. "Oh, no. She says the boat trip with that fisherman was a bust. They didn't catch anything, and the fisherman told them he's spending the next few weeks on a different island."

"Maybe they can go back to that spot themselves."

"No, she says it was too dark for them to see how they got there, and he wouldn't give them directions. They're back to square one." He crumbled up the note and tossed it in the trashcan. "Just like us."

Lucy reacted angrily. "We are *not* back to square one. We got the journal back, right?" She waved it around. "Besides, I got a really good look at that torn page before I lost it, and you'll never believe what was written on it."

It was, she explained, a description of how the *Miner's Revenge* struck the reef and sank to the bottom of the sea, losing all its cargo. Le Moyne and his crew escaped to the island on lifeboats with nothing but their clothes.

"So that's why those men are searching the sea for the pirate ship," she concluded. "They think the gold must've been onboard when it sank."

Paddy considered that for a moment. "Then why would he have left those clues we found? None of it makes any sense." He adjusted his glasses and frowned.

Lucy flipped through the pages. "Why don't you read this? We can take a few days before bringing it back to the museum. Maybe there's something else in there. Something those two men missed."

Paddy took the journal, feeling its weight. Other than brief moments during the chase the night before, this was his first chance to hold it and it sent a tingle rippling through his fingertips. "Okay. But the librarian and the museum lady were both certain it was a fake."

"But it might be real, too. There's no harm in reading it, right? After all, we went to all that trouble to get our hands on it."

It took two days.

On Thursday afternoon Lucy was stretched on the couch, reading, when Paddy emerged from his room.

"I'm done," he said, holding up the journal.

Lucy shut her book. "Well, what's in it? Don't keep me in suspense."

"Sometimes his handwriting is difficult to read, but I got most of it. He wrote about daily activities, members of his crew, visits to different ports for supplies, fights—everything that happened. And get this—he would sometimes chop up the pigs he kept on board for food and toss their guts into the sea."

"Eww, that's disgusting. Why would he do that?"

"To attract sharks. It would frighten the sailors of captured ships into cooperating with him. Isn't that clever?"

"No, it's gross."

"But it worked. One time they attacked a ship called the *St. Augustine* and set it on fire. The other sailors just gave up and decided to join his crew after he threatened to throw them in the water after the pig parts. He wrote that he wouldn't have done it, though. He only wanted to make himself seem scary and thought it was funny that everyone always believed him."

"I don't care about any of that. What happened to the *Miner's Revenge*? Did it sink with the gold on board?"

"I thought it was interesting."

"Paddy!"

He sighed. "Okay, okay. The journal tells how he stole the gold. The whole story, from the beginning. He said it was the cleverest job he ever pulled."

"*Paddy*! What happened to his ship? Does it say?"

"It later ran onto the reef around Janaconda Island while being chased by the British Navy, and it caught fire and sank. Black smoke filled the sky, and the navy boat sailed off without even bothering to search for survivors. After they were safe, he told the crew not to tell anyone he got away. The rest of the details were on the page with the map you lost."

"I guess it's true—the ship sank with the gold on it," said Lucy, dejected, "and our treasure hunting days are over."

"Oh, I don't know about that. I think he snuck the gold off the ship before it was destroyed."

"Why do you think that?"

"In another part, he said his plan 'worked' and not even his crew knew the full truth. I think he set his ship on fire on purpose so the British would stop hunting him." He opened the journal and flipped through the pages. "Here, let me read you the very last entry, which he wrote years later when he was an old man."

As to the question of what really happened to the Venezuelan gold, which I am often asked, I can answer truthfully that the Gold will forever remain on board the Ship. But where that is—now that is the puzzle. After all, a pirate Captain is allowed his secrets. To discover the solution to my little game, a treasure hunter need only climb aboard the Ship, stand on deck, and feel his feet tremble and the wind rush from below.

"I don't get it," said Lucy. "How are we supposed to stand on the deck of a ship that's on the bottom of the sea? And why would he even write that if he had already gotten the gold off?"

"Maybe it's another clue."

"If those things we found really *are* clues. Maybe all this was just his idea of a joke or something."

Paddy tightened the corners of his mouth. "You can believe what you want. I think his final entry was meant as a challenge, and confirms the treasure is hidden somewhere on the island. That means those other men are looking in the wrong place."

"Only if the journal is real, not a hoax. And we have no way to know for sure."

"So what do we do next?" Paddy asked. "I'm out of ideas."

"I don't know. Maybe something will turn up."

☠ ☠ ☠

What turned up was a dinner invitation for the twins with Chi-Chi and his family. Sunday afternoon, Lucy and Paddy rode into the village and parked their bikes at the elementary school, where Chi-Chi was waiting. He led them into a neighborhood swarming with kids playing soccer on unpaved streets, down a narrow side street, until they reached a blue house with a red door.

"*Hola*," greeted a woman with long black hair. She had a pleasant, round face, and wore the bright-colored clothes that were popular among the island's women. "You must be Lucy and Paddy. Welcome."

"This is my mom," Chi-Chi said. "And that's my little sister," he added, as a naked toddler darted between them, giggling.

"Come here, you," called a deep voice. A man crossed through the room after the girl. "It is time for her bath, but she will not stay still long enough to catch her." He ambled off in pursuit. "Bonita? Where did you go?"

"She likes her bath," Mrs. Flores explained, "but we must chase her first. It is a game to her."

The door opened and a young man entered, maybe four or five years older than Chi-Chi. He cradled a basketball in one arm and his shirt was stained with sweat. He glanced at Lucy and Paddy and cocked the side of his mouth into a partial sneer. "*¿Quiénes son ellos?*"

"English when there's company," Chi-Chi's mother demanded. "And be polite. These are Chi-Chi's friends, Lucy and Paddy."

"Hi," Lucy said.

"This is my brother Joaquin," Chi-Chi explained.

"No balls in the house," Mrs. Flores scolded.

Joaquin flipped the ball toward his brother, who caught it an inch before it connected with his face. "Put this away for me."

Chi-Chi tossed it back, harder. "Do it yourself."

His mom planted her hands on her hips and glowered. "I don't care, boys. Just get it out of my house."

Joaquin snorted, opened the door, and dropped the ball on the grass. Then he reentered and smacked Chi-Chi on the back of his head as he walked past. "*La próxima vez.*"

"English!" Mrs. Flores shouted as Joaquin disappeared down the hall.

"Come on, let's go outside," Chi-Chi said. He led the twins into the yard, where he kicked the basketball across the grass.

"Dinner in a half hour," Mrs. Flores shouted after them. "I won't come get you."

Chi-Chi looked at Paddy and sighed. "Don't mind Joaquin. He can be a jerk, but he is my older brother. The two often go together here."

They joined the soccer game, which was more like a free-for-all with a ball. When they returned to the house, Bonita was in pajamas and the rest of the family was ready to eat, including Chi-Chi's grandmother, who sat down next to Lucy.

Chi-Chi's mother brought out several bowls and handed around utensils. As everyone reached for different dishes, Mr. Flores asked the twins about their stay.

"We love it here," Lucy answered as she scooped some food into her bowl, a mixture of rice, beans and vegetables in a reddish-brown sauce.

"Where are you residing?"

"They're in that big run-down house on the cliff outside town," Chi-Chi said between bites. "You know, the one that has been empty forever."

Chi-Chi's grandmother perked up. "The house on the hill? Mr. Stephenson's old house?"

"Yes!" said Paddy in surprise. "You know about our house?"

She smiled. "More than most. I remember playing in that house when I was a little girl."

"Really?" Lucy exclaimed.

"*No otra historia*," Joaquin muttered.

"English!" Mrs. Flores said. "I won't tell you again."

Grandma Flores glared at Joaquin before continuing. "I thought it has been empty since Mr. Stephenson died."

"We think it's been empty for a long time," Lucy said. "We were allowed to stay there because our dad's work is so important. But how did you get in?"

"Ah—now there's a story. My mother was Mr. Stephenson's housekeeper."

"I didn't know that," Chi-Chi's mother said, looking a bit surprised.

Across the table, Joaquin groaned.

"Quit it!" said Chi-Chi, hitting his brother on the shoulder. "I want to listen."

Chi-Chi's grandmother nodded. "She was his housekeeper until he passed away. I was a sick girl and often stayed home from school. On those days my mother would take me to work with her. Goodness! I couldn't have been more than nine or ten when he passed. I haven't thought about those days in years. I especially remember all the beautiful paintings on the walls. I'm sure they're all gone now. Oh well, what a shame; many of them were painted by Mr. Stephenson himself."

"No," Lucy said. "The paintings are still there, along with the rest of his things. You actually knew him?"

"Oh, yes. What a sweet man. He called me his little treasure and always was happy to see me. Sometimes he'd even bring me to the big hotel, the one in the middle of the jungle. It had the most wonderful playground made of wood. I loved climbing around on it. But that was a long, long time ago."

The twins glanced at each other before Paddy said, "We heard he used to be a pirate."

Chi-Chi's grandmother laughed. "Yes, I suppose he was. But that was before I met him, and I'll always remember Mr. Stephenson as my friend. I would go upstairs into his study while my mother was working, and we'd play cards, or he'd tell me stories about pirates. He even wrote some down for me." She laughed again. "I used to think he was making them up, that they were only stories to entertain me, but later I learned they may have been true. I can show them to you if you're interested. I think he was simply a lonely man who enjoyed having company."

Lucy's head was spinning. "Wait—his study? Don't you mean his library? That's downstairs."

"No, it was definitely upstairs. He used one of the smaller bedrooms as his personal study. Yes—I am certain of it. I think it was the second one on the right."

Lucy's stomach lurched. "That room's locked now. Do you remember what it was like inside?"

"There was a desk and some cabinets. A couch, too. Oh, and he kept a telescope pointed toward the window. Sometimes he would let me look when there was a ship near shore. That's about all I can remember."

"Oh," Lucy said. Another dead end.

"What I really liked most about the days I spent there," Grandma Flores continued, "was playing in the cellar."

That brought the twins back fast. "Uh, what cellar?" Paddy asked.

Grandma Flores smiled. "It was a storeroom. I used to call it my secret room, because Mama didn't know about it and I would use it to hide from her. Mr. Stephenson stocked it with toys and games for me to play with. I remember taking the child's elevator to get down there."

This was too much for Paddy to absorb. "Um . . . there's an elevator? A *child's* elevator? Inside the house? To a *secret room*?"

"Well, it isn't really an elevator," admitted Grandma Flores. "I just called it that. It's a dumbwaiter. Do you know what that is?"

The twins shook their heads.

"It's a shelf that moves inside the wall between the kitchen and other floors. It's meant for food, not people, but as a child I could squeeze inside and ride it safely. One thing I could never figure out, though, was how Mr. Stephenson got down to the cellar himself. There must be another way, but he never told me how. My mother didn't know either, so it must be hidden. What memories! I wonder if those old toys are still there."

"We'll let you know, Grandma Flores," said Lucy, as Bonita threw a handful of rice across the table, causing Mr. Flores to knock over his drink. "I think we may go look and see for ourselves."

TWENTY

Jean-Pierre Le Moyne watched as Captain Charles Forester strode into the dark tavern, his military boots scraping the dirt floor. Other than the footwear, the British naval commander had disguised himself for this trip ashore. Perhaps, Le Moyne mused with cynicism, they were his only pair. He scanned the soot-stained walls and the grim faces of the dozen or so patrons scattered throughout the room. No one was paying attention to the stranger with the ramrod posture who'd just strolled through the door. He motioned for the English captain to join him.

"About time you arrived," Le Moyne grumbled as Captain Forester slid onto a wobbly chair across the table. "I've been waiting for nearly three weeks."

"I see you received my message."

"I assure you, I would not be here but for my curiosity."

Forester nodded. "I despise these out-of-the-way port towns. Filled with rogues and thieves. You never know where an enemy might lurk." His hand, Le Moyne noticed, moved to the bulge at his hip that could only be a small pistol hidden beneath his shirt. Either it was a subconscious gesture or the captain was sending a message.

Le Moyne signaled and the proprietor, a short, dark-haired man with a pronounced limp, approached carrying a pair of tall glasses. He placed them on the table between the two men, and, with a nod, withdrew without a word.

Forester took a long drink and wiped his mouth on his sleeve. "The secrecy of our meeting extends to my own officers. As British soldiers, they are duty-bound to arrest known pirates, regardless of whether they are enjoying a round of ale with their commander."

Le Moyne held his glass aloft. "I salute you for your caution."

"But I have told them a good lie," Forester continued, taking another sip. "We have a naturalist on board, a man named Thibodeaux. As we speak he is tramping through the jungle, searching for lizards and frogs. A total nitwit." He laughed. "My admiral demanded I grant him passage to carry out his 'scientific discoveries,' and so I have brought him here, to this miserable hunk of rock in the middle of the ocean. Let's see if there's anything of interest he can find. Somehow, I doubt it."

"I rather like this place," Le Moyne contested. "But you didn't ask me here to discuss frogs. I suppose it's about that business we discussed earlier."

Forester sighed and ran his fingers through his thinning hair. "You did it, didn't you? You stole it all before you sank that transport."

The scene repeated in Le Moyne's mind. After commandeering the trailing convoy ship, he and half his crew had snuck up on the Venezuelan transport in the dense fog and boarded her. "I am the notorious pirate Jean-Pierre Le Moyne," he announced to the frightened crew, waving a pistol in each hand. "Join me or die." They chose the former, in part due to the sound of sharks tearing pig meat off the port bow. His offer to share some of the gold with them hadn't hurt, either. For the gold *had* been there, as Forester had said, and even with the help of the Venezuelan sailors it took most of the night to move all of it to the hold of the stolen convoy ship. Then the transport's hull was lined with explosive charges and blown up. By the time the rest of the convoy realized what had happened, the transport was gone, submerged under the depths, and Le Moyne was miles away.

Of course, his crew had no idea what was inside those heavy crates; to them it was merely another job. But he couldn't risk keeping the gold onboard forever. At some point they'd get curious and pry the lids off the crates to look for themselves. So before Captain Forester was expected to arrive on Janaconda Island, Le Moyne quietly transferred the gold into barrels and unloaded them onto a bluff overlooking the sea, a spot not far from the tiny village. With the help of the Venezuelan sailors, he buried the barrels deep in the ground. He had led them by a roundabout route and taken the precaution of blindfolding each of the men for a portion of the journey; there was no way any of them would be able to find their way back alone. Then, before they could talk to his regular crew about the affair, he'd provided each with a pouch of gold coins and arranged for them to sail to Haiti on a ship about to leave port. Now he was the only one who knew what had happened to the gold shipment. He could always return for it later, at his leisure.

Before Le Moyne could answer, Forester shook his head. "No, no, I don't want to know; it's better that I didn't. Tell me, Le Moyne, do you understand why I asked you to disrupt that shipment? I think it's important you know the full story."

"You mentioned it had something to do with politics. I don't care much about politics. An advantage of being a pirate."

"You'll care about this." Captain Forester took another swig of ale, leaning forward to lower his voice. "A few years ago, a large deposit of gold was discovered in the jungles of British Guiana, near Venezuela.

"It was possibly the biggest find in South America. Our colony would become rich—but Venezuela claimed the vein was discovered on their side of the border. They mined for the gold themselves—illegally, we believe—while their government sought international support. When British spies discovered a ton of this gold scheduled for transport to Spain, we saw an opportunity to discourage future mining. That's where you came in."

"You expected Venezuela to abandon their claim to the mine after I disrupted the shipment," said Le Moyne. "But they didn't, did they?"

"No," Forester admitted. "They dug in their heels and kept mining. So now the British government has decided to pursue a different tack to end the dispute: peaceful negotiation. To demonstrate our good faith, Admiral Cornwell, who remains blissfully unaware of our earlier arrangement, has ordered the fleet to increase regional security, beginning with the capture of a certain pirate. There are a dozen British frigates looking for you right now, and they *will* be successful. The British fleet will never tire, will never stop, until you've been captured or killed. You're a marked man."

"I see. And you're telling me this because—"

"Because, as of this moment, our deal is off."

Le Moyne felt the hair rise on the back of his neck. "You double-crossing worm! You intend to arrest me?"

Forester placed his hand on his pistol. "Settle down. If I were here to arrest you, I'd be in my uniform and there'd be a dozen marines standing behind me with their bayonets pointed at your head."

Le Moyne lifted his palms to prove they were empty. This wasn't the place for a showdown. "What do you want from me, then? You want me to negotiate for my freedom? Is that it?"

Forester laughed. "You can keep the gold, for whatever good it will do you. We'll get it eventually."

Now Le Moyne knew he was done. Greed, he could understand, could barter with, but this devil captain didn't want the gold for himself. Everything was honor and duty to him.

"If you're not here to arrest me, and you're not here to take the gold for yourself, then why are we sitting together in this tavern?"

Forester smiled. "I thought it was the sporting thing to do. In every fox hunt, the fox hears the sound of the trumpets and feels his heartbeat race as the hounds close in. Consider this meeting to be the blowing of the horns."

"So this is nothing but a game to you."

"Of course; what else would it be?" He leaned close. "Now here's my advice to you, Le Moyne. You're full of tricks, aren't you? The only way you can escape this old hound is to disappear off the face of the earth. You think you can manage that? Because anything less and the British Navy *will* find you. Commit another act of piracy anywhere in the Caribbean, and we will find you. Show up in any of our colonies, and we will find you. Spend any of the gold, and we will track you down. Somehow, I think not even you are up to that trick."

He leaned back in his seat, raised his hand, and the proprietor returned with two more mugs of ale.

Captain Forester lifted his glass. "This one's on me, Le Moyne. Let the hunt begin."

TWENTY-ONE

"**P**addy! Get up!"

Paddy groaned and rubbed his eyes. Lucy was standing over him, shaking him by the shoulder.

"What is it?" he mumbled. "I thought I told you never to wake me."

She yanked the blanket off his body. "Mom and Dad have already left. We don't have any time to waste; we've *got* to find that dumbwaiter and explore the cellar before they get home."

That got his attention. Usually he stayed in bed as long as possible, but not today. "Okay—I'm up. I'll be downstairs in a few minutes."

After Lucy left, he got dressed as various thoughts ran through his mind. *The cellar.* What they would find there he could only guess. Maybe the cellar—the secret room, as Chi-Chi's grandmother called it—would contain one more clue to the location of the treasure. *The final clue.* Maybe the treasure itself.

There was another possibility, too: that the room contained nothing but a few old, rusty toys. But he'd never find out just by ruminating about it. He slipped on a shirt and headed downstairs.

Lucy was pacing in the hall when he found her.

He grinned. So he wasn't the only one who was excited. "I'm ready now."

The twins scurried into the kitchen. Two of the walls were covered with wallpaper and were partially blocked by appliances and the table. The entrance cut through the third wall, which was too narrow for someone to climb inside. The fourth wall, though, was lined with wood panels that swung open to reveal shelves crammed with food and household supplies that had been purchased by their parents.

"I bet it's in there," Lucy said. "Let's take everything out and have a look."

They opened all the panel doors and emptied the shelves. Soon the floor was littered with plates, silverware, forty-three cents in change, fourteen cans of vegetables, six dead spiders, a pound bag of sugar, assorted spices, a yellowed roll of shelf paper, several bottles of dirty fluid, and a box of uncooked macaroni (among other things), leaving little space to walk.

Paddy tripped over a bag of flour, sending a white cloud into the air like a puff of snow.

Finally they found a metal shelf behind a panel in the corner, wide enough to hold a large box. The shelf was scratched and dotted with small pin dents. Lucy rapped on it with her knuckles, producing a noise like a rock dropped into a steel bucket and causing it to wobble slightly.

"That must be it," Lucy said, looking inside.

Paddy peered around her. "It's smaller than I thought."

"We could probably get on one at a time." She rapped again. "It seems sturdy enough to hold us."

Paddy ran his fingers through the thin layer of dust. "How does this thing work?"

"Pulleys, I think. Someone tugs on a rope and the shelf moves between floors."

"Then where is the rope?"

"I don't know." Lucy banged on the adjacent panels, but they didn't pop open.

"Grandma Flores said she used to ride up and down herself," Paddy mused. "That would only make sense if she could reach a rope from inside."

"Good point."

"Go ahead; reach in," he prodded. "See what's in there."

"You're just afraid of spiders."

He shrugged. "Not my fault your arms are longer."

"Sometimes I think you enjoy being the short one," she muttered as she reached inside and probed with her hands. Her fingers touched a knob next to the shelf. She slid it toward her, opening a narrow space with a pair of ropes hanging down. "Eureka!"

Paddy nudged her out of the way and slid a chair against the wall. "I'm going first."

"Wait." Lucy held him back. "It's probably dark down there. Why don't you get the flashlights?"

"So you can go first? No thanks."

"You're impossible. Look, while you're doing that, I'll get my notebook. We'll meet back here."

Paddy ran off, climbing the stairs two at a time. When he returned, Lucy was sitting in the dumbwaiter with her feet dangling.

She shrugged. "I guess I had already had my notebook with me."

"Figures."

"Hand me one of the flashlights. I'll yell when I'm off so you can bring the dumbwaiter back up."

Lucy curled her feet inside and Paddy gave her a flashlight. She tugged on one of the ropes. Almost instantly there was a loud grinding sound and the shelf jolted twice.

"You sure this is safe?" Paddy asked.

"Pretty sure. It just hasn't been used in a while. Let me try this one." She chose the other rope and pulled.

"It's working! You're going down!"

"About time! My feet are falling asleep!"

Slowly the dumbwaiter descended, disappearing from the open niche. The grinding noise continued. About half a minute later Paddy heard a soft *thump* and nothing more.

"Lucy?" he called through the wall. "Are you all right? What happened?"

"The elevator won't go any more," she called back. "I think I'm at the bottom. But I can't see anything."

"Use the flashlight."

"I can't—I'm too scrunched up. Hold on."

She tried to climb off the shelf, but discovered another panel blocking her way. She felt a momentary panic as her legs began to ache. *Don't be a baby*, she thought. She kicked hard with her feet. The panel swung out on a hinge and her face was hit by a whiff of stale air.

Lucy hopped down and flipped on the flashlight. She took a deep breath, calming her nerves, and stretched her limbs before turning around to examine the wall. Next to the dumbwaiter a small section of the wall was cut away, through which she could reach the ropes.

"Hold on," she called up the chute. "I'll send the dumbwaiter back up." She pulled on one of the ropes, sending the shelf back where it had come from. After a short delay, the grinding noise began again. Soon the shelf reappeared. Paddy climbed down, laughing.

"What's so funny?"

"Did Chi-Chi's grandmother really think she was sneaking down here without her mom knowing?" He snickered some more. "That sound would wake the dead."

"At least it still works," Lucy said. "Come on."

The cellar was cold and damp, and smelled like wet laundry. They swept the room with the beams, causing eerie shadows to shift across the floor like wraiths. On top of a nearby cabinet rested an old lantern next to a metal tin containing a handful of matches.

"I wonder if there's still oil in it," Paddy said. He lifted the lantern and shook it. Something sloshed around inside. He struck a match and lit the wick. The lantern began to glow, brightening the room.

They flicked off the flashlights and glanced at the shelves and dressers that bordered the walls. In the middle of the floor, a group of toys littered a piece of carpet.

"These must have belonged to Chi-Chi's grandmother," Lucy remarked.

She picked up a doll with long yellow hair, dressed in a flowery gown with a ribbon around its waist for a sash. "I'll bet this was one of the dolls she played with as a little girl. Maybe we should take it back to her. It might make her happy to see it again."

"That thing? Why would she want it? It's falling apart."

Instead of answering, Lucy placed the doll inside the dumbwaiter. "We should check those cabinets first," she said. "Maybe he put some personal stuff in there. Then we should look for any hidden compartments—in the walls, in the floor. We can't overlook anything—I just *know* we'll find a clue down here."

She marched over to one of the shelves and tugged at a cardboard box draped with cobwebs. There was a tearing sound as the side ripped. Lucy fell to the ground and the box slid off the shelf, spilling its contents.

It was nothing but rags and bottles of chemicals to clean the floor and furniture. Lucy's hands were now filthy, and her hip ached. She glanced over at Paddy, who was standing near one of the far walls, smirking.

"Aren't you going to help?" she asked.

"Maybe we should look over here first." He held the lantern higher so Lucy could see the large mural of a ship painted across the wall. "Sometimes you need to see the *big picture*, Lucy."

"Oh, be quiet."

Together the twins stood in front of the mural. It was a pirate ship, its sails unfurled and billowing in the wind. On the deck, between the two tall masts, a great treasure was piled in a heap, with colorful jewels and necklaces mixed among gold and silver coins. To emphasize the extent of the riches, the painter had added a shining aura that lit the sky above the ship's sails.

"Wow," said Lucy. "That's some painting."

She tapped the wall below the ship, where a small 'T.S.' was inscribed adjacent to a square with the letter 'X' inside of it. Once again, a circle was drawn over the point where the lines crossed. But this time both the three stars and four moons were missing.

Lucy asked, "What do you think it means?"

"I don't know," said Paddy, "but did you see this?" He touched the hull of the boat, where the word 'GEMINI' appeared in block letters. "Gemini—that's the constellation we've been looking for."

"How could I forget?"

"And do you remember what was written at the end of the journal? It was something like, 'The treasure will always remain on the ship.' There's got to be a connection."

Lucy's eyes flashed. "Maybe the treasure is on a ship called the *Gemini*."

"The journal didn't mention any ship called *Gemini*. I'd remember something like that."

"Then maybe it means the treasure is behind this wall."

The twins kicked and pushed, but the wall was rock solid, and with their hands smarting from all the banging, they gave up in frustration.

"This is ridiculous," said Lucy. "We started by looking for a real pirate treasure, and all we've found is a painted treasure on a painted pirate ship in some smelly cellar. Let's look around some more. Maybe there's something else down here."

But after rifling through the boxes and cabinets, the only things the twins discovered were more ammonia and polishing cream, some old clothes, and a few boxes of toys.

In one of the corners of the room, though, three rotting barrels sat in the shadows. Lucy peeked inside; they were empty. Then she noticed something nearby on the cement floor. She turned on her flashlight and shone it along the ground, walking back and forth as Paddy watched. She returned to the barrels and slid one a few feet across the floor. She smiled.

"Look at this." She aimed her flashlight at her feet and swept the beam in a tight arc, tracing the outline of a faint reddish-brown circle.

Paddy squinted. "Looks like the barrel left a stain on the floor. Maybe rust or the paint rubbed off the edges. It's probably been there forever."

"It's not the only one." She walked a few feet away and pointed at the ground again with the light. "There's another one, over here. And there, and there, and there." The faint reddish-brown circles covered half the floor. "There are probably two dozen of them! What do you think Thomas Stephenson could have stored in that many barrels in a secret cellar under his house?"

He blinked. "You think the treasure used to be here? Because there are some faint reddish circles on the floor? That's nuts."

"No, it's not. All those circles are the same size and color as the three barrels still here. Look for yourself if you don't believe me."

"That doesn't mean anything. Maybe he kept water in them or something."

Lucy reached her flashlight into the barrel. Narrow streaks of light shot around the room.

"They're not watertight."

"Maybe they got warped."

"Argh! You're impossible. I'm telling you, he must've built this cellar to store the gold, and then eventually moved it somewhere else, leaving that clue as to where he put it." She gestured toward the mural.

"If you're right, then how did he get those barrels out of the cellar? There's no way something that big and heavy would fit into that tiny dumbwaiter."

Lucy swung her flashlight, settling on a pair of large windows near the ceiling so caked with grime they were nearly indistinguishable from the wall.

"There, I'll bet." She aimed her light higher, illuminating a thick metal hook connected to a wood beam. "Pulleys. Wonder why we didn't notice those windows outside the house."

"Probably behind those big hedges," Paddy said. "But it still doesn't explain how he came down here when he wanted to check on Chi-Chi's grandmother. Let's keep looking around. Maybe there's still something to find."

They inched along the perimeter of the room, holding the lantern close to the wall. Lucy began to get antsy. The place stank of mildew and ammonia, and thick cobwebs hung from the walls, some with bugs still stuck in them. Making matters worse, Paddy began making up stories about nasty things happening to children slinking through cellars of old houses, about the frightening creatures that might live there and the disgusting things they do at night. She was ready to bite his head off herself if he didn't stop.

Finally, near one of the corners they found a thin, even crack. They knocked on the wall—it sounded different, almost hollow. Lucy looked up. Above their heads, a small block jutted from the wall. She reached up and tugged, and a large panel swung open, revealing a dark flight of stairs.

Paddy was ecstatic. "A secret passage! I knew there had to be a secret passage in this house somewhere."

"Come on. I just want to get out of here already." Holding the lantern in front of her, she climbed the staircase. Paddy followed, shutting the door behind them. The stairs turned partway up the flight, before ending at another door, this one with a knob attached at a normal height. Lucy twisted and pushed, but nothing happened.

"Help me," she said. "It's really heavy."

She moved aside to make room, and together they leaned against the door, pushing hard. After a few seconds the decades of crust gave way and it swung open. The twins stepped out, blinked, and looked around.

They were back in the library!

"That's fantastic!" exclaimed Paddy. "So that's how he came and went."

They turned around. One entire bookcase was attached to a hinge. Lucy swung it back to its original position, where it shut with a soft *click*. Paddy tugged, but it refused to reopen.

"There's got to be a latch somewhere," Paddy said. "We didn't find one when we took all the books off the shelves. Maybe it's on top where we can't reach. Oh, well."

"It's okay. I don't think we need to go back down there again." Lucy rested her hand on the bookcase and gave a small snort. "He must've built this library to hide the stairs to the cellar. It all makes sense. I'm sure of it now; the treasure *was* there."

Paddy nodded. "Okay, I'm convinced. Now we just have to figure out where he moved it."

"That's where we'll find *Gemini*, whatever that means," said Lucy.

TWENTY-TWO

Eight weeks had passed since the twins and their parents had arrived on the island, and soon it would be time for them to return to Maryland. The thought of leaving made Lucy and Paddy miserable. It was impossible to recall their feelings when first seeing the run-down, decrepit mansion, but now they couldn't imagine living anywhere else. Their parents had been right—this *was* a summer they would never forget.

As the end of summer grew close, the Hendricks family spent their time trying to solve their respective mysteries. Lucy and Paddy reviewed the clues to the treasure that they'd recorded in Lucy's notebook, while their parents desperately tried to locate a living, breathing heliomanth. Despite their best efforts, they had still been unsuccessful at finding the elusive fish.

And they were running out of time. Less than a week of their trip remained.

The morning of the summer festival Lucy and Paddy awoke to a cloud-filled sky. They popped out of their beds, got dressed, and ran downstairs.

"Are you excited?" asked their mother, handing them breakfast.

"Are we ever!" answered Lucy, grinning. She took a bite of papaya, the juice dripping down her chin. "We've been looking forward to this for weeks."

"It's going to be really neat," Paddy added. "Chi-Chi told us there's gonna be lots of rides and games. I can't wait!"

"We'll see," their mother said. "Just try not to be disappointed. I'm sure it will be different from the fairs you're used to back home. I only hope the rain will hold off until evening."

She was referring to the tropical storm approaching from the east that threatened to douse the island with several inches of rain. Warning signs had been posted in the village, but no one seemed concerned. The librarian told Lucy that during most summers at least one hurricane passed overhead, and compared to those this storm would seem nothing more than a shower. Besides, as far as anyone could remember, it had never rained during the festival itself.

Off in the distance, storm clouds thickened into a gray mass while the twins and their parents biked into town. They chained their bikes and entered the main square to watch the footrace signaling the beginning of the festival. As runners stretched on the grass, a group of children danced to a steel drum band. Everyone seemed oblivious to the approaching foul weather. A long red banner hung over one end of the square flapped in the growing wind. Then the runners lined up and a flag was dropped. As the spectators cheered, the competitors surged across the starting line.

Once the runners filtered through the square, the twins and their parents followed the crowd through the cobblestone streets until they reached the marina, where the race would end after looping around the village.

The twins had never seen the dock jammed with so many boats. Whether due to the festival or the oncoming storm, every slip was full. Paddy studied their sails and rigging and counted the pelicans perched on the deck railings. He had always loved boats, loved the clanging rhythm when the ropes banged against their masts. As he glanced from hull to hull, he tried to imagine what it would be like to sail across the ocean to faraway lands as Le Moyne once had. Then he did a double take, and grabbed Lucy's sleeve, tugging hard.

"Look," he whispered, his eyes wide. "There's the yellow boat."

Lucy turned. The boat with the blue wave on the hull was docked in one of the last slips at the far end of the marina. From their position, it was impossible to tell whether the two men were still onboard. "We can't take any chances," she said in reply.

"Yeah," said Paddy, frowning. "They're trouble."

But their fears were forgotten as the first runners streamed past, drenched in sweat. The twins cheered with the other spectators as the winner crossed the line with his arms raised in victory. A cascade of bodies followed, until the last athletes huffed their way to the finish.

Now it was almost time for the parade. Their father handed them some money and said, "That should keep you for a few hours at least. We'll see you back at home this evening. But if the storm gets bad, find shelter and come home when it's safe."

After giving their word, Lucy and Paddy darted back to the town square, cutting through the packed streets. Up ahead, at the far end of the block, Lucy spied the old man from the square, deep in conversation with Officer Ernst. The old man was gesturing with his hands, and Officer Ernst tilted his head up as if he was laughing about something.

"Come on," she said, grabbing Paddy's arm and leading him down a side street. "This way."

Two blocks later they returned to the main street and continued ahead. As they forged through the crowd, Lucy felt a hand grab her from behind.

"Paddy!" she screamed.

She squirmed, expecting the worst, but it was Manuel Vargas. With him was his niece, Katarina, looking bored.

Manuel smiled warmly. "Hi kids. How has your summer been?"

"Great," Lucy said.

"How about you, Paddy? I remember you were worried there wouldn't be anything fun to do."

"You'd be surprised what there is to do around here," replied Paddy, as both children laughed.

"Well, I just wanted to say hello. Enjoy the festival." He glanced up at the sky and furrowed his brow. "I hope the rain holds off. You never know this time of the year."

Then the crowd shifted. Lucy heard Katarina yell, "Let's go shopping again!" as Manuel and his niece disappeared in a sea of bodies.

"Come on." Lucy grabbed Paddy's arm and together they ran off until they were able to find a good spot along the parade route.

Crowds of people wandered through the street, chatting and laughing. Some wore home-made costumes as if it was Halloween. Then a half-dozen adults strutted down the street in full pirate gear, complete with boots, black hats, and swords dangling from their belts. Several wore bright blue coats. They were booed good-naturedly by the crowd and several children pelted them with candy.

Minutes later a symphony of horns blasted. The street cleared to allow the parade to come through. First was the town's brass band, marching to a steady drumbeat. As musicians strolled past in their red and black uniforms, the twins were joined by another familiar face.

"*Hola, ¿Qué hay?*" said Chi-Chi. "Neat parade, huh?"

"*¿Qué hay?* yourself," Lucy responded. "You were right; it is pretty swell."

"Wait a bit; it'll get even better."

The musicians were followed by a dozen men and women who ran down the center of the street, throwing candy and flowers. They wore bandanas across their foreheads and executed cartwheels and flips to entertain the crowd.

As they passed, a new rhythm erupted from down the block, growing until it echoed off the buildings like the rumble of thunder. Four dancers emerged through the crowd-lined street wearing rainbow-colored striped shirts and baggy black pants, their faces masked. Following them were a quartet of percussionists, beating on drums slung across their shoulders. The dancers jumped and flew through the air as the drummers beat louder and faster and faster and louder until their arms were blurs.

Other groups followed, some performing their own dances. Eventually came the mayor and other elected officials, waving and shaking hands. The twins noticed they received significantly less applause. They were followed by several clusters of kids wearing different sets of uniforms, trailed by the town's only fire truck.

When the fire engine passed, the street filled with older kids on bikes. The spectators began milling around. "I guess that's the end of the parade," Paddy said. "Let's get something to eat. Then I want to check out the games."

They wove among several dozen food booths. The aroma of the frying meat and spices made their mouths water. At Chi-Chi's insistence, the twins each got a pocket of dough stuffed with rice, beans, and vegetables, mixed with a spicy sauce that dripped through their fingers.

"Not bad," said Lucy, taking a bite. "But I prefer hot dogs."

"Soon you'll get hot dogs again," Chi-Chi replied.

"I know," said Paddy, "but I can wait a little longer."

They ran through the streets, past salesmen hawking shirts and souvenirs, past a man drawing portraits. The twins tried all the carnival games but only managed to win a realistic-looking cap gun. Knowing their mother would never allow them to keep it, they gave it to Chi-Chi, who was thrilled with the gift, never having had a toy gun before.

Chi-Chi mentioned that some rides were set up in an empty field on the other end of the village, and the three friends headed off to find them. Unable to contain his energy, Chi-Chi ran ahead, periodically firing the cap gun into the air.

As they walked down the street, Paddy felt something tug on his shirt. Small pinpricks rose up his back. He flinched, startled, before feeling a tickle at his neck like a feather duster. A loud chatter cut through the air.

Lucy laughed. "That monkey sure likes you."

Paddy tried to turn his head but the monkey grabbed his ear. He flinched, remembering the old man's explanation of how he lost part of his own. "Okay, okay," he sighed, afraid to disturb the animal. "You can stay. Just don't bite me or anything."

Paddy noticed several people staring at him as they continued on their way. The monkey appeared content on his perch, but then suddenly started to hoot and grind its teeth. Paddy flinched, and the monkey leapt off his shoulder and scurried off. "I wonder what spooked it," he started to say, but stopped as a hand grabbed him by the upper arm. "What the—"

Next to him, Lucy spun as something latched onto her shoulder, expecting it to be Manuel and his niece again. But instead it was one of the men from the yellow yacht.

Lucy shrieked and tried to twist away, frantic. She struggled, then bit down on the man's wrist, hard. He yelped but only squeezed tighter. The crowd was thick with strangers, none paying any attention to what was happening. A woman frying bananas briefly caught Lucy's desperate gaze, then looked away as a customer handed her money. She looked at her brother, who was also being restrained. Up the street, Chi-Chi had already disappeared.

"Well, well," said the man holding Lucy. "See what we've caught in the street. Two little mice that like to take things that don't belong to them."

"Two little mice—ha, that's a good one!" exclaimed the other man. "I guess the birds always get the worm in the end."

"Birds? *Birds*? We're not birds. Cats. We're cats. They're mice. *Cats* catch mice. Idiot. You should say something like, 'the cats have caught the mice.' *That* would make sense. There's no drama with worms; they just slither around in the ground like little slithery things."

"Oh," said the man holding Paddy, the guy who had chased them into the woods. His face was lined with confusion. "But don't birds catch worms, too?"

The man gripping Lucy rolled his eyes with frustration. "You're hopeless."

A band with a full horn section began to play at a nearby corner, making it hard to hear.

Lucy set her jaw. "Who are you? What do you want with us?"

The man holding Paddy blurted out, "I'm Jack and he's Sid."

"Shuddup!" Sid yelled, slapping Jack across the cheek. He pulled Lucy close. "Now what should we do with you two? You've caused more than enough trouble already."

"We don't have that stupid journal anymore," Lucy spat. "We gave it back to the museum. It's useless, anyway—a forgery."

Next to her, Paddy tried to hide his shock: for the first time he could remember, Lucy had *lied*. The journal wasn't a fake; they had gotten the proof from

Chi-Chi's grandmother, who loaned them one of the stories that Thomas Stephenson had written for her long ago after their dinner together. Both story and journal contained the same looping 'L's, the same lopsided 'P's and 'B's, the same swooping line through the top of the capital 'T's. There was no doubt the handwriting was the same.

"Did you hear that?" said the guy holding Lucy, the leader, the guy named Sid. "They says it's useless. Now, why d'ya suppose they'd say that, unless they already know where the treasure is?"

"Maybe they know where the treasure is," repeated Jack, still gripping Paddy's arm, one step behind.

"Well, they'll have to show it to us then."

Lucy screamed "Help!", but her voice sounded tiny and blended in with the clamor of the festival. A group of women walked by, close. For a moment Lucy caught the attention of one, who smiled at her before vanishing in the crowd. No one seemed to notice their distress.

"We don't know where it is," Paddy pleaded. "Honest! Just let us go, okay?"

"Quiet!" shouted Sid. He raised his hand as if to strike him, only to lower it when an older couple nearby turned their heads. "I won't hesitate to hurt you," he said quietly. "If you cooperate and do what we ask, it'll all be over soon. Understand? This doesn't have to be hard. It's up to you."

Lucy and Paddy stopped resisting. The men pushed them ahead, not giving them an opportunity to run off. Soon it became clear that the twins were being led to the marina, toward the yellow-hulled yacht moored at the dock, and then . . . then where?

As the twins stumbled forward, looking for a way out of their predicament, they heard a voice calling their names. It was Chi-Chi, oblivious to the danger.

"Hey, *amigos*, there you are," he said. "*¿Que paso?* I've been waiting at the rides." Then he glanced up, and for the first time noticed the two men standing behind them, looking as if they wanted to be somewhere else. "Who's that?"

Paddy was unable to keep quiet. "Chi-Chi! They're kidnapping us! Get help!"

But his warning came too late. Sid reached out and grabbed Chi-Chi by the wrist. "We might as well take this one with us, too," he said. "All of you now, keep walking." He shoved Chi-Chi in the back, hard.

Retaining his balance, Chi-Chi tried to run off. But Jack was too quick for him, locking one of his meaty arms around the boy's neck. Chi-Chi struggled against the grip without success.

"What's going on?" Chi-Chi whispered as they hustled along.

"They're after the treasure," Lucy whispered back. "They think we know where it is. I don't know where they're taking us."

"Don't worry," he said back. "I'll get us out of this. No one knows this island like I do. I'll figure out how to escape." But the two men paid no attention to this talk and pushed them forward until they reached the slip with their boat.

"Get on," said Sid. "We've got somewhere to go. Together."

TWENTY-THREE

The yacht sped through the water, the sky a frightening dark green. The kids stood in the center of the deck with Jack watching them from a distance. When the boat had gone about a hundred feet, they heard the engine shift into neutral. The door opened and Sid came out. He argued with Jack, quietly, so the kids couldn't overhear, then disappeared again. He returned with a coiled line, which he used to tie the kids' hands behind their backs.

This time both Sid and Jack went through the door, leaving Lucy, Paddy, and Chi-Chi alone on the deck. The motor growled, masking the thunder rumbling in the distance. The sea rose and fell in great swells as if it were one final never-ending carnival ride. Unable to keep their balance, the kids fell, banging against the cabinets and nautical equipment.

The air tasted of salt and the wind parched their lips. The children rolled like bowling pins. Paddy, tasting bile at the back of his throat, tried not to vomit as his shoulders and back bounced against the hard floor each time a wave slammed into the boat. The vessel was lifted over a crest and Lucy slid into Chi-Chi, accidentally kicking him in the chest and head. Their wrists were already chafed raw.

Fear and anxiety rose in Lucy's gut. She twisted her body so her back faced Chi-Chi's. "Try to untie my hands," she yelled, struggling to be heard.

She felt Chi-Chi momentarily fumbling with the rope. "No, can't get a grip on the end. Too much movement."

The boat fell and Lucy rolled the other way, kneeing Paddy in the stomach. He groaned and retched. At that, she gave up thought of escape, instead focusing on breathing and remaining still to reduce the bruising and pain in her arms and shoulders.

After about ten minutes, the engine roar dropped to a soft-pitched whine. The boat slowed. Lucy and Paddy scrambled to their feet and looked over the side. They gasped as the miserable truth sunk in: the men had gone to the festival intending to abduct them. They'd prepared for it. How else would they have known to take them . . . *here*?

For they were coasting toward the little dock behind the old mansion.

They must've been spying on us, Lucy realized.

The motor cut out. The boat bounced through the surf and banged against the dock. Then, just as Paddy reached his limit and finally vomited over his shoes, the door to the wheelhouse was thrust open and the men stormed onto the deck.

"Don't worry," Sid said. "You'll be back on dry land soon enough." He laughed and tossed a rope around one of the wooden pilings and pulled it tight.

"Come on," he said. "Off we go."

The three children climbed over the edge of the boat and onto the dock. Sid and Jack pushed them over the grass until the five of them stood on the porch.

"I don't understand," said Lucy. "Why'd you take us here? What do you want from us?"

Sid chuckled. "Imagine my surprise when I learned you were staying in the pirate's old house. I finally figured out why you snuck on our boat and stole that journal: to keep us from discovering what you already know."

"What are you talking about?" Lucy retorted.

"Don't you get it?" said Paddy. "They think the treasure is inside the house."

"How perceptive," Sid sneered. "So now open the door so we can get on with it."

"You're wrong; the gold isn't here," Lucy insisted. "We've looked. You're just wasting your time."

"You wouldn't blame me for not believing you," Sid replied. "The treasure is here—I'm sure of it. But if you're so certain we're wrong, I can't imagine you'd be upset if we took a peek inside. Now open the door!"

Lucy sighed. "We keep the key under that large stone near the flowers."

Sid found the key and unlocked the door. It swung open with a bang. Lucy was yanked through the entrance and tossed onto the floor like a doll, the wind knocked out of her. She heard the door slam and looked around to see Paddy and Chi-Chi lying next to her, groaning.

She exhaled hard. Her hands and fingers were starting to tingle from the rope. "We've got to figure out how to get out of here," she blurted out. "And warn Mom and Dad."

Paddy nodded as Sid and Jack strode past. Their bodies aching, the three friends scrambled to their feet and followed the men into the living room.

"Tear this place apart," Sid instructed. "The gold has to be here somewhere."

"Right," said Jack. Then, after a long pause, he asked, "Where, exactly, do you think?"

"Idiot!" Sid clenched his fist, and Lucy got the sudden impression he was tired of having to explain everything to his partner.

"*Think*, man! The treasure is big—*really* big." Sid stretched his hands apart. "It could be gold bars, could be coins. It's gotta be stored in barrels or a large safe, maybe even inside the wall behind one of those ugly paintings. Start there."

Jack's gaze shifted between all the artwork hanging on the living room wall before fixing on the painting of the castle on the cliff.

"I really like this one, boss." He traced the outline of the ramparts with the tips of his fingers. "Do you suppose that's a real castle somewhere?"

"Jack, *now*." Sid's face was turning red and looked like it was ready to explode. "We don't have all day."

With an indifferent shrug, the stocky man reached up and the painting was gone, ripped from the wall as if it were nothing more than a piece of cardboard. Beneath the spot where it had hung for more than half a century was just more wall. Not a safe, not a container embedded in the plaster, not even a keyhole.

Jack twisted his hips and his fist was through the wall, making a jagged hole in the plaster and scattering dust and bits of debris on the floor. Inside was an empty gap between two beams of wood. He tugged on the broken edge to widen the hole, releasing a shower of white particles. He got on his knees and reached in.

"Nothing there, Boss."

"Do the rest," instructed Sid. "I'm gonna get a drink and look around the rest of the house." He strode from the living room.

Lucy, Paddy and Chi-Chi stared in stunned silence as Jack moved from painting to painting, studying them as if he were at an art gallery before ripping them from the wall and tossing them into the corner. Then, as if he was shadow boxing, he held up his hands, twisted his hips, and bam! There'd be fist-sized holes where the paintings had been. Already the pile of splintered wood and canvas was nearly three feet high. Two walls of the living room were bare, pockmarked with gaps in the plaster, and still no sign of a safe.

Jack stood before the group of five paintings of ships that corresponded to the tiles upstairs, stroking his chin. Lucy heard Sid banging around in the kitchen, and she tried to remember whether they had removed the doll that once belonged to Chi-Chi's grandmother from the dumbwaiter.

"You don't have to break everything," she said quietly.

Jack carefully removed the painting of the ship in the rainstorm. He held the thick gray frame in his meaty hands, studying the image. "Almost makes me feel like I'm there," he said.

And he squeezed.

The frame snapped, tearing the canvas in half. Jack spun on one foot and heaved the pieces in the corner. The sound slashed through Lucy's heart.

"Why are you doing this?"

He turned, and in his eyes Lucy saw no malice or anger, only loyalty to Sid. "It's my job. It's what he asked me to do." He removed another painting, the one of the ship sailing under a starry sky, and twisted his hands until the frame began to snap.

"But it's art! Don't you care?"

Jack tugged the canvas from the remains of the frame and showed it to Lucy. "You can keep this one." He rolled it up and placed it on the couch, out of danger. Then he tossed the splintered pieces of wood into the corner.

"Are you enjoying this?" she asked.

Jack swung his fist, and a hole appeared where the painting had hung. He pulled apart some remnants of wallboard to widen the gap and reached in, feeling around. "When I was younger," he said, "I once tore an entire house apart with my hands and a sledgehammer, just to see if I could do it. Unfortunately, the house belonged to my ex-wife's new boyfriend, and the guy wasn't impressed." He pulled out his arm and stood straight, facing Lucy. "Or maybe he *was* impressed, because next thing I knew, the guy had called the cops and I was being stuffed into a police car. That's how I ended up in jail the first time."

"Is that how you met Sid?" Paddy asked.

"Nah." Jack removed the next painting, the one of the ship anchored near the shore. "You want this one?"

"Uh, sure."

"Lemme take it out of the frame for you. So Sid doesn't know I didn't destroy it."

Then Jack went to work, using his fingertips like pliers to snap open the edges of the frame without damaging the artwork, a true craftsman with his hands. "I didn't meet Sid until my fourth term." He held the canvas, now free, toward Paddy.

"My hands are tied."

"Oh, yeah." Jack rolled up the painting and placed it on the couch next to the one for Lucy. "It'll be there for you later."

"You just fell in with the wrong people, that's all," Lucy said. "You don't have to do this. You don't have to do what he says."

He shook his head. "You're wrong about me." He punched at the wall, scattering dust and more debris on the floor. "I never thought I'd have another chance to tear a house apart with my bare hands." He flexed his muscles. "You know, they built houses strong in the old days, but you've got to keep challenging yourself if you want to succeed in this business." He pulled the last painting off the wall and tossed it into the corner, where it hit the wall with a loud crash.

A sob escaped from Lucy's lips.

Moments later Sid returned. "You still in here?" he said. "We don't have all day. Let's move things along."

Jack's path of devastation continued into the formal dining room, and then the regular dining room. When he reached the library, Jack didn't even need to ask his partner what to do. Without hesitating he swung his massive arms like clubs, sweeping all the books onto the floor into a great pile. Then he reached up and grabbed the nearest bare shelf, and pulled. The whole bookcase came crashing down, breaking apart when it hit the floor. When that revealed nothing, he pulled down the next bookcase with a loud crash, and then another, as the three children watched the destruction, the ropes digging into their wrists. One of the bookcases smacked into the piano, lengthening the crack across the soundboard and snapping one of the piano legs. The piano tipped, its corner banging into the floor with a cacophony of sound.

In the momentary noise and confusion, Chi-Chi tried to bolt out the door but Sid caught him by the shirt collar and yanked him back.

"You're the tricky one, huh?" he said. "Why don't you sit down here so I can keep an eye on you." He pushed Chi-Chi onto the piano bench, twisting his arm in the process, and stood behind him. "Rip down the rest of those shelves, Jack. Let's go. We don't got all day."

Lucy and Paddy held their breath. Would Jack discover the secret entrance to the hidden cellar? Upon reaching the critical bookcase, Jack pulled and pulled, but it didn't budge. Jack paused, his brow curled in thought, then gave up. He stood there, panting from his hard work, not realizing that only a few feet away was a stairway leading underneath the house, to a mural that possibly revealed the treasure's location.

"See, I told you," said Lucy, breathing deep. "There's nothing here. It's just a stupid, run-down house. Can't you leave it alone?"

"Not yet," said Sid. "Jack—check upstairs."

Jack marched up the staircase, followed by the three kids, closely guarded by Sid. He walked into the nearest bedroom, Lucy's, and proceeded to tear it apart. He upended the bed, dumped her clothes out of the dressers, pulled the drawers from the desk, and punched a hole in the closet wall with a swing of his massive fist, setting loose a shower of white dust. He gave the same treatment to Paddy's room, followed by the empty bedroom and their parents' room. In each he found nothing that might lead to the Venezuelan gold, and his only visible reaction was yet another shrug of his broad shoulders. Finally he reached the door next to Lucy's room and jiggled the knob.

"What's in there?" asked Sid from behind his partner. "Why is it locked?"

"We don't know," Paddy answered. "That door's been locked since we moved in."

"I see." Sid frowned, then nodded toward Jack, who took a step back and kicked at the doorknob with all his strength. Then he kicked a second time, and a third—and then the doorframe broke apart, sending a storm of splinters across the hall. The door flung open with astonishing force; it rebounded with a loud bang, smacking Jack hard in the face. He cried in pain as blood began to drip from his nose, which looked broken. Paying no attention, Sid pushed past his partner and entered the room.

It was roughly the same size as Lucy's and Paddy's bedrooms, and the walls were covered with the same wallpaper. Instead of a bed, though, an old couch was jammed against one of the walls. A small brown wooden desk, scratched and coffee-stained, was positioned against the wall opposite the couch. Above the desk hung a cork board with scraps of paper tacked onto it, lists of addresses and now-useless reminders to pay bills in swooping, regal handwriting.

In the center of the room stood the telescope Paddy had seen from the tree limb, aimed at the window, toward the sea. Its purpose was obvious: Thomas Stephenson obsessed over the fear that the British Navy was on its way to capture him, and the telescope was his early-warning system. Now, though, the ocean could hardly be seen at all through the dark green sky and the spraying waves pounding the shore. The storm had nearly arrived.

Above the couch hung another painting, quite different from the landscapes on the first floor. While those images were mostly of majestic ships at sea and peaceful island scenes, this painting was almost frightening: it was Jean-Pierre Le Moyne's grave, his name etched across the headstone, followed by various aliases, including 'Bully Blue-Coat' and 'Thomas Stephenson.' But this was not his actual grave, the twins realized. He had been buried on a hill in the middle of a vast clearing, while this version was located in a busy cemetery, and the engraving didn't include the poem and symbols.

"How morbid," Lucy said. "Imagine sitting under a picture of your own gravestone! There was definitely something strange about this fellow."

"The date of death isn't right," whispered Paddy, pointing at the picture, where underneath Thomas Stephenson's name appeared the numbers 03-13-34.

"That isn't even close to when he actually died. He would've been over a hundred."

"Maybe he was being optimistic, or it was an important day for him, like some anniversary."

"Maybe," Paddy agreed. "But what do you think about that?" He pointed toward the top of the painting, where a handwritten scrawl read: *Upon Death Great Riches Shall Be Reached.*

"It's about going to heaven," Chi-Chi volunteered. "Got to be."

"I don't know," Lucy said, studying the picture carefully. "He doesn't seem religious to me. Maybe the whole thing is the missing—"

She didn't have a chance to finish her thought. Nudging the children out of the way, Jack reached up and tore the painting off the wall, tossing it across the room where the frame shattered into long splinters.

"No safe behind this one either, Chief."

"Hey!" Lucy shouted. "We were looking at that!"

Jack turned, and the kids could see the blood still trickling from his nose and the red stains on the front of his shirt.

"You know, you could simply tilt the paintings up a little to see underneath them," criticized Lucy. "There's no reason to destroy everything."

"Too late for that," said Sid, who had rifled through the desk and dumped the drawers on the floor. "Looks like we're done here. There ain't no treasure."

"We could've told you that an hour ago," grumbled Paddy.

"We did," Lucy added.

"All right," said Sid. He grabbed the arms of each of the children and dragged them to the couch, forcing them to sit. "So you kids were right. But I still think you know where the gold is. So spill it."

"This is ridiculous," cried Lucy. "Why should we help you? You kidnapped us and destroyed our house and everything in it. I've had enough of this."

"Because of this." Sid smiled, and it wasn't a happy smile.

He reached into his pocket, extracted a small square of paper, and flipped it toward the couch, where it landed on Lucy's lap.

It was a photograph, a photograph of Lucy and Paddy walking through Santa Elena. With their parents.

Where *were* their parents anyway? Lucy realized they should have been home way before now, especially with the storm brewing. There was no way they'd want to be caught in the rain, especially their mom.

"If you want to see them alive again," Sid said, "you'll cooperate with us."

"Where are they? What have you done with them?" Lucy shrieked. Paddy tried to rise, but Jack held out his huge palm and pressed it against Paddy's chest, forcing him back onto the couch. Chi-Chi leaned forward and tried to bite Jack's wrist, but the man casually reached behind Chi-Chi's back with his other hand, grabbed his thumb, and twisted. Chi-Chi howled and curled away until the pressure subsided.

"It's easier if you just sit like he wants," Jack said, sounding apologetic.

Sid's eyes shifted between the faces of each of the children. "We've got them stashed somewhere safe and sound where you'll never find them. So one more time: where is the treasure?"

"We don't know!" Lucy insisted.

"For some reason I don't believe you." Sid walked over to the window, through which the waves could be seen crashing over the shore line. "Jack—come here."

With Jack standing next to him, Sid said in a low voice, "Take them to the boat with us. We'll decide what to do with them later. I'm sure I can figure out a way to get them to talk."

"You're pretty creative, boss," Jack agreed.

"I know where the treasure is," whispered Chi-Chi. "I'll tell you. But first you got to untie our hands."

"What?" Paddy stared at his friend. "What are you talking about?"

Chi-Chi's eyes erupted with a look Paddy had never seen before.

"Yeah," Paddy added. "We'll tell you where you can get it. Untie our hands. And—and tell us where our parents are so we can make sure they're okay."

"Well, aren't we little negotiators," laughed Sid. "You have any other demands?"

"Yeah, Boss, maybe they want half the treasure for themselves," Jack chuckled.

Ignoring his partner, Sid walked back to the couch and pointed a single finger at Paddy's face. "Let me explain how this will work, kid. You tell me where the treasure is, and I untie everyone's hands. But no one leaves and I don't tell no one where your parents are until we get the gold. Then we let you go. That's the deal, take it or leave it."

Before Paddy could formulate a response, Chi-Chi said. "The treasure is buried in the jungle. At the ancient temple. Inside the big dirt mounds." He twisted his body. "Now untie."

Instead Sid reached down and grabbed Chi-Chi by the collar. "Liar." He lifted Chi-Chi up, then tossed him on the floor like a doll. Lucy screamed as Sid pulled back his foot to kick Chi-Chi in the ribs.

"I'll give you one more chance," Sid said. "What's it gonna be?"

"Okay, okay," Paddy said. "I'll tell you." He paused, taking a deep breath. "You're right, he was trying to trick you. But I won't." Turning to Chi-Chi, he added, "We're all in this together, right?"

"Right," said Chi-Chi, still bent on the floor in a fetal position.

Sid pulled Chi-Chi to his knees. "Any more monkey business, your parents get it. Understand?"

"I understand."

"So let's have it. Tell me where the treasure is! You used the journal to find it and stashed it somewhere in the house, didn't you?"

"No, my sister told the truth," said Paddy. "It's not here. The treasure . . ." Here he stumbled, before hit by a flash of inspiration. "The treasure is in the cave. You know where that is, right?"

"I don't know about any cave," Sid said.

"It's in the jungle, on the other side of Santa Elena," Paddy said. "A few miles away. People used to live there a long time ago and nowadays folks are superstitious about going inside. Tell them, Chi-Chi."

"Yup. Truth."

"See?" Paddy nodded. "It's the perfect place to hide something that big."

Sid was still suspicious. "Why haven't you gotten it yourselves?"

"We've tried, but we don't know where it is, exactly. We've looked for it but it's a big cave."

"Then how are you so sure?"

"He left a marker—a symbol indicating it's there."

"If you're lying . . .," Sid started. He stared deep into Paddy's eyes as Paddy held his breath, trying not to blush. This was the moment of truth. He thought about baseball games and the neighbor's dog back in Maryland, about his friends in school and his old room. Then Sid said, "You can't fool a con man, son."

Uh-oh, thought Paddy.

". . . But it seems like you're telling the truth. Okay, then—looks like we're going caving. All of us." He turned to Jack. "We're going to need shovels. Go look in that shed near the dock." As Jack left, Sid said, "Okay, I'll fulfill my part of the bargain." He untied each of their hands. "Anyone tries to escape, the others get punished."

"We understand," said Lucy.

As they went down the stairs, Lucy pulled her brother close. "What are you doing?" she whispered. "The treasure isn't there."

"We're just going to have to find a way to escape," he whispered back, as Chi-Chi nodded resolutely next to them. "It's our only chance of coming out of this alive."

Then they were out of the house, being hustled across the yard. Sid clenched Chi-Chi's shirt with one hand and Paddy's with the other, allowing Lucy to walk next to them unhindered. The wind kicked up, blowing twigs and leaves into their hair.

"Shouldn't we wait until this storm is over?" Lucy said.

Sid snorted in reply. "We'll be dry in that cave of yours."

As Jack returned with shovels, Sid herded the kids onto the yellow boat. By now the waves splashed over the dock and the tiny rowboat had overturned. Paying no mind to the approaching storm, Sid unhitched the rope and started up the engine. A rumble followed and the yacht began to vibrate underneath their feet.

"Head east," instructed Paddy, screaming to be heard over the howling wind. "The entrance to the cave is a few miles past the marina, near the water."

Sid turned to Paddy and said, "You better not be leading us astray. I won't have patience for no tricks."

"No tricks." Paddy touched his cheeks; they were cool. "That's the right way."

As the boat pulled away from the dock, there was a flash of lightning and the rain began to fall . . .

TWENTY-FOUR

T he yacht cut through the water. All five passengers were crammed in the wheelhouse, protected from the nasty weather, but not the stomach-tossing ride. In the distance a fork of lightning flashed, then another. Following Paddy's instructions, Sid maneuvered the boat along the coastline and past the marina, toward an uninhabited part of the island.

Everything looked different in the rain, and Paddy scanned the shore for a landmark near the cave's camouflaged back entrance. The raindrops splashed against the windshield, fogging the glass, making it difficult to see.

"Look!" he said, pointing at a pillar framed against the darkened sky. "Up there!"

"That's Lion Rock," explained Lucy. "It's watching over the gold. Remember the poem on his grave?" She shut her eyes and recited the relevant lines. "A lion in the summer's heat, with heart as cold as stone, stands guard with mask of rock . . ."

". . . Over treasure, and ancient bones," Sid finished. "Sure, I remember. But I thought the lion referred to him."

"That too," Paddy said. "You better steer the boat close to shore and find a place to drop the anchor. The entrance isn't much farther."

The yacht slowed and entered shallow water. The rain fell harder, cloaking the land in spray and cloud. The boat jolted and lurched as it scraped over rocks and submerged logs, sending shivers grinding through the hull. At one point the vessel got stuck on some underwater obstacle, and Sid had to throw it in reverse to pull free.

Sid cursed. "We'll never navigate through this."

"A good spot ahead," Chi-Chi shouted over the rain. "I've been here before. Fishing with my dad. Between those two tall palms."

"I see it." Sid steered the yacht through the gap and into a small cove. He slowed and dropped anchor a few feet from shore before getting Jack's attention. "Get the shovels and some flashlights and meet us on land."

Sid left the protection of the wheelhouse cabin and slipped over the side. The kids followed, the water reaching their chests. When they reached the shore, they huddled under a lone tree until joined by Jack, carrying a duffel-sized gear-bag.

Sid pulled Paddy close. "You lead the way, son," he said. "Remember—no tricks, or someone will get hurt."

"Don't worry," said Paddy, his glasses dripping. "I know what I'm doing."

I hope so, Lucy thought.

With Paddy in front, they trudged along the rocky shore, their clothes drenched. The storm had turned the trail into a muddy path. Each step was treacherous. Branches whipped their faces and the wind threatened to force them back. Lucy slipped, and Paddy fell on his backside trying to help her up, covering them with ooze and grime.

Sid showed no mercy. "Let's go," he said, his authoritative voice piercing the roar of the downpour. He gave them a light shove. "Weather's only going to get worse. Only way to dry off is to reach this cave of yours. So pick up the pace."

"We're going as fast as we can!" Lucy shouted over her shoulder. She shivered, and it wasn't from the cold.

"I got to pee," said Chi-Chi.

"In the cave," Sid replied, pushing him in his back.

Fallen branches and leaves made it difficult to determine the right direction. Paddy led them one way, then changed his mind and backtracked. After a few false leads, he located the correct trail, which rose in a slight incline. Unable to prevent themselves from slipping in the mud, Lucy, Paddy, and Chi-Chi bent down, using their hands and fingers to pull themselves up the path. Sid's and Jack's boots provided better traction. They herded the children along the path, seemingly oblivious to their suffering.

Soon the five of them stood outside a great slab of stone. A swollen river flowed swiftly through a narrow gap toward the sea.

"That's it—the entrance to the cave," Paddy said as the rain ran down his cheeks. "This is probably a good time for the flashlights."

"Wait one second," Sid complained. "You're telling me the treasure is in *there*? That's nothing more than a hole in the ground. I'm not going to follow you in there. I can smell a trap when I see one."

Lucy stepped forward and pushed some of the brush and ivy from the rock above the cave entrance.

"There's the proof," she said. "Those stars match the ones on his grave. He carved them there himself as a marker."

"Wow, *chévere*," said Chi-Chi.

Sid turned to face Paddy. "Is that true, kid? You didn't put that there yourselves? Remember, I can tell if you're lying."

"Yeah," answered Paddy. "It's true. See his initials?"

"Okay then," Sid said. He reached into Jack's bag and handed out the flashlights. "No tricks."

Paddy exhaled. "Follow me." He flipped on his light and disappeared through the fissure, into the gloom.

They trekked single file through the flooded tunnel: Paddy first, followed by Lucy, then Chi-Chi. Behind them came Sid and Jack, who spoke to each other in low voices. The rush of water upset their footing, making it difficult not to slip.

Chi-Chi attempted to jump onto a large stone that protruded through the surface. The rock tottered, causing him to lose his balance and tumble into the river. The current began to drag him out, toward the sea. He reached with his hands, trying to grab hold of the tunnel floor, anything, but continued his slide until Jack grasped his shirt, lifting him to his feet. A trail of blood oozed down Chi-Chi's leg from a long cut.

"Let's go," said Sid. "Don't stop until we get there." Jack glanced at Chi-Chi sympathetically, but didn't say anything.

They dug their fingers into narrow crevasses in the rocks for balance. After about forty feet, the tunnel expanded and the adults could walk without hunching over.

Lucy noticed Chi-Chi glancing around nervously. "It's okay," she said. "We'll find some way out of this."

"Not worried about that," he answered. "It's just I don't like bats."

She took his hand. "There's nothing to worry about. Bats don't hurt people. It's only a superstition."

He looked down at the blood on his leg. "You sure?"

"I'm sure. They won't bother you. They mostly eat mosquitoes and other bugs, at least when they can't get any strawberry jam. Look, some are over there."

Lucy pointed her flashlight near the ceiling, at some small dark blotches. As they watched, several blotches dropped and flew a short distance through the tunnel, coming to rest on another rock face. Chi-Chi whined, but as more bats skittered along the walls at a distance, he muttered, "Guess you're right." Still, he eyed them with distrust.

They waded through the water until reaching a second narrow passageway. Continuing ahead, they struggled against the current until it ended at the mouth of the next, larger antechamber. Paddy scrambled up a ledge littered with stones with the others following him. Here, above the river, the ground was dry and cluttered with stalagmites crammed together like a battalion of miniature soldiers.

Lucy stopped and turned. "There's some ancient pottery and human bones up here. Don't touch any of it, okay?"

"Is any of this stuff worth anything?" asked Jack, reaching for a partially-intact clay pot.

"Don't," Lucy started. "You'll break it. Touch it and we won't take you any farther, I swear. It's a big cave."

"Leave it," said Sid, shaking his head. "It's all worthless garbage anyway. We're here for something much bigger. It'll just weigh us down."

Jack shrugged, as if he didn't care one way or the other.

They continued along, past the pottery. When he saw the human skulls and bones, Chi-Chi's mouth dropped open and he crossed himself. At the far end of the ledge they slid back into the water. After passing through another narrow tunnel, the walls gave way to the empty expanse of the huge central cavern.

"Wow," said Jack, swinging his flashlight at the stalactites that hung from the roof like giant icicles. "I never seen nothing like this before. I wish I had a camera. You kids really came here yourself?"

"Stuff it," growled Sid. "We're not here to sightsee." Turning to Paddy, he said, "So where's the treasure, kid? You said there was some marker."

Instead of answering, Paddy glanced at the narrow ledges ringing the cavern high above the floor. When he saw the blue jacket draped around one of the stalagmites, he lit it with his flashlight until Sid noticed it, too. Then he took a deep breath. This was the part he'd been mentally practicing since they began their slog through the cave. As is usually the case, the lie began with a kernel of truth.

"Do you see that? That's Le Moyne's blue coat—*the* blue coat. It's guarding the treasure, like the poem on his grave says. That's the signal."

"That's it?" Sid's voice squeaked. "A *coat*? You think the gold's in this miserable place because of a *coat*?"

"That's not all. There's something carved on the rock under the jacket—the letter 'X', like on a pirate's treasure map. Climb up yourself if you don't believe me. You have a rope, don't you?"

Sid thought for a moment, then nodded. "Okay. So the gold's here somewhere. Where do we dig? It's a big cave and half is underwater. We could be here for a month."

Paddy shrugged and looked away. "We don't know. Like I said, that's why it's still here. We came a couple of times but couldn't find it. Maybe you could get a metal detector or something." He smiled. "Well,

I've done my part. I've led you to the spot like I promised. Can you let us go now?"

"No way. You'd go straight to the cops. No, you two and your friend are gonna stay with us until we find it. We got enough shovels for each of you. If you're lucky, it won't take more than a few hours." He turned to face Jack. "Start looking around. Maybe there's something else written on one of the rocks in here."

As Sid and Jack split up to inspect the walls, the three friends waded into the water to talk to each other without being overheard. Although Paddy's lie had stuck, he felt deflated. They were still confined in the cave without an obvious method of escape.

"What now?" Lucy asked.

"I don't know," said Paddy. "We need to find some way to get out of here. Maybe some sort of diversion, but I'm out of ideas."

"Maybe you should have thought of that before you got us trapped in here with those two lunatics," she responded. "When they discover the gold isn't here, they're going to kill us, or worse."

"It was the only thing I could think of!" Paddy shot back. "I didn't hear you come up with a better plan."

The argument would have continued, but at that moment a loud thundering noise reverberated through the cavern, as if a cannon had been fired. Almost instantly the echoing boom was replaced by the ominous sound of rushing water as the river began rapidly rising.

Lucy shrieked. "Out of the water! Out of the water!"

They pushed their way toward the edge of the cavern, fighting the current. It pulled at them like a magnet, trying to sweep them away. Chi-Chi reached a large boulder near the base of the wall and wrapped one arm around it, extending his other hand toward the twins.

"Grab me! *¡Vamonos!*"

Paddy grasped Chi-Chi's hand and, with thick branches surging past, they pulled Lucy toward them. The three of them scrambled to a narrow ledge some ten feet above the base of the cavern floor as the two men climbed up from the other direction.

"Thanks," Lucy said.

"No problem," Chi-Chi said. "We're in this together, *si*?"

"*Si*," Lucy repeated.

They looked down into the chasm. The river was now a torrent, pouring through the cave with the sound of a steam train. Already the narrow passageways on each end of the large cavern were completely filled with water.

"It's a flash flood," said Jack from beside them. "Looks like we're stuck for now."

Sid swore loudly. "We're gonna have to wait it out," he said angrily. "At least no one else is gonna come through here for a while."

The twins tried to calm their fluttering nerves and assessed the new reality of the situation. Now there was no difference between captor and captive. Along with Chi-Chi, they were trapped with Sid and Jack, with nowhere to go, no way out. But at least the water had stopped rising. It continued to rush through the cave like a dam had broken upstream, a maelstrom of turmoil and power, but had reached its apex a couple of feet from the base of the ledge. All they could do now was sit with their legs dangling over the side and wait for the current to calm and the water to recede.

"We could be here for hours," Lucy complained. "Or even days."

"Trapped in a cave with a couple of criminals and a hurricane blowing outside. This is just like that movie we saw last year," remembered Paddy. "But they were stuck in an old hotel with a bunch of gangsters."

"*Key Largo*, right?" Jack asked. "I love that movie."

"Yeah," said Paddy. "That's it. How does it end, anyway? Our mom made us leave when it got scary."

Sid stared into Paddy's eyes. "The gangsters kill everybody, one by one."

"Everybody?"

"Everybody," Sid said with a sneer. "Good thing this is real life and not a movie. Hate for that to happen to you kids."

"He's making that up," Lucy said to her brother. "I heard Bogart stops the bad guys and rescues everyone."

"You should ask about *Treasure of Sierra Madre*," Sid added. "In that one Bogart goes crazy while looking for buried treasure. Like *us*." He shouted that last word and made his eyes bug out, causing Paddy to flinch.

"That's not funny," Lucy said.

"You kids don't know what you're in for," Sid said. "This is just the beginning."

Just then there was a splash below them. The twins looked into the churning water and screamed.

"Chi-Chi!" cried Paddy. "Help him!"

"Oh no!" Lucy shouted. "He fell in!"

But it was too late. As they watched in horror, Chi-Chi was taken by the current, spun around in circles, and swept through the cavern and out of sight. He was gone.

TWENTY-FIVE

T he *Miner's Revenge* sped across the sea. Captain Jean-Pierre Le Moyne paced along the deck, his blue coat fluttering in the stiff wind. He glanced to the south. Several miles away sailed the British frigate, the *Vanguard*. Over the past six days it had gradually gained on the *Miner's Revenge*, and now was nearly within range.

As Le Moyne watched, a small wisp of smoke puffed from a starboard porthole and a muffled boom echoed across the water. Moments later there was a small splash about a quarter mile away. Yes, still out of range. But not for much longer.

The *Vanguard* outgunned his schooner and was sure to be the victor in any firefight, which is why Le Moyne was fleeing. But the *Vanguard* was just a little faster. Not much, and not at all when the sea was smooth as glass, but when the wind kicked up and the waves churned it was a tiny bit quicker and that's all that mattered. Eventually the British warship would catch up, and it would be good-bye *Miner's Revenge*, because the *Vanguard*'s cannons were more than just a little bit better. They were a lot better, with a half-mile more range and double the accuracy.

But Le Moyne had one trick left. He checked the sea chart a second time, then called to the wheel.

"Fifteen degrees to starboard."

Such a course correction would allow the British frigate to gain even more ground. Now it would only be a matter of hours before the *Vanguard* would be able to turn broadside and blast the hell out of his ship.

"That will take us close to Janaconda Island," the wheelman shouted back.

"I'm counting on it," Le Moyne replied. "Stay the course."

They'd be stuck between the seventy-four gun frigate on one side and the razor-sharp reef on the other. Le Moyne smiled briefly. At least that's how it would seem to someone not familiar with the secret to navigating the narrow channels. If the *Vanguard* tried to follow, well, that would be bad news for Captain Forester, because it would run aground and the *Miner's Revenge* would simply circle around and fire on its portside, where the frigate didn't have any guns. Three days earlier he had shifted bearing, hoping against hope they'd reach the island before being caught by the faster frigate, where he'd finally possess a strategic advantage in this chase to the death. *Janaconda Island.* What was it about that place that kept drawing him? Maybe it was time to start believing in fate.

An hour went by, then another. The *Miner's Revenge* stayed on its course toward disaster. The *Vanguard* fired another test shot, and this one passed through one of the sails. The ragged edges of the tear whipped in the breeze. Now they were within range. It would be a matter of minutes before the British frigate would unload all its guns. Through the light fog Le Moyne could barely see the island in the distance. Almost there.

There was a thump, followed by a low-pitched rumbling sound, sort of like the sound of an earthquake. The ship tilted, first one way and then the other, before grinding to a halt. They had run aground.

Le Moyne grimaced. He had misread the chart and been caught in his own trap.

A man ran onto the deck; it was O'Brian. "We're taking on water," the second mate announced. "Fast. The hull is crushed, and the ship's gonna sink. Ain't nothin' to be done about it, neither."

At that moment another shot rang across the sea and a cannonball blew apart the foremast, sending a shower of splinters flying. Le Moyne felt a sharp pain in the side of his head and reached up with his hand. His hair was wet and warm. Strange; it didn't seem to be raining. He looked at his fingers, saw they were covered with blood. From somewhere on the ship another man cried out in pain. So this was it, then. The end of everything.

What have I done, a voice cried inside Le Moyne's head. *What have I done?*

"Abandon ship," he announced. "Drop the rowboats!"

There was a round of fire and the *Miner's Revenge* shuddered under his feet. It was being torn apart.

No, correction: it *had* been torn apart.

The last volley had broken the ship in two. Both masts were ripped off their steps as the ship tilted. Maybe half the crew killed, and probably half of the rest trapped below deck in the rising water. In less than an hour the ship would sink forever, but perhaps there was a chance to save those left, including himself. All he needed was time. The ship vibrated again, and his knees buckled.

He was dimly aware that the first longboat had already been lowered with a dozen men onboard. He'd have to act fast. If they rowed away now, the *Vanguard* would see the long rowboat, even from this distance, and destroy it with a few well-placed shots. Somehow, he'd have to make it appear that everyone aboard the *Miner's Revenge* was dead. Conceal the escape. Create a diversion. He tried to focus through his pounding headache.

More screams. Le Moyne coughed and choked on the black smoke that filled his lungs. His head spinning, Le Moyne staggered across the lurching deck. An arm poked out from a pile of debris. He paused to kick at the wreckage, to push it away, to help the crewman trapped underneath. He pulled at the arm and nearly lost his balance as it came free. There was nothing attached to it; it was just a stump, ripped from the body of an unlucky sailor. Le Moyne flung it aside like a piece of trash. *Must focus.*

Grasping the wooden rail, he stumbled down the staircase into the upper hold, three steps at a time. The water was waist-deep and pouring in fast. He pushed through the seawater, making his way to the shelves against the far wall.

A moan. He turned his head, fighting dizziness. A boy, no older than thirteen or fourteen, was huddled against the side wall, his hands clenched against the wound in his stomach. Le Moyne recognized him as the cabin boy who'd joined the crew at a recent port. Riley, or Sully, or maybe Willy.

"Help," the boy cried out.

No time. "Hold on." Le Moyne forged forward and reached around the boy's back, lifting him by the armpits. After helping the young crewman to the stairwell, he laid the boy across the steps and ripped open his shirt. A fragment of wood jutted from the boy's stomach like a stake. No time, there was no time. The boy was as good as dead; he had to focus on his job.

"Bite down on this," he heard himself say. He shoved the torn shred from the shirt into the boy's mouth. "This will hurt." He grasped the wood and yanked. The boy moaned. He yanked again; the shard came free, releasing a flow of blood.

Le Moyne jerked the fabric out of the boy's mouth and jammed it against the wound, then pressed the youngster's hand against it. "Hold it there. Now, can you move?"

The boy groaned, nodded. "Yes."

"Then go! There is still time to catch the longboat."

"Thank you"—a whisper. Then he was gone, up the stairs and out of sight.

Le Moyne entered the water once again, fighting against the cotton in his head, his exhaustion. A boy— there was a boy here. A minute ago, an hour ago, or was it last week? *Focus.* He searched the shelves and soon located what he was looking for. Gunpowder. He yanked the box off the shelf and watched it splash into the water amidst the floating debris, before hoisting it onto his shoulder. He lost his footing and slid into the water, slow to get up. A wave of nausea and dizziness coursed through him, and he pressed his hand against his forehead. It came away covered with blood. He vomited into the water, twice, and the dizziness passed.

Somehow Le Moyne still held the box. He trudged ahead until he reached the stairs and climbed back to the deck. The air stank of death. A boy—was there a boy? No time. *Need to focus.* He threw the box down, opened the flaps, reached in. The gunpowder had remained dry. To his distorted sense of touch it felt raw, like sawdust, and it clumped to the wet blood smeared across his fingers.

Only one thing left to do. He reached into his upper jacket pocket and pulled out a tin of matches. It was the box he'd taken during his meeting with Captain Forester all those months ago. He picked a match, dropped it, took another, then a third. *Focus!* He struck the match once, twice, then watched it burst in blue flame. Reaching down, he lit the corner of the nearest flap. When he was sure it had caught, he turned and ran, ran as fast as he could to the edge of the ship, the side from where the longboat had been lowered moments earlier. Or was it yesterday? His head hurt too much to think now. Behind him was a loud whoosh as the sky erupted in reds and oranges.

Le Moyne was thrown over the rail. The wind whistled as he fell, fell, fell through the air until he met the cold sea with a splash. Salt water filled his mouth, burned his nose. He lifted his head and gasped for breath. *Where was that boat?* His head went under once again, and all went dark.

TWENTY-SIX

"Chi-Chi! Chi-Chi!" Lucy and Paddy shouted over and over, tears streaming down their faces.

"Maybe he's holding onto a rock or something," Paddy said, hope dripping off every syllable. The twins swept their flashlights through the cavern, but the light hardly made a dent in the gloom.

"You see anything?" Lucy asked.

"No, it's too dark. *Chi-Chi*! Where are you?"

A huge branch swept past, scraping against the walls. The host of bats, unsettled by the noise, circled the roof overhead.

Lucy's lower lip trembled. "I hope he's all right."

"I'm gonna go in," Paddy announced. "I'll find him."

He prepared to slide down the ledge when Lucy grabbed him by his shirt, holding him back.

"Are you nuts? You'll get lost in there, too."

"I have to know—I have to know if he's all right!"

Sid stood on the edge of the precipice and peered into the black depths, his flashlight reflecting off the foaming water. "Forget about him; he's already dead," he said. "Those narrow passages are filled with water. No one can hold their breath that long."

"Dead?" Lucy began to sob as the river continued to wash through the cavern, carrying broken branches and loose debris.

"Don't listen to him," Paddy said. "He's just trying to scare us again." But he was crying now, too.

"It's all our fault," Lucy continued. "He didn't want anything to do with the treasure from the very beginning."

Paddy nodded, grimacing. "I should never have said it was in this stupid cave to begin with. We'd be home safe now if it wasn't for me."

Lucy sniffled. "You don't know that. Mom and Dad would be dead if you didn't do something."

They hugged, letting the tears flow down their cheeks.

"He's a really good swimmer," Paddy said, as much to convince himself as to console his sister. "If anyone can make it through there, it's him. Remember how—"

He was interrupted by a large crash, followed by a loud roar. A boulder or some debris deeper in the cave must have washed away. Lucy sobbed.

They both knew the truth: they'd never see him again. But there was nothing they could do other than try to stay alive themselves.

One hour led to the next. At some point the tears ran out. The sound of the water rushing through the cavern made them sleepy. Giving in to their exhaustion, they dozed off on the rock ledge. Eventually—it could have been three hours or seven, there was no way to know—they woke to near silence. The storm outside must have died out. Now they had to wait for the water level to drop low enough for them to get out of the cave, but that could still take hours.

Paddy took one of the flashlights and climbed up to the stalagmite that was draped with the blue pirate coat. From her position below, Lucy could see him glancing back and forth between the carved rock and the tourist map, which he held in his hands. Then, after about a half hour, he stuffed the map into his back pocket and clambered down.

As they sat in the darkness, Sid and Jack talked among themselves, showing no remorse for what had happened.

"Once the water goes down," said Sid, "we can start to dig. We have plenty of time . . . plenty of time." He rambled faster and faster. "The treasure's here; I can feel it. We'll be able to buy a new boat! Can you imagine that? One hundred—no, make it two hundred feet long, with big cabins and velvet couches. We'll be kings of the sea."

"I like the boat we have, boss," answered Jack.

"Fine, you can keep it. Mine will be bigger—a whole lot bigger. I'll be able to go anywhere I want . . . anywhere!"

This sort of talk continued for a while, alternating between how they planned to remove the gold and how they'd spend it. In addition to the new boat, Sid wanted a mansion in France and lots of fancy cars. Jack, though, was content to purchase his own piece of land, where he could live alone with some dogs and a vegetable garden.

Eventually Sid's anxiety overtook him, and he ordered Jack to check if the water level was falling.

Jack frowned. "What do you want me to do—get in the water?"

"Yes," Sid answered. "That's exactly what I want you to do."

"But it's dangerous. That boy floated away. I could get hurt."

"Oh, you're right; how selfish of me," responded Sid. "You're much more valuable than he was." Then, in the darkness, Lucy and Paddy heard someone shout, "Hey!" followed by a splash. They shone their flashlights down into the flooded cavern, where they saw Jack treading water.

"You pushed me," accused Jack.

"No I didn't," Sid replied. "My foot slipped, and I grabbed you for balance."

"Oh. I guess that's okay then. It sure seemed like you pushed me, though."

"But while you're in the water, see if the water level has started to recede. The water's probably shallow enough now for you to put your feet down where you are."

"Uh, okay . . . I guess." said Jack after a moment. "I could use some light."

The twins aimed their flashlights toward the water, and Jack raised his arm in thanks. Then the concerned look on his face shifted to a wide smile. "Yup. It's about five feet deep here. Can stand with my head just above the surface." He gave everyone the thumbs-up sign and began to swim his way across the cavern.

Twigs and leaves drifted by. The beams from the flashlights illuminated Jack as he reached the far side of the cave, where he was able to stand once more.

"Looks like the water level is down three or four inches," he shouted after examining the moisture on the wall.

"Excellent!" Sid called out. "Good work. Get back here and I'll help you up on the ledge to dry off."

He turned to Lucy and Paddy. "You two are pretty smart, right? How much time we got 'til all the water's gone and we can start to dig?"

"Start to *dig*?" cried Lucy. "Are you crazy? That could take days. We'll starve to death!"

Before Sid could respond, their discussion was interrupted by a loud shriek. They trained their flashlights on Jack, who was standing near the far side of the cavern with his hands in the air, the water swirling around his armpits.

"Ah!" He slapped at the water. "Something bit my leg!"

He spun in circles, as if trying to see in all directions simultaneously. There was a small splash a few feet to his left, then another.

"What is it?" Sid yelled out. "Do you see anything?"

"It's those big ugly-looking fish again!" Jack shouted back. "Like the one that bit me a few months ago. There have got to be at least a dozen of them, and they're huge! I'm getting out." He started swimming toward the ledge where the others were sitting.

"Hold on," called Paddy. "What do they look like?"

"They look like fish. What do you think they look like?" There was another splash and one jumped out, flapped its wide tail along the surface, and slipped back under.

The hours spent collecting bones at Rita's Café had paid off. "It's the heliomanth!" cried Lucy. "We found it!"

"I don't care what it's called," Jack answered. "Is it dangerous?"

"They're vicious," replied Lucy. "They'll rip your skin off in chunks." She winked at Paddy. "I heard one guy had to have his leg amputated."

"You're kidding, right?"

"Stay in and find out," Paddy called.

"The heck with this," Jack said, moving toward the ledge.

"I'm getting in to take a closer look," said Paddy. "Mom and Dad would kill us if they knew we had a chance to study the heliomanth and didn't do it."

"I'm coming in too," Lucy said.

Together, the twins slid down the rocky slope and into the water.

Until now, Sid hadn't been watching them, but that got his attention. "Hey!" he shouted. "Where are you brats going? Get back up here—*now*."

"No way," Paddy said.

"Jack—get over here and grab them."

"Where do you *think* we're going?" Lucy shouted, exasperated. She pointed toward the far end of the cavern. "There's no way out. Not with the water level this high. We're all stuck here."

"Well—I'm not going to let you go wherever you want down there. *Jack*!"

"Yeah, Boss?"

"Stay close to them."

Jack stared from across the cavern. "Not with those bloody fish swimming around. You come in if you want. I'm getting out where it's safe." He continued the rest of the way and clambered up the ledge, with Sid refusing to help his partner.

Lucy and Paddy swam toward the center of the pool, to a spot too deep for them to stand. They treaded water, looking around.

A shape flashed. "Look!" Paddy cried. "Over there! I see one!" Holding his glasses in place, he put his face under the surface to get a better look, and Lucy followed his example. The fish swam between their bodies, close enough for them to grab its tail.

They raised their heads and inhaled sharply.

"Wow," said Lucy. "That's neat." I wish Mom and Dad were here to see this."

"We can come back and show them when we get out of here. There are still a few days before we have to leave for home."

"They won't have a chance," Lucy replied. "Once the water level drops, the fish will probably swim out to the ocean again. It's either us or no one."

"I guess we better do a good job of it," said Paddy. "Try to remember everything."

For the next fifteen minutes all thoughts of escape vanished. They treaded water, periodically sticking their heads under the surface. Soon they spied a second fish, then a third—and then there were too many to count.

After a while, Lucy turned to Paddy and whispered, "We have to think about getting out of here."

"What do you mean?"

"Sid and Jack are still up on the ledge. They're not watching us. I'll bet we could swim out of here before they could catch us."

Paddy eyed the distance to the end of the cavern. "I don't know, Lucy," he said. "It's pretty far and Jack's a real good swimmer. Remember how he kept up with our rowboat? Besides, the water is still pretty rough down at that end. We could drown."

"Just like Chi-Chi," Lucy whispered.

"I don't want to think about it."

She grabbed his arm under the water. "We have to get out of here. The water level's going down. Maybe Chi-Chi's hurt and needs our help. We've got to do it, and soon."

"But—"

"You can't be afraid. We've got to do it."

He sighed. "You're right. But let's wait a little longer, just to be safe."

"Not much longer. This is our best chance, while we're in the water and they're not."

So the twins stayed in, studying the heliomanth and eyeing both the water level and their captors on the dry ledge. Then without warning there were a number of small splashes around them. The fish scattered and vanished. A moment later, the rhythmic sound of oars stroking against the water echoed through the cavern.

"Someone's coming!" shouted Jack. "It's a boat. Ahoy! We're in here!"

"Shut up!" Sid replied.

The twins pointed their flashlights upstream. As they watched, a small rowboat emerged through the entrance of the cavern and turned in their direction.

"*Hola, ¿Qué hay?*" cried a familiar voice from inside the boat.

"Chi-Chi?" screamed Paddy in amazement. "Chi-Chi? Is that you?"

Chi-Chi waved his arms over his head. Lucy and Paddy laughed, and cheered, and then laughed some more. Everything was going to be fine. Then they noticed that there was another person in the boat sitting behind him.

It was the old man from the town square. And he had a gun.

TWENTY-SEVEN

"Chi-Chi!" Lucy shouted as the rowboat inched toward the ledge. "Thank goodness! We thought you'd drowned!"

The boat reached the edge of the cavern, and the twins recognized it as the one from the dock behind their house. The old man must have stolen it.

Chi-Chi jumped to the rock and the twins hugged him hard. "No way. I told you I could hold my breath underwater a long time. It was just like free diving at Shark Alley."

Paddy laughed. "I just didn't believe it. I've never heard of anyone holding their breath that long."

"No more than a minute at a time. Only ended up with a few scrapes." He held up his arms, which were covered with red welts. "After I got out, I went for help."

"And he found me instead," said the old man, stepping out of the rowboat. He looped the rope around a stalagmite and followed Chi-Chi onto the ledge, still brandishing the gun.

"More competition for the gold," Sid muttered. "This is turning into a real party."

"Don't shoot!" Lucy raised her arms. "Are you still after that stupid treasure? We don't know where it is—I swear!"

"Hey, wait a sec," said Jack. "You said it was buried here in the cave."

"Shut *up*," yelled Sid. "You idiot."

"You're right, Lucy," said the old man. "I *am* still after the treasure. But that doesn't make me a bad guy. Let me finally introduce myself. My name is Robert McNeill. I'm a retired policeman from Des Moines. And you two," he said, waving his gun at Sid and Jack, "you two are coming with me. Based on what this young man has told me, I'm taking you in on charges of burglary, destruction of property, assault, and kidnapping."

"You can't arrest us," Sid scoffed. "You're no cop. Not no more."

"Once a cop, always a cop," said Mr. McNeill. "I'm making a citizen's arrest."

"Like hell you are." Sid rushed at Mr. McNeill, only to slip on the slick rock and fall against the older man's chest. Mr. McNeill punched Sid across the jaw, knocking him to the ground where he remained, glaring, a thin ribbon of blood dribbling from the corner of his mouth. From the far side of the ledge, Jack eyed Mr. McNeill warily, but made no attempt to move.

"Wait a second," said Lucy. Everything was happening too fast. "You're a police officer?"

"Surprised me, too," Chi-Chi said.

"I thought you were terrified of him. Why did you go to him for help?"

"I didn't."

"It was still raining when Chi-Chi reached the center of town," Mr. McNeill said. "The worst of the storm had passed, but the festival was over and the streets were empty. I went out to stretch my legs when he ran into me. I saw the cuts on his arms and demanded answers."

"I told him you were trapped in the cave and needed help," added Chi-Chi. "So here we are."

"You're awesome, Chi-Chi," Paddy exclaimed. "You know, you scared us when you fell into the water."

Chi-Chi looked hurt. "Fell? I *jumped*. I thought you were creating a distraction by talking about that stupid movie."

At that moment, Sid rose and leapt from the ledge into the little boat, attempting a getaway. But he misjudged the distance and landed off-center, causing the craft to flip over and dumping him face-first into the water.

"That's enough, now," said Mr. McNeill, pointing the gun. "Don't make me use this, you hear?"

"That's the cap gun you gave me at the festival," Chi-Chi whispered, grinning.

Mr. McNeill slipped into the water and grabbed Sid's wrist, pinning back his arm. "Don't make me use my cuffs."

"He doesn't have any handcuffs," whispered Chi-Chi. "It's a trick. He told me he'd threaten it if he had to and not to say anything. He must've been a great policeman."

"Okay, okay," said Sid.

"What about you, Sonny?" Mr. McNeill turned to Jack. "You need cuffs, or you wanna try without?"

"Nah, I'm fine," came the reply. "I'm too exhausted to fight. I just want out of this place already."

"Terrific," said Mr. McNeill. "It'll be easier this way. I bet the water's low enough so we can wade out of here now. We'll have to leave the rowboat behind, though." He looked at the twins. "We can come back for it later."

Everyone plunged into the water. They pushed their way through the tunnels, following the current of the river, until they passed through the final barrier and into the fresh air. The sun was beginning to rise in the east. The storm had moved off, leaving branches strewn across the path. Lucy looked up at the soft glow in the sky. They'd been in the cave all night.

They walked along the beach, with Mr. McNeill always pointing the cap gun toward the backs of Sid and Jack. It was nearly 6:00 in the morning when they arrived at the police station.

Lucy turned to her brother. "I guess it's over. We'll never find that treasure now. All that work for nothing."

Paddy's face twisted into a strange smirk as they reached the front desk, which was manned by a very surprised Officer H. Douglas Ernst III.

TWENTY-EIGHT

An officer departed to inform Chi-Chi's parents that he was safe. The policeman returned a half hour later with news that the storm had flooded Chi-Chi's street, but his family was fine. His father sent instructions for Chi-Chi to remain with Lucy and Paddy until the water subsided. But no one knew what had happened to Mr. and Mrs. Hendricks. As Lucy and Paddy fretted, a police cruiser was sent to look for them.

Sid and Jack were fingerprinted and thrown in a pair of holding cells in the rear of the station. It turned out they had committed a series of crimes in Florida before coming to the island, including stealing the yellow boat from a family in Pompano Beach, and a reward was offered for their capture. Mr. McNeill refused to accept it, saying he was only doing his job.

When reminded he was retired, he laughed and said, "Once a cop, always a cop."

"I think the reward money should go to Chi-Chi," he said. "He's the reason these crooks were captured."

"But I didn't do anything special," Chi-Chi argued. "I'm a regular kid, not a hero."

"Son," said Mr. McNeill, "heroes are just regular people who do extraordinary things. You risked your life jumping into that current to save your friends. Whether you believe it or not, you *are* the real hero here."

"I agree," Lucy said. "Chi-Chi deserves the reward money."

Chi-Chi reluctantly accepted. When he was told the size of the reward—five thousand dollars—his jaw dropped.

"Wow—what are you going to do with it all?" Paddy asked.

"Well . . . I kind of want to go to college when I'm old enough."

Mr. McNeill clapped him on the shoulder. "I think that's a terrific idea. What would you like to study? I think you'd make a fine police officer."

Chi-Chi blushed. "It's silly, but . . . I think I want to become a scientist. Maybe . . . maybe I'll learn about bats."

"*Bats*?" Lucy exclaimed. "But you hate them!"

"They're not so bad when you get used to them," Chi-Chi said. "I figure there are plenty of fish scientists, but no one has ever studied the bats here on the island."

"Chi-Chi Flores, bat scientist," said Paddy. "I don't think I'll ever get used to that."

"Well you better, 'cause in about twenty years, you'll be calling me *Doctor* Chi-Chi!"

The conference room door opened and a policeman entered, followed by Mr. and Mrs. Hendricks.

"Lucy! Paddy! Thank goodness you're all right!" Their mom ran over and gave them a long hug as tears of joy ran down her face. "We were so worried about you."

"Us?" Lucy said. "We were worried about *you.* Weren't you kidnapped? How did you get away?"

Their mother frowned. "What are you talking about? We were playing bridge in the rec center. When the rain started, we decided it was safer to wait there until the storm passed. When we got home, the house was a total wreck and you weren't there. We've been up all night frantic with worry. Then we heard a noise outside and saw a truck pulling out with the rowboat stashed in the back."

"That would've been me," Mr. McNeill interrupted.

"What happened?" their mother finished. "Where have you been? What—"

"Let them talk," their father interrupted. "From the beginning."

So Lucy and Paddy told of their adventure from when they first encountered Mr. McNeill in the square weeks earlier. When they finished, their parents were silent. Then, unexpectedly, their father laughed—a long, slow laugh until tears ran down his cheeks. Lucy and Paddy straightened at the shock of it until they too began to smile and giggle.

"Well," their father said, "it sounds like you had an eventful summer after all."

"There's one more thing," Paddy said. "We found the heliomanth!"

Their father's eyes widened. "What? Where? Tell me!"

"There were at least a dozen of them in the cave with us. We recognized them straight off."

"That's my kids," said their mom with pride.

"In a *cave*?" Their father frowned. "That doesn't sound right. The size of their teeth and eyes suggest they live in the open water."

Lucy replied, "One of those crooks said he saw them in the sea a few months ago."

"Yeah," Paddy added. "When we were exploring the cave several weeks ago, they weren't there. But the water was shallower then. Maybe they were trying to escape the storm or something."

Their mother became visibly angry. "The two of you went exploring a cave without telling us first? We need to have a talk about this when we get home."

"Margaret," said their father. "That can wait—first things first." He turned to Officer Ernst. "Do you think we could talk to those men?"

Mrs. Hendricks bristled. "Now you want to *talk* to them?"

"*Margaret*. The children are safe. This could be our only chance to learn where the heliomanth lives."

She shook her head. "Scientists."

Officer Ernst exhaled hard. "It's a bit unusual, but I don't see why not."

He led them to the holding cells, where their mother immediately stepped forward.

"You should be ashamed of yourselves! Kidnapping and scaring two young children like that! I hope you rot in prison for the rest of your—"

"Margaret!"

"Mom, we're fine," Lucy said. "Really."

"I give up," their mother said under her breath, stepping back.

"So," said Mr. Hendricks, speaking to Jack. "Can you tell us where else you saw the heliomanth? It's important."

"You know," prodded Lucy. "The fish you said bit you."

"Don't answer that," Sid shouted. "There's no reason to help them."

Jack stared at his partner through the bars. "I'm through listening to you. These people have done nothing to us we didn't deserve, and these kids have been nicer to me than you ever have."

He looked up at their father. "It was about a half mile offshore, in a shallow place with a lot of underwater grass. I remember 'cause I wanted to cool off, but your fish bit me in the . . . well, one just bit me. I ran the motor and banged on the side of the boat to chase them off. Every time we went back there I did the same thing."

"You must have anchored directly in the middle of their habitat. That may be where they lay their eggs. No wonder we haven't been able to find them—you scattered them throughout the bay. You think you can show us the spot?"

"He couldn't find his head if it wasn't attached," Sid said. "Don't know why you're talking to him at all. He's an idiot."

"Sure," answered Jack, ignoring his partner. "If I ever get out of here."

Mr. Hendricks looked toward Officer Ernst. "You think the judge would let him out for a few hours?"

"You've got to be kidding."

Lucy, Paddy, and their father all spoke together. "It's *important*."

Mrs. Hendricks shrugged. "There isn't anything as bullheaded as a scientist."

"You're telling me." The officer shrugged. "Okay. I think the judge might agree if I vouch for him."

"Would you?" asked Mr. Hendricks.

"I ain't gonna escape," said Jack. "I jus' wanna do something good for a change, that's all."

Officer Ernst threw up his hands. "If that's what you want, I'll talk to the judge."

"Terrific," said Mr. Hendricks. He turned back to Jack. "We'll make sure to tell the judge how helpful you've been. Maybe it'll make a difference in your sentence."

"Hey!" called Sid from across the hall. "I can be helpful, too! I can even pilot a boat to that spot and kill one of those fancy fish so you can dissect it and stuff it to take it home with you. Tell the judge I wanna help, too, willya?"

☠   ☠   ☠

"Well then," said Mr. McNeill after they had reconvened in the conference room. "That ends that. The only remaining question is, where's the treasure? I suspect you were pulling a fast one, and it isn't in the cave at all. Is that right, son?"

Paddy nodded. "I sure fooled Sid and Jack, though, didn't I?"

"Yes, you did," Lucy agreed. "But we're no closer to finding it ourselves."

"That's the way it often is with secret treasures," said Mr. Hendricks. "Everyone thinks they can find them, but they're only legends that don't actually exist."

"Lucy and Paddy found clues," Chi-Chi said. "Lots of them."

"I'm sorry," replied the twins' father. "Someone was probably playing a trick, or maybe it was merely a collection of coincidences. Either way, I'm certain there's nothing out there to find."

"Hold on," said Paddy. "I'm not so sure about that. I had a lot of time to think it out while we were stuck in that awful cave. For a long time I was stumped. It's a tricky puzzle, but every puzzle has a solution, right?"

He reached into his pocket and pulled out the partially torn, still-wet brochure that the librarian gave him weeks ago. Paddy carefully unfolded it, wary not to tear it further, and spread it across the conference room table with the full island map facing up.

"I need a pen," he said, glancing around the room.

Officer Ernst took a fountain pen from his pocket and handed it to Paddy.

"So where is it?" Chi-Chi said. "You gonna show us?"

"In a moment. I need to explain first." Paddy took a breath and squeezed the pen between his fingers. "Let's first go through all the places we found clues. I think there were four."

"There was the cave," said Lucy. "I don't think I'll ever forget that place."

"Right," agreed Paddy. "The cave is one. We went right to the center, where we discovered Stephenson's blue pirate jacket hanging over a stalagmite. Underneath, we found a square carved with an 'X' through it, along with three stars."

"He also put his initials and three stars over both entrances," Lucy explained. "That's how Paddy tricked those crooks into believing the gold was inside."

"That's right." Paddy paused to study the map. "The cave isn't marked, but I think the big cavern is right about here." He drew a circle with Officer Ernst's pen. "Next?"

"The ancient temple?" Chi-Chi asked. "You asked me to take you, but we didn't find anything."

"Good one," Paddy said. "We didn't find the clue there because it had been moved to the museum."

"Huh," said Mr. McNeill. "That's some good detective work."

"It was a lucky accident," said Lucy. "But it wasn't much of a clue. It was only Stephenson's initials next to four moons. It was on a block of stone that was moved from the temple years ago. I don't see how that helps."

"Don't forget about the square with the 'X' through it."

"I thought that was just his personal mark. I don't see why it's important."

"I'll get to that." Paddy scanned the map again until he found the ancient temple, and circled it. "Two more to go."

"Well, I'll guess one of them was the house," said Mrs. Hendricks, "because there are so many things written on the walls."

"The house—thanks, Mom."

"It's over here," said Lucy, pointing to an empty spot on the map near the sea.

She lifted her finger and Paddy made a third circle.

"The last one," said Mr. McNeill, "has got to be Stephenson's grave. The poem on his gravestone is definitely a clue, even though no one understands it."

"That's all four," said Paddy. "Lucy figured out he left clues where they wouldn't be destroyed over the years. That's how she guessed there'd be one at the temple, even though we didn't see it at first. Making sure his house wouldn't be painted or redecorated was harder, but he took care of that through his will. You told us that when we first ran into you, Mr. McNeill, although I don't think you meant to."

Mr. McNeill chuckled. "You kids remember everything, don't you?"

"Lucy remembers stuff. I just think things out."

"Okay, so circle his grave already," Lucy prodded.

"Not yet. Lucy, do you remember our trip to the town cemetery? I went ahead to look for the grave while you rested on the grass."

"I was exhausted and frustrated. You found the office and learned he wasn't buried there."

"Right. But I didn't tell you what the man in the office told me. I didn't think it was important at the time. What he said was that Stephenson *insisted* on being buried in that big field. His dad owned that plot of land, and he told me that Stephenson offered more and more money for it until his father gave in, as if he'd already decided he had to be buried there—that's what he said, pretty much his exact words."

Lucy cocked her head. "Wait—you think that's where the treasure is? In his grave? Or on the hilltop next to the grave? That doesn't make any sense. Then what's the point of the poem?"

"No, no. The treasure isn't *in* his grave; the grave *itself* is a clue—or rather, the *location* of the grave. Look!"

As everyone watched, Paddy reached across the map and drew one final circle, this time around the numbered box designating the location of the gravesite. Then he drew four straight lines, one passing through each circle.

"You see?" he said.

"A square. So what?' said Mr. McNeill.

"Nearly a *perfect* square," Paddy responded. "What's the chance of that?"

"Go on," Lucy said. "We're listening."

"Okay. What's more, those four locations match the phrases and symbols on the bottom half of his gravestone under the poem." Above the square he had just drawn, he wrote 'Remember Me,' underlining it twice.

"There are four things on his gravestone below those words: the phrases 'In Death' and 'In Life,' and two sets of symbols: Three stars and four moons in different phases. If you look at them right, together they form a square."

"I'm with you so far," said Mr. McNeill.

"Well, what represents death better than a grave?" Paddy asked. To emphasize his point, along the edge of the square passing through the location of the grave, he wrote the word 'Death.'

"And a house is where a person lives their life, right?" Across the bottom edge of the square, he wrote the word 'Life.'

"The other two are more difficult. First, there's the cave. On both entrances, he carved three stars with his initials."

"He also put three stars on the stalagmite under his jacket," interjected Lucy. "Next to one of those squares."

"Right—that confused me for a long time. I finally figured out he was showing us that the three stars on his gravestone stood for the cave. So, let me add that detail to the map." He reached with the pen and crudely drew three stars vertically down the right edge of the square, adjacent to the first circle he had drawn.

"One left," he said. "I guess everyone knows what's coming."

"I do," said Lucy. "The moons at the ancient temple. May I?"

Paddy handed the pen to his sister, who drew four moons along the upper edge of the square.

"You see?" said Paddy in triumph. "It matches."

"That's a good theory, but it doesn't completely fit," Lucy said. "On the grave, the word "Death" appears on top, while on your map you've written it on the left. Also, the stars and moons are in the wrong places."

"I think that's part of the puzzle. He wanted us to discover that the important thing was the relationship between the four places. It wouldn't make sense unless you had found all four clues."

"Let's say you're right. I still don't see how that helps. We're still back where we started, without the treasure."

"Don't you get it? The square connecting these places is *itself* a treasure map! A map leading to *Gemini*."

"Oh, the mythological twins," their mom said. "What does that have to do with all of this?"

"Well, that's one thing I'm not sure about yet. But it popped up several times."

"You're thinking of the mural," Lucy said.

"What's this about a mural?" asked Mr. McNeill.

"A giant mural of a pirate ship with the name *Gemini*," Paddy said. "We found it in a secret cellar under the house. We didn't tell you about it because we were frightened of you then. Not anymore."

"Sounds more and more like you didn't need my help after all," said Mr. McNeill, smiling.

Their mother frowned. "Wait—there's a secret cellar under the house? How on earth did you get in there?"

"Mom—just listen, okay? Next to the mural, Stephenson painted his initials and a square with the letter 'X' inside of it. What Lucy called his personal mark. Just like in the cave and carved on the ancient pictographs from the temple. In each case, the spot where the lines of the 'X' crossed was circled, like the word 'and' in the center of the gravestone inscription."

Paddy reached down and touched the pen to the middle of the square he had drawn across the map. "Do you get it now?" As everyone watched, he drew two diagonal lines inside the square, connecting opposite corners.

"X marks the spot," he said with a shrug. "Isn't that the way it always is on pirate treasure maps?"

The lines crossed over one of the little brown boxes, which Paddy circled. Everyone leaned over the table to read the map's legend.

"You're kidding me," Mr. McNeill said. "You think the treasure is *there*?"

Paddy nodded.

"The old hotel," said Chi-Chi.

"That's where we'll find it," Paddy agreed. "The old hotel."

Officer Ernst cleared his throat. "I have something that may interest you. It's an old police file. Wait here; I'll get it."

A few minutes later he returned carrying a small folder. He sat down between Lucy and Paddy and opened it across the table.

"This is our oldest unsolved case," he said, flipping through the yellowed pages. "A few years after that hotel was built, a couple of thieves robbed it and all the guests. The owner of the hotel repaid his guests in full, but refused to cooperate with the investigation, saying he didn't want any publicity. The thieves were never caught, which is why this file still exists."

He continued to scan the documents. "Ah, here we are." He pressed his finger against the page. "I was right. I thought I recognized the name. Look here. The owner of the hotel was your very own Thomas Stephenson."

"That's why he used to take Chi-Chi's grandmother there to play on the playground," Paddy said. "He owned it."

"You think those thieves were after the gold?" asked Chi-Chi.

"No," Lucy said. "I'll bet it was just a coincidence. They didn't know what was there, and Stephenson wouldn't have wanted to publicize the fact he lived on Janaconda Island. Remember, he was hiding from the British Navy. There were probably already rumors about who he used to be. He only wanted to live the rest of his life in peace."

"Maybe," said Officer Ernst, "he was also afraid that if people learned he owned the hotel, someone would eventually guess the treasure was there."

"Chi-Chi," Paddy interrupted, "you said you've been to that old hotel. Can you take us there?"

"Yeah, sure. Same road as the one we took to the temple, until it splits. Might be flooded from the rainstorm. Haven't been there in a long time."

"If you don't mind me tagging along, my truck could get us there," said Mr. McNeill. "But we'd have to get to it first. It's still down by the riverbank."

"You can come," Lucy said. "You deserve to see how this treasure hunt ends."

"Terrific," responded Mr. McNeill.

"I'll give you a lift," said Officer Ernst. "Now that the sun's up, I'd like to assess the damage to the residential neighborhoods anyway."

He left the station with Mr. McNeill, who returned forty-five minutes later in his mud-splattered pickup. The kids climbed into the back, with Mr. and Mrs. Hendricks in the front seat. Soon the truck was bumping along the unpaved road, splashing puddles left by the storm.

Chi-Chi banged on the back window to direct Mr. McNeill to turn down an unmarked path that was little more than a long driveway. After a short distance, the jungle gave way to a field overgrown with weeds and bushes. Scattered throughout the clearing were twenty or thirty buildings. Mr. McNeill drove over the grass next to one of the old bungalows and turned off the motor.

"Okay, kids," he said after they'd all gotten out. "It's your show. Where to?"

"I don't know," said Paddy, looking around. It wasn't like any hotel he'd ever seen before. He'd expected a few buildings surrounding a swimming pool, but this hotel was more like a luxurious campsite, with cabins and cozy restaurants instead of tents.

He frowned. "The gold has to be here somewhere—I'll bet my next flavored ice on it."

"That's the one I still owe you," laughed Mr. McNeill.

Lucy exhaled hard. "Sid was right about one thing. The treasure is huge. It would have to be stored somewhere like a giant safe or even underground."

"Plenty of space around here," Mr. McNeill said, looking around.

They split up, with Mr. and Mrs. Hendricks, Mr. McNeill and Chi-Chi, and Lucy and Paddy together in pairs. While the others wandered through the hotel grounds, the twins entered the reception building, which led to a web of offices. The floor was covered by a thin layer of dust and littered with curled-up skeletons of long-dead lizards and rats, but other than some empty desks and cabinets the rooms were bare. Disappointed, they returned to Mr. McNeill's truck, where the rest of the group were already waiting.

"Anything?" asked Chi-Chi.

"Nope," Paddy answered. "How about you?"

"We found a restaurant and a couple of shops," said Mr. McNeill. "No safe."

"Nothing promising from us either," said Mrs. Hendricks.

"Let's keep looking," said Lucy. "It's a big resort."

The sun rose higher. They walked through the compound, dodging puddles and downed branches. As sweat formed on their foreheads, they discovered a paved path leading to the remains of an amphitheater, where several horseshoe-shaped tiers of bleachers were constructed around a cobblestone floor. On the open side was a large platform several feet above the ground.

"Should we look under the stage?" asked Mr. McNeill, after they'd examined the rest of the arena. "You could probably fit a large container under there."

"What do you think, Paddy?" Lucy asked. "Paddy?"

But her brother had climbed to the upper row of seats, where he sat with his head in his hands, thinking.

"Okay then," she said, taking charge. "Let's look. Is there a hatch somewhere?"

There was. A small trapdoor in one of the rear corners of the wood stage swung up on a hinge. Because he was smallest, Chi-Chi was chosen to scramble around below. Mr. McNeill handed him a flashlight, and down he went. For the next few minutes, they heard sounds of grunting and scraping from under their feet. Then Chi-Chi's head popped back up through the hatch.

"Some mice," he said as Mr. McNeill helped him out. "And old socks and costumes. That's it."

Lucy sighed. "I'm out of ideas."

"I'm not," said a faraway voice.

They stared up into the highest part of the bleachers, where Paddy stood, peering into the distance.

"I think," he said, "we should go to the playground."

"Now?" Lucy asked. "Be serious. We can keep searching."

"I *really* think we should go to the playground," Paddy said in the same soft voice.

Chi-Chi sprang up the stairs. "Why? That place is all rundown."

"What is it?" Lucy asked, climbing. Upon reaching her brother in the topmost row, she turned. Jutting up in the distance were the upper sections of two ship masts. "Oh," she said. "I see."

"The gold will forever remain on board the ship," said Paddy, repeating the phrase from the end of the journal. "I think we've found our treasure. Come on."

The three adults and three children left the amphitheater together. As they pushed through the overgrown brush, the immense ship gradually became visible until it loomed over them. Twisted, curving ladders led to the deck, and poles had been erected along the hull to slide to the sand below. It was the greatest playground the twins had ever seen, the product of the mind of an old man who missed his days at sea.

"Could the treasure be buried in the field next to that ship?" Mrs. Hendricks asked.

"No—not in the field," Lucy answered. "On the ship itself. It's all so obvious now."

"Yes," Paddy agreed. "It looks exactly like the mural in the cellar."

"And you think that mural marked the location of the treasure?" asked their father. "A model of a boat used as a playground?"

"I can think of one simple way to check," Paddy said. He pushed through the tall grass, where the gold letters were still visible on the ship's base despite decades of dirt and mildew. *"Gemini."*

"So it wasn't a real ship all along," Lucy concluded.

"Remember the piano music?" Paddy asked. "A boat was sketched around the words '*Castor & Pollux*' in the title. Castor and Pollux—the Gemini twins. This is it."

Mr. McNeill laughed. "Anything else in that mural that might help us?"

"There was a pile of gold coins painted between the masts," Paddy said. "Maybe there's something on the deck."

"Let's climb up," Chi-Chi suggested.

While the three adults watched, the children scaled one of the curved ladders until reaching the top.

"Surely, there's another way," Mr. McNeill grumbled.

"Come on, you can do it!" Lucy called down.

The twins' father sighed as he grabbed hold of the nearest ladder and started to climb, with their mother following behind. Mr. McNeill, though, turned and headed back toward the amphitheater.

About twenty minutes later he returned and climbed up, carrying an axe from his truck. When he reached the deck, Lucy greeted him with a long sigh. "There's nothing here," she said, disappointed. "No box, no container, no nothing. Just some bars and nets to climb on."

"Of course not," Mr. McNeill said. "He wouldn't leave his gold out in the open. I think the mural was symbolic—and we need to look *inside* the ship."

"We looked for a door or hatch, too," said Lucy. "There isn't a way inside."

"There aren't going to be any doors for this one," he said gruffly. "We're going to have to do this the old-fashioned way. You say the treasure was between the masts?"

"That's where it was on the mural," Lucy answered. "Why? What are you going to—hey!"

Mr. McNeill swung the axe at the deck. The others shielded their faces as splinters flew. He swung again, and again, until he had made a wide hole in the flooring.

"Stairs!" exclaimed Chi-Chi.

The stairway led down into the center of the ship, into a large box-shaped room. Contained in one wall was a metal door with a large combination lock, like a bank vault. It was locked.

Mr. McNeill rapped hard on the door with the flat edge of the axe, producing a loud boom that echoed through the room.

"Now what?" he said. "I doubt even dynamite would have any effect on this. Unless we figure out the combination, we're out of luck." He spun the tumbler absent-mindedly. "No way in. What a shame. This door is all that stands between us and a lifetime of riches."

Riches . . . Chi-Chi jumped forward. "That's right!" he shouted. "It's *death*. Upon *death* great riches shall be reached."

"Death," repeated Paddy. "Of course! The painting in his study. The numbers weren't a *date*—they were the combination! Lucy, do you remember?"

"I do," she said. "They were 03-13-34." With her hand trembling, she reached to twist the dial—first one way, then the other, then back in the first direction once more. Holding her breath, she pushed hard on the handle. There was a soft click as the lock released. Slowly, and with the others peering over her shoulder, she pulled open the door to reveal the piles of gold bars stacked in cubes.

TWENTY-NINE

Thomas Stephenson took a long look at the weathered leather binding and flipped through the pages covered with his familiar scrawl. Over the years he'd recorded details of his pirate life—leaving out that covert business with Captain Forester of the *Vanguard*, of course—and now that the last page had been filled, the puzzle was complete. It was time to put his plan in motion. He reread the note he penned over breakfast.

Dear Sir,

Enclosed please find a personal journal that describes my life and career in some detail. With this letter, I hereby instruct you to deliver this journal to the Historical Museum of Janaconda

Island upon the tenth anniversary of my death, where it shall remain available for inspection to all interested parties. Please make a donation to the museum on my behalf in the amount of $1,000 to ensure its continued display. In addition, I direct my estate to provide periodic funding to the Janaconda Public Library for the purchase of materials and related equipment as is required, and for such contributions to be made anonymously.

I also reaffirm the instructions contained in my will, executed three years ago. After my death, my House, including the gardens, Hotel, and Grave shall receive periodic upkeep indefinitely, to be paid for through a monetary trust established in my Name. Yet my house is <u>NEVER</u> to be renovated, redecorated, or altered in any way or form, inside or out. Upon a proper request, however, any respectable and decent peoples may visit and stay within the house, so long as they comply with the above restriction. I have enclosed a set of keys.

These instructions to you shall remain secret, and shall not be revealed to anyone, not even the MUSEUM.

Thomas Stephenson
July, 1904

He signed his name, then opened the middle drawer of his desk and removed a thick envelope, sliding the journal inside. At that moment, his arthritic fingers stiffened and the book dropped to the floor, where it landed on one of his bare feet. Thomas Stephenson swore loudly.

"Is everything all right?" It was the housekeeper.

"Yes, fine," he replied. "Just cleaning up."

"You let me know if you need help with anything. I don't like it when you lock yourself up there in that room. I can't help you if you fall. You're not a young man anymore."

"I'll be only a minute. And then I'll have a package for you to take to the post office."

"That reminds me—a telegram arrived from your friend William Sullivan. He's a captain now."

"That so? You know I saved his life when he was a boy?"

"So you've told me."

He opened the door and poked his head out. "How's that daughter of yours this morning? Is she better?"

"Yes, much better. She was able to go to school today, although I think she prefers spending her time here in this house with you."

"Are you afraid I'm a bad influence? Don't worry; she'll forget all about me when she gets older."

"Somehow, I doubt that."

He smiled. Spending time with the little girl almost made him feel young again. As he rubbed his aching fingers he glanced up at the painting of his grave that hung on the wall, and remembered what he was supposed to be doing.

He bent down to pick up the journal and slipped it inside the envelope with the note and a set of keys. After sealing the envelope shut, he flipped it over, and in the space for the address, wrote:

Mr. M. Chittenden
Law Firm of Boggs & Patterson
Post Office Box 1041
Belize City, Belize

Then he stood and tucked the envelope under his arm. "I'm ready."

"Good, because I've brewed some tea."

THIRTY

The small airplane streaked through the clouds scattered across the endless blue sky. Lucy peered through the window, wondering when the flight would finally end. She'd lost interest in her books hours ago, and sat with her chin resting on her palms, staring at the sea. Then she saw something in the ocean below. She reached over and grabbed her brother's shirt, tugging hard.

"Quit it," Paddy complained. The air turbulence was making him sick and Lucy knew it.

Lucy ignored his plea. "Look!" she cried, pointing out her window. "There it is!"

Fighting nausea, Paddy squinted and scanned the water. Ahead, off in the distance, was a greenish-brown smudge about the size of a wood chip. As the plane flew, the smudge grew until there was no doubt: they had returned to Janaconda Island.

"It's hard to believe it's been a year since we left," Lucy remarked. "It feels like we've only been gone a week. I wonder if everything is the same."

"Somehow, I doubt that," said their mother with a smile.

"I can't wait to see Chi-Chi again," Paddy exclaimed. "I've got so much to tell him. I wonder what he's been up to all this time."

"Me, too," agreed Lucy.

They didn't have to wait long. The airplane began to descend until the island filled the entire window. The twins could observe roads and buildings, and a few minutes later the plane landed.

The Hendricks family stepped out and walked down a mobile staircase that had been wheeled to the door of the plane. Waiting at the bottom was Manuel Vargas.

"Hello and welcome back! It's wonderful to see you again." He picked up their luggage and carried it to a nearby van. "I'm sure you'll want to freshen up. But before I take you to the hotel, I've got someplace to show you first. I just hope we won't be late."

"It's probably not what you had in mind for your vacation," said Manuel as they raced through the jungle, "but you must visit the lab while you're here.

There are a half-dozen scientists studying the heliomanth! What's more, the spot where they lay eggs has been declared a protected area and is now off-limits to boats and swimmers."

"Is that so," said their father, smiling.

The twins stopped listening and instead stared out the window. Eventually they realized Manuel was taking the shore road, and they'd soon pass their old house. They peered through the glass, hoping to catch a glimpse. But they needn't have worried. The van slowed and turned onto the long stone driveway where, almost a year earlier, a taxi cab had dropped them upon their initial arrival.

They were shocked at the sight, for the house had been completely transformed. Its walls had been covered with a fresh coat of blue paint, and the grounds landscaped with tall coconut palms and lush fruit trees. But this was only part of the surprise.

"My goodness," said Mrs. Hendricks. "I hardly recognize the place!"

Manuel turned off the engine. "Come on," he said. "They'll be so excited to see you." He hopped out and proceeded down the path, motioning for the family to follow.

Lucy and Paddy ran after him, wondering what—or who—they'd find. Above the door hung a sign that read, 'The Thomas Stephenson House & Museum.'

Manuel opened the door and the twins entered, eager to see the house again.

"Welcome to the museum," greeted another familiar voice. "Lucy! Paddy! My goodness! It's so good to see you!"

Chi-Chi's mother, Mrs. Flores gave them each a big hug. "Today's the Grand Opening, of course—we couldn't open it to the public before you got here, since it was your idea to turn this place into a museum—not to mention your money that paid for it."

"It was never our money," Lucy interjected. "It was always Thomas Stephenson's. We just helped find where he put it, that's all. We thought it would be nice for people to remember him for more than just as a ruthless pirate captain."

"And that's exactly what we've done. We've restored the house to the way it was when it was built. Let me show you around." Mrs. Flores took their hands and led them into the living room, where the paintings, now restored, once again hung from the walls.

As they passed through the arch separating the living room and the formal dining room, Lucy pointed at the equations carved in the woodwork and asked if anyone had ever figured out what they meant.

"Yes, as a matter of fact," answered Mrs. Flores. "We contacted a mathematician in Boston, who helped us with them. It turned out that the solutions are the global coordinates of his hotel."

"Wow," Paddy said. His gaze shifted to the corner of the living room, where Chi-Chi's grandmother sat talking to a small group of people.

Mrs. Flores smiled. "My mother will be giving talks while the museum is open. She's prepared a whole presentation about what Mr. Stephenson was really like. I'm sure it'll be a huge hit. She's one of the few people left who knew him."

At that moment, Grandma Flores noticed the twins and smiled broadly.

"I haven't seen her so happy in years," Mrs. Flores added.

She led Lucy and Paddy through the house while their parents remained behind to listen to Grandma Flores. The twins couldn't get over how wonderful everything looked. The rooms were filled with exhibits on Thomas Stephenson's life as a pirate and his time spent on the island, with an emphasis on his paintings and other interests.

When they reached the study, Paddy's eyes widened. There in the corner, draped over a mannequin, rested the old pirate's ragged blue coat.

"We found it in the cave, right where you said it would be."

Paddy stared at the jacket, a physical reminder that their adventure wasn't just his imagination. It had been cleaned and pressed, with the buttons polished. "Wow," he said, stroking it with his fingertips. "I don't suppose I could . . ."

"Try it on? Of course."

Tentatively Paddy lifted the jacket and slipped his arms into the sleeves.

"You want me to get the camera from the van?" Lucy asked.

"It's okay," he answered. "There's a mirror here."

For a full minute he stood gazing at the image reflected back at him. Then he removed the jacket and replaced it on the mannequin. He smiled. "I'm through playing pirate. I'm happy just to be me."

"Being a detective and a treasure hunter is better than being a pirate anyway," answered Lucy.

They descended the stairs and entered the library, where the piano had been repaired and the staircase leading to the cellar was wide open. Someone had found the secret latch.

The twins bounded down the stairs. On the floor stood a few dozen barrels containing a reproduction of the gold bars. The exhibit described where the treasure originated and how it was stolen, and that it was probably stored here in barrels just like these for many years. Also in the cellar, protected by a thin sheet of glass, was the mural of the ship *Gemini*, along with a sign indicating it was the 'final clue' to the location of the treasure.

The twins grinned when they read the last line of the sign: 'This cellar and the lost gold were discovered by Lucy and Patrick Hendricks.'

When they finished touring the house, Manuel took the family on a short driving tour of the village. Lucy and Paddy saw all the old familiar locations: the marina, where they watched the fish bought and sold each morning; the library, where they were given the map that helped them in their adventure; the town square, where Mr. McNeill scared them half to death the first time they ran into him. Then Manuel stopped in front of a single-story brick building.

"Look at that!" exclaimed Mrs. Hendricks. She pointed at the wall, where 'Lucy and Patrick Hendricks Elementary School' appeared in large letters.

"I thought it was going to be named after Thomas Stephenson," remarked their father.

"Well, it's like this," Manuel started. "The town council figured enough stuff had already been named for him, and something should be named for Lucy and Paddy, too. After all, it was their generous gift that made all this possible."

For the first time, Lucy was speechless.

"We just figured the best way to use the treasure was to help the island as much as we could," Paddy explained.

"And help it you did," said Manuel, driving off. "The library is being expanded, as you wanted. And you won't believe this, but a team of archeologists arrived a few months ago, and they've begun to excavate near the ancient temple. They're amazed at how extensive and well-preserved the site is. They think tourists will come from all over the world to see it once it's restored."

"Wow," said Lucy, getting her voice back. "Could we see it while we're here?"

"Of course! The entire island is open to the two of you, you know that. There isn't much to see quite yet, though—it'll take years before they're finished. But it will eventually get done."

"What about the bones and pottery we found in the cave?" Paddy asked. "Will they be preserved, too?"

"They will stay where they are," Manuel said, "so visitors can see them as they were left if they wish. But guides will be instructed not to disturb anything."

As Manuel spoke, he turned down a newly-paved road that wound through the jungle. He drove on, and twenty minutes later they emerged in a large clearing.

"We're here," Manuel said.

Lucy and Paddy looked and realized they had arrived at the old hotel. Extensive renovations were in progress, and the grounds had been landscaped. It looked magnificent.

The van came to a halt and an older man ambled up and opened their door. It was none other than Mr. McNeill.

"Howdy, folks. Welcome to the new Stephenson Jungle Lodge. You're our first guests! We haven't quite finished fixing it up yet, but we worked extra hard on the Grand Suite for your visit. You'll be staying there."

"Thanks, Mr. McNeill," Lucy said. "It's great to see you again! The Grand Suite? Won't that be a little fancy?"

Mr. McNeill winked. "Nothing's too good for the owners of the hotel." He laughed. "But if you've got any suggestions on how we can improve the place further, you let me know, okay?"

"We thought you were retired," said their father. "Don't tell me you came all the way here just to welcome us."

"Not exactly. After that adventure last summer, I figured I'd been retired long enough. So I signed on to manage this place for when tourists return. We're going to have a couple of restaurants and set up all sorts of activities. We even bought that old cable line out in the jungle, which we're planning to repair. Good thing no one has been using it; we discovered it was ready to snap."

Paddy was about to say something about *that*, when he noticed someone coming toward them, waving.

"Look!" he cried. "It's Chi-Chi!"

The twins ran off to greet their old friend.

"*Vamos*," Chi-Chi said after they had hugged. "Let's go play." He turned and sprinted across the lawn, with Lucy and Paddy following, laughing. They ran past the amphitheater and toward the *Gemini*, which had been restored and repainted, and was now the centerpiece of a huge playground.

Paddy grabbed hold of a ladder. "Race you to the top," he said with a grin.

"You're on," shouted Chi-Chi, as he began to climb.

Acknowledgements

My journey to becoming a writer started with this story, although I hardly knew it at the time.

Back in 2006, my then-four-year-old daughter Sophie turned to me and asked, "Can you tell me a story about Lucy and Paddy?"

"Um, sure," I said, without any sense of what she was talking about. "Who are they?"

"They're twins," she said. "They're ten years old. I made them up."

I must've been quiet for some time, because she spoke again. "Here, I'll get you started. Lucy and Paddy are twins. They are ten years old. Now, you finish."

I suppose I could have made up a quick five-minute tale on the spot, but something about her expression persuaded me that she deserved more. So I told her I'd think about it and get back to her.

A day turned to a week, a week into two. After about three weeks, she asked, "Do you have a Lucy and Paddy story yet?"

"No," I replied, "I'm still thinking about it."

A month, two months, three months went by, but she never forgot. Every so often she'd ask if I was ready. I would tell her there were simply too many distractions; my wife was applying to graduate school, we would have to sell our house and move to who-knew-where, I was focused on my job and taking care of Sophie and her one-year-old sister, Elena, during my wife's night classes. But I reiterated that I'd get to it eventually.

We moved to Florida. Sophie turned five. We settled into a new life in a new state. Still no story. But she never forgot. Every few weeks she'd ask, and she happily accepted my answer: not yet, but I promise.

Finally, roughly a year and a half after her initial request, life had calmed and I was ready to proceed. But so much time had passed that my daughter, a voracious reader, was now ready to tackle longer chapter books. Although I'd never written anything very long, I decided to attempt an 80-page adventure story, planning to complete it in time for her birthday six months away.

The plot came quickly. A few months earlier, Tampa had held its annual Gasparilla pirate festival, so pirate treasure was fresh on my mind. That spring, my wife and I went on vacation to Belize (leaving our children with their grandparents), and I brought a notebook, planning to work out the details and begin to write. That trip ultimately inspired many locations that appear in these pages. The cave, for instance, is based on the remarkable Actun Tunichil Muknal (called locally ATM), an extensive underground cave system which still contains ancient stoneware and skeletal remains similar to those described here.

While there, our guide told us of an incident several years earlier when a flash flood caused the river passing through the cave to suddenly rise, trapping his tour group on a ledge for eight hours. Throw in a couple of bad guys, and I knew I had the story's climax. The ancient temple is based on one of the many Mayan sites scattered through the country. Shark Alley exists as well, and is a popular snorkeling site off the coast near Ambergris Caye, where you can swim with and touch rays and nurse sharks.

The story got longer and longer. I increased my self-imposed 80-page limit to 120, 160, and then I stopped counting. At some point I became fixated on understanding how Jean-Pierre Le Moyne obtained the gold and why he hid it on Janaconda Island, inspiring me to script the "flashback" chapters. To prepare, I devoured the Horatio Hornblower novels by C. S. Forester, the Lord Ramage books by Dudley Pope, and the Aubrey-Maturin series, which includes the famous *Master and Commander*, by Patrick O'Brian, all of which I highly recommend for older readers interested in 19th century seafaring adventures (I'm partial to the Hornblower books, myself). The names of Forester, Pope, and O'Brian were used in those chapters as a subtle reference.

The heliomanth was premised on the coelacanth, an ancient species of fish rediscovered in 1938 by a young South African museum curator, an event wonderfully described in the book *A Fish Caught in Time: The Search for the Coelacanth* by Samantha Weinberg. The scene at the café where the heliomanth is grilled was completely invented—or so I thought. Several years after writing that chapter, I discovered that Charles Darwin once had a similar experience. While conducting a survey in South America, locals informed Darwin of a rare flightless bird, one of several species related to the ostrich. After searching unsuccessfully, he returned to camp and was in the middle of dinner when he realized the cook had prepared it for their meal! Darwin then grabbed the plates from the crewmembers to recover as many bones as possible. The animal is now known as Darwin's Rhea. So in this case fiction is based on a kernel of truth, if unknowingly.

I finished the story in time for my daughter's seventh birthday, a year and a half after I started. I gave her a copy, and after she read it, it sat for years, undisturbed, until in early 2015 I decided to take another look at it while between projects.

I read the first few chapters and quickly realized that the story was horrible. Not the plot (or so I hope; you can e-mail me your own opinion), but the quality of the writing itself. In the years since drafting the first version, I had continued writing stories, and my skill had improved. I recognized poor prose when I saw it. But I still loved the plot and the characters. Instead of giving up on it, I set out to rewrite the story from the beginning.

This process lasted about eighteen months. I took the first chapter to the members of my writing group, who immediately had two suggestions: make the kids older, and set the story in the 1940s. They wanted a prologue, too. Then I got to work and edited the heck out of it. You hold in your hands the result.

In total, I spent around three years on this book, not including the time Sophie unsuccessfully pestered me after her initial request. Was it worth it? You can be the judge, but for me the answer is yes. Lucy and Paddy had become real people, and I felt the need to complete their story—at least *this* story, because they may eventually have further adventures. (At some point, years later, my daughter admitted that Lucy and Paddy were the names of two characters in a cartoon she had watched, although she remembers nothing else about them or what the name of the show was. Now you know.)

Through the entire process, I was guided by a simple vision: to write a complex story that would be both interesting and age-appropriate for seven-to-ten-year-old kids who are advanced readers. As a child, Sophie was one such advanced reader, and it was difficult to find books on her reading level not aimed at teenagers. I never strayed from that vision, and hope I accomplished that goal. If you're an elementary school-age child who loves to read, I hope you'll think so, too.

I'd like to thank all the wonderful and immensely talented members of my writing critique group, Safety Harbor Writers & Poets, who freely gave their time and energy to ensuring the success of this project: Nancy Bruckner, Amy Bryant, Nicole ("the adverb lady") Caron, Stuart Dwork, Barbara Finkelstein, Carrie Granato, Laura Kepner, Deb Klein, and Chris Shaun. Also, my longtime friend Douglas Ernst Helmreich reviewed a draft of the first version of this story, and I named the police officer after him.

Finally, a shout-out to my family for their unending support: my wife Dawn, and our two daughters, Sophie and Elena, without whom this would never have been completed. I love you all dearly.

To my readers: Nothing thrills me more than hearing from you. If you enjoyed this story, have a question, want to complain about an anachronism, or simply want help with your math homework, please e-mail me at warren.firschein@gmail.com.

ABOUT THE AUTHOR

After growing up in New Jersey, **Warren Firschein** graduated from the University of Rochester in 1989 with a degree in political science, followed by a law degree from the University of Pittsburgh and an MBA from Carnegie Mellon University. He is the author of *Out of Synch* (Chapter Two Press, 2015), as well as the coauthor of *A Brief History of Safety Harbor, Florida* (History Press, 2013). He is also the cofounder and managing editor of *Odet*, a literary journal based near Tampa Bay. When not writing, he is an attorney for the Federal Communications Commission. He lives in Safety Harbor, Florida with his wife, Dawn, and their two daughters, Sophie and Elena. Visit him at www.warrenfirschein.com.

9 781942 679042